It is said that with the end of times, an unlikely ally will betray the world to save it. He who is this dark warrior of vengeance must dispatch his own demons of the heart, before he can rid the shadow of darkness from this realm, once and for all.

Queen Bonna Min

AuthorHouse™
1663 Liberty Drive
Bloomington, IN 47403
www.authorhouse.com
Phone: 1-800-839-8640

Published by AuthorHouse 8/20/2012

ISBN: 978-1-4772-5240-6 (sc)
ISBN: 978-1-4772-5239-0 (e)

Two years ago...

Margarite, she prefers Margaret, Renee Stanford, daughter of Antonio Callistone, stumbles into her Boston penthouse, highly intoxicated, with an anger level to match. She is the epitome of the self made success story, taking her small television cable company to the height of a major media conglomerate. Tonight her anger stems from her father's interference, and conspiracy theories about his involvement with the evening's celebration. How dare he intrude on her moment of glory?

Even in her unsavory state, she is a creature of beauty moving through the moonlight that cascades into the room from the balcony doors. As if backed by years of practice, her shoes are flung one at a time across the living room, with one taking out a flower vase, while the other topples a lamp in the opposite direction. Surprisingly, Margaret's primary goal at the moment is to keep from spilling her champagne, while all the while venting about her father's interference with her time in the spotlight, again. Why the worry about the champagne is beyond comprehension. Perhaps it is an unconscious action associated with her intoxication. It's not like she needs any more and if she did, there are six more bottles over in the living room bar, neatly lined up along the mirrored backdrop, should a refill be needed.

Again, she begins to pace back and forth while arguing with herself as she sips from her champagne. Her chaperone for the evening waits at the door as a distinguished gentleman would do. He watches as she continues her temper tantrum, whipping her jet black hair around to catch the beams of moonlight, while stomping her feet. Needless to say, the wild hair effect only adds to her sultry, seductive, appearance, which he approves of even more. A smile crosses his face that bears a two day's growth of beard that somehow adds to his devilish charm. His attire is that of a black tie affair, well groomed and debonair. Obviously, he is a man of class and sophistication, and yet young enough to appreciate the wilder side of life. Admiring her silhouette with a devilish grin as she struts back and forth in the moonlight, he states, "I'm not sure if I should wait for you to invite me in, or do I presume that my duty is to close the door behind myself after entering." When Margaret begins to unzip her dress, the handsome man finds reason to add, "Because you are starting to undress!" Acting quickly, he enters the home and quickly closes the door as her dress hits the floor around her ankles.

With the alcohol taking full effect, Margaret states, "Your duty is to get over here and make me forget about my father's intrusion." Tripping over the dress around her feet, she bumbles around for a second, and bounces off the grandfather clock stationed beside her bedroom door. All of this and she doesn't spill a drop of her precious champagne. "Come hither, Marcus," she commands before sipping from her glass. With her head slightly bowed over her glass, Margaret gives him a seductive stare as she purses her lips around the rim of the glass.

Trying to be the voice of reason Marcus points out, "If you took a moment to think about the situation, you wouldn't be so angry. After all, his donation will fund the expeditions that you want to film for your broadcast company. The advertising alone will take your company through the roof, because you won't have to pay your father one dime of it as a return for his contribution." Marcus Dupree, the assistant curator of a local up and coming museum, and former acquirer of antiquities, walks over to Margaret and takes her in his arms to kiss her long and hard. For the past six months, he and his team of colleagues have been in league with Margaret's Television Broadcast Company, filming archaeology documentaries in Egypt and South America. Pulling his mouth away from hers, he looks into her eyes and says, "You play me, woman. And yet, I cannot deny you."

"Why Marcus, I don't know what you mean by that." She finishes off her drink, and then throws the vessel to shatter in the fireplace. Turning away from him, she pushes open the eight foot double doors to her room, revealing the posh decadence of her sanctuary. "Bring that firm body over here to me. I want you to talk to me some more. What is that sexy accent that you sport?"

"Why, it is part French," he answers, "part Cajun," he adds, as he takes off his coat. "But I do declare that it is all me, Cheri." Then, as if teasing her, he stops and retrieves a small package from his coat pocket. "First, I have something for you to commemorate the evening. It's just a small memento, really, from the dig site in Egypt." Carefully, Marcus opens the small box and carefully dumps the item out into his hand. He slowly pulls the silk handkerchief from the gift to reveal several more layers of tissue paper, as if all of this protected something precious within the layers.

Her intoxicated state plays off the child in her as her anxiety of her anticipation starts to build. To Margaret, he isn't trying to be cautious or careful. She thinks that he is just trying to tease her. "What is it? Tell me what it is," she stammers, while staggering back across the room.

Marcus smiles at her, and then motions for her to stop. "Ah, ah, not until I am finished," he suggests. Being the intellectual executive that she is, Margaret quickly decides to sit right down in the middle of the plush carpeting, believing that she is safer, having a shorter distance to fall. "First," he parlays, "you must promise me that you will drop this issue with your father's generosity. If it will make you feel better, I promise that I will make sure that all of his money is well spent." Marcus pulls away the last sheet of tissue paper from around the object to reveal a small glass orb the size of a golf ball, fractured, shattered, and poorly put back together.

No longer impressed, Margaret implies, "Really Marcus? I actually believed that you thought more of me than that."

But when he kneels down beside her, Margaret sees how the orb seems to reflect light in a way that it casts off a pink aura. "Like I was saying, it was found at the dig sight, but was determined to be not part of the original burial treasure. Someone had discovered the tomb, perhaps centuries before us, and had this bauble with them at the time." Marcus smiles at the effect the orb is having on Margaret. His plan is working out perfectly, as he expected. "One of the assistants for the dig had made the discovery, and sifted through the sand to find every piece. When it was deemed unessential to the inventory by the senior archaeologist, the assistant painstakingly reassembled it. It wasn't until the last sliver of glass was put in place that it started to give off the pink illumination." Marcus holds out his hands to offer it to Margaret. "Like the chief archaeologist, Mr. Van Buren, at the museum, deemed it unworthy of the exhibit, so I decided to give it to you."

Margaret's eyes twinkle, reflecting the pink glow that entrances her. She takes the fragile orb in her hands and says, "I feel so horrible about this."

"And why is that, my petite?"

"Because, I think I am going to be sick, and here you've brought me a gift." She doesn't appear to be ill, but Marcus rises all the same. Casually he walks back over to the chair and gathers his coat, as if he doesn't plan on staying. "Are you sure? I could stay and watch over you," he suggests, but his words are patronizing, as if he already knows the answer.

"No, no, that won't be necessary. I think I'm just going to lie down until it passes." She never looks up at Marcus. Her eyes never leave the glowing glass orb resting in her hands, as Marcus slides back into his over coat.

This lack of attention prevents her from seeing the mischievous smile Marcus was giving her, or the red hue around the pupils of his eyes. "Very well, my sweet petite, I shall be off, but thank you for accepting my gift."

Entranced by the effects of the aura, Margaret doesn't even see Marcus exit the room, much less leave the penthouse. But when she hears the front door close, she quickly leaves the floor to move to the bed, where she can inspect her new treasure more closely. Even drunk as a skunk, she can see that it was ancient in origin, which intrigues her even more. Who made this curious little trinket? When was it made? She is positive that the time was long ago, but how? After further inspection Margaret realizes that it's not a simple glass orb, but a global representation of Earth, complete with the continents raised slightly across the sphere's surface.

Her gaze is suddenly interrupted by the overwhelming sensation to relieve herself, which is not surprising after the champagne intake of earlier tonight. With no reason why, Margaret treats the simple piece of glass as if it is the most precious thing on earth. Carefully, she lays it down on her thick feather down comforter. She then jumps up and almost falls down twice as she hurries over to the bathroom. As she sits down, she thinks about what Marcus said. Who is he to be laying down terms of agreement to her? Once off her throne, she giggles a little recalling Marcus' proposition, "You have to drop this issue about your father's generosity," she mocks.

She stops at the sink and props herself up on the counter to take a couple of deep breaths. Margaret isn't going to be sick, but it wouldn't hurt to have a little cold water splashed in her face to sober up. "What does he know, any way?" Never turning the light on, she doesn't notice the mirror's distorted view, or the image of another woman in the reflection.

"I know, child," a voice proclaims, causing Margaret to look up at the mirror. Shocked by the image, she stumbles back away from the vanity until she is stopped by the wall behind her. Then, she simply slides down the wall, pulling the towels from their bars, and taking them to the floor with her. Frightened, and sobering quickly, she can't help but look up at the mirror, hoping it is all just a bad hallucination. Instead, she sees the image of a dark haired woman, looking very regal with her adornment of gold and jewels.

"Child?" Margaret can't believe what she is seeing, but at the same time she isn't seeing everything visible in the reflection of the mirror. "Are you my mother?" She doesn't see the dreadful surroundings of the woman in the reflection. She doesn't see the remnants of suffering at the woman's feet. All Margaret sees is the woman's face, and is mesmerized by the close family resemblance. Unsure if this whole episode is a result of her intoxication, Margaret decides to indulge in this hallucination by asking, "Tell me, are you the spirit of my mother? This is a perfect example of when someone has one of these episodes. But why did you come to me this way, right now." Then, as if something takes over her rational state of mind, Margaret becomes fixated with the thought of this being her mother coming back to her from the beyond. She looks herself over as if ashamed by her present state, and then adds, "I'm a wreck, and embarrassed to see you like this."

"Do not be, my child, I have been watching over you for quite some time. You are a very powerful woman, Margarite, but I come to you this night, to offer you so much more."

Margaret blinks her eyes and declares in a quiet voice of awe, "I don't believe this!" The spell has been cast, and now Margaret must follow this course.

"But you held the proof in your hands, did you not? It is your little trinket, the gift bestowed to you this night that allows us to connect. But if it is proof that you need, then go and gather your bauble and tell it what you want. But be warned, to pursue this offer, you must vow to avenge me, and carry out my plan to do so."

Not quite sober, and hearing what she wants to hear, Margaret pulls herself together to welcome the opportunity to avenge her mother's murder. Oh, and in the process, she will become the most powerful woman in the world? Of course Margaret would jump at the chance. Rushing from the bathroom, she hurries over to the bed and collects her treasure, holding it cupped with both hands. Not knowing whether she should believe all of this or not, she holds the glass orb up in front of her face. Staring at the pink aura she whispers, "I want the power, I want it all."

Immediately, Margaret's body takes on the same glow as the orb as she begins to feel euphoric, while her body, mind, and soul, are enveloped by the overwhelming sensation. If this is what true unlimited power feels like, there is no way she can refuse the bargain. Reveling in the glory of her newfound addiction, Margaret is taken to her limits and passes out from being unable to handle it any more.

Her fall to the floor will suffer no damage to her, or the glass orb that rolls across the carpet and under the edge of her bed. In fact, it now appears somehow, as if it had never been damaged centuries ago, in the Egyptian tomb.

North & South: Lines Drawn

The End Of Times Part II

Stacy A. Wright

authorHOUSE®

"Not again,"

Billy Ray McBride stands on the balcony of Darien Callistone's downtown Atlanta condo, and stares at the would-be mobster standing over by the railing. Focused on his phone call, Callistone doesn't realize that Billy is standing there behind him. Billy doesn't bother to interrupt the conversation, to let Darien know that Billy was standing there. He will find out soon enough.

"Why have the dreams returned?"

"...yeah, and I think you worry too much, Smithers. If he ever shows his face around here again, he'll have the devil to pay." Darien hangs up the phone, laughing at the old man's paranoia. Staring out at the Atlanta skyline, Darien feels like the king of the world, especially now that his father has returned to New York. He throws his cigarette over the railing and turns to enter the condominium.

"I know the night this happened."

"Holy Jesus, where did you come from?" Darien staggers back a step, shocked and scared by Billy's presence, dressed as a black specter of death.

Billy answers the question with a flurry of punches, followed by a kick to Darien's chest that sends Callistone flying across the balcony. Dazed and confused, the mobster's son scrambles to right himself, and retrieves his pistol from the nearby table. It offers him a little confidence as he takes aim, but Billy is already on top of him, slapping the gun free from Darien's hand. "I hate guns," Billy declares while staring down at his prey. This leaves Darien Callistone helpless against the beating that Billy gives him. In a matter of just a minute or two, Darien is reduced to a wasted lump of flesh covered in blood. Billy stares at Darien, seething with rage that has been brought to the surface. "Your father will be the lucky one. His end will be quick and easy. Tell him I'm coming for him, when you are able to talk again." Billy turns away from Darien as if the mobster's son was nothing more than an annoyance, and never offered a threat to Billy in the first place.

> "It's the night I thought all of this came to an end."

Darien rolls over to a seated position, resting himself against the balcony railing. He knows that he can reach his gun, but he isn't sure if he can pick himself up, much less the massive automatic pistol. He mumbles through swollen lips, "Who are you?"

> "An eye for an eye,"

Too stupid to stay down, Darien does his best to stand against Billy, believing that his Callistone name can protect him. Billy watches Darien's efforts in the reflection on the balcony doors, and simply waits for the opportunity to strike. When he sees Callistone struggling to raise the gun, Billy spins around and pulls his mask off his head. "The name is Billy Ray McBride!" With that, Billy kicks the gun free again with one foot, and then follows his motion through to deliver another kick to Darien's chin, with his other foot. The force sends the mobster's son over the railing and onto the sloped glass of the building's exterior.

"I lost my father. Callistone lost his son."

Darien slides down the first section of glass, before he is able to find a toehold on the glass mullion. "Oh my God, oh my God, oh my God!" His breathing becomes rapid and shallow as he lays there thirty stories above the street. "Hey, are you still up there?" He tries to pull himself up, but the blood soaked glass becomes more and more slippery with each attempt. Panic sets in as he sees that his struggles to save himself from certain doom are all in vain. When the leather sole of his shoe slips from the mullion, Darien is sent sliding down the next section of glass until he is able to catch the framework of the glass with his fingertips. He realizes that he has just seized his last chance to stop himself, before going over the edge, but Dairen doesn't know how long he can hold on. "Wait, you can't just leave me here. I can pay whatever you want!""

"I wanted all of this to end."

Billy appears over the railing to look at Darien's predicament. "Yes I can. I don't need your money." Happy with the outcome of the situation, Billy turns to walk away again.

"You son of a bitch, my father will make sure you pay for this!" Darien develops a sinking feeling in his stomach, when his fingertips slip from the window trim. "I'm slipping," he warns.

"That's not my problem…" Billy declares as Darien is heard screaming when he goes over the edge, "…Any more." He adds, before entering the condo.

The dream ends with an image of Antonio Callistone's face appearing, causing Billy to suddenly sit up in bed, soaking wet with sweat. He looks over at Taylor sleeping beside him and wonders, "Why is this happening again?"

North & South: Lines Drawn

Chapter 1

Three months ago, A New York Mobster was shown the mortality limits of his lifestyle, when his life was threatened by a man who had vengeance in his heart. When Antonio Callistone proved to be untouchable, the vigilante set his sights on Antonio's son, Darien. The death of his son has dramatically changed his life, and his future plans. Episodes like this have a tendency to weaken a man...

A black Bentley rolls up the driveway of the palatial estate in upstate New York, owned by Antonio Callistone. The driver, a young woman in her late thirties looks at herself in the mirror, as if she expected to see someone else. As of late, she has taken on a new personality, being outspoken and in the limelight more often. This will be just another example of the new Margaret. After checking her makeup, she stares into the mirror. "Everything is coming together, Mother. The time has come to really get this ball rolling." The words, "most powerful woman in the world," ring in the young woman's ears, as she recalls the euphoric addiction that drives her actions.

Slipping her black sunglasses onto her face to hide her eyes, she climbs out of the car and starts for the grand entrance of the home. Wearing a long, low cut, black evening dress with heels to match, she walks up to the open front doors of the lavish estate, as if she was a debutant making her entrance at the ball. "Daddy, I'm home," Margaret Stanford declares, entering the family estate. She drops her bag in the foyer, and waits for a second before continuing inside. Almost immediately, she is confronted by her father's associates and employees making their way into the formal dining room, bidding Ms. Stanford their condolences. Being the daughter of the largest crime syndicate on the east coast, she has grown up accustomed to having such riff raff wandering through the main house. It is no surprise that Margaret has been summoned to return home to find the largest "family" turnout, since her father was handed over the reins to the syndicate. The overwhelming sense of mourning is because the gathering is being held for her younger brother's wake.

Looks are not deceiving in this young woman's case. She is not here because she wants to be, nor does she want to renew her affiliation with the family business. Sometimes, we must do the things we hate the most, so that we can get what we want.

There is a deep rooted hatred for her father alive and well inside her. It started long ago, when a young father to be, Callistone, discovered that his wife had given birth to a healthy baby girl. He was told all along that this child conceived was to be a healthy baby boy, his heir to the family throne. A proud papa, Antonio believed that he had been given his first born son, the one that would someday take control of the family empire. In a blind fit of rage, Antonio strangled his wife to death, and then shot the midwife. She was the unfortunate one who broke the news to him, that a daughter had been born. Coincidentally, the day after Margaret's birth, the doctor's office who originally told Callistone that Margaret was a boy, blew up in a raging inferno. The doctor, two nurses, and four patients were killed in the fire.

Deep inside, he felt cheated. A daughter was nothing to him, when he expected the heir apparent for the Callistone Empire. Sooner than later, Antonio's anger subsided, and the realization of what he had done finally set it. His anger quickly turned into guilt, and shame, forcing him to make amends through his daughter's life. Antonio vowed to give the girl everything she could ever need, or want, as long as it was as far away from him as possible.

Callistone soon after married Margaret's wet nurse, who cared for Margaret until she was old enough to be shipped off to boarding school. The wait for Antonio to receive his son wasn't a long one. It was Antonio's second wife who bore her brothers, Robert and Darien. Once the boys were old enough to stand beside their father, Angelica, their mother and Margaret's wet nurse, soon after became the subject of a self imposed exile of booze and depression. The only time she is seen, which is very rarely, is hiding behind some kind of veil, as she moves through the house like a specter in the night.

But even with the poor breeding stock, Antonio believed that his first son was going to become a great man. That is, until Robert's cousin Jonathan, accidentally shot Robert in the head. The boys had found the keys to Antonio's hunting case and were playing with the guns when one went off. The loss of Robert traumatized Antonio to no end. His only recourse was to latch onto young Darien and personally groom the lad into a true mobster's son. Confident that he could not fail, this firm belief allowed him to overlook Darien's shortcomings. Now, Antonio can sit around and make all of his claims to fame about the little bastard, and Darien will never have to live up to them.

With everything that Margaret has accomplished with her life, Antonio has never shown any interest whatsoever. At her College graduation, instead of being the proud father of her, Antonio had the audacity to outweigh her achievements by bragging about Darien's first trigger job. Out of anger and spite, Margaret stood up at her banquet and raised a glass to her brother. She then proceeded to tell everyone present that Darien would never be worth more than the bullet it would take to kill him. Then again, here she is, taking time away from her busy corporate schedule, to attend this morbid gala in honor of poor Darien's passing.

This lifestyle of hers that occupies her time stems from the one thing Antonio was able to give to his daughter, or at least it was the one thing she didn't reject. He had "acquired" a small cable broadcasting company, and signed it over to her, to give her communications degree purpose, claiming it was simply a graduation present. At first, Margaret was going to decline the gift, believing that it was another attempt of him buying her off. Finally, after a long debate, she gave in to her vices by deciding that it was something she deserved, due to the lack of a real family that she had growing up. It may seem like a pathetic justification, but it has served her well since then. To start her career and new life, Margaret's last act as a Callistone was to change her name, taking her mother's maiden name as an insult to her father. To prove that she was superior to her brothers, Margaret took the little company, on the verge of folding, and turned it into one of the world's leaders in Media corporations; The Silverline Corporation.

Alas, over the past two years, certain bridges have been mended, allowing Antonio to bring her back into the family fold, or at least as far as she would let him. Some saw this as strange, but Antonio dismissed their accusations because of his need to seek his forgiveness. He may soon be surprised at how far she wants to be back into the family business.

Into the formal dining room she strides, making her presence known with the clicking of her heels on the granite tile floor. The heads of her father's syndicate sit around the large rectangular table, at their respective places, with her father sitting at the opposite end, impatiently awaiting her arrival. Once she is sure that everyone has looked at her, Margaret walks over to her seat and places her briefcase on the table. Then, instead of sitting, she walks to the other end and gives her distraught father a kiss on his cheek. "It pains me, Father, to see you in such sorrow." It pains her even more to put on this façade, but sacrifices must be made for the betterment of standing. Out the corner of her eye, she can see the outline on the wall, where a picture had been removed from the family collection, to be replaced by a smaller, cheap, dime store frame containing a snapshot photo of Margaret from her college graduation. What a pathetic attempt to show his intentions. She gives him another kiss and rises from her bent over position. "My brother will be missed by us all," she adds, looking around the table with a glare. Immediately, her gaze at the men prompts quick responses and replies from the rest of the attending party to concur. This display of compassion of hers is merely for the audience to sway their allegiance and obedience her way, if and when the time comes, and means nothing more. Satisfied that she had convinced everyone of her stand, Margaret starts for her seat once again.

Displaying the class and sex appeal of a socialite, she struts back to her chair, and then stops. Everyone around the table watches as she slowly takes a few steps back to stop behind Salvador Marcotti's chair. Her true dark nature is visible to few, especially the man seated in front of her. Salvador Marcotti is a heavy set man who occupies the entire chair, and cares nothing about what people think of his size. Balding and overweight, he resembles a heavier Marlon

Brandau with out the mustache, but no one ever seems to notice the resemblance. "Mr. Marcotti, aren't you the one in charge of my father's security?" Margaret nonchalantly reaches down into her cleavage and retrieves a small derringer, keeping it hidden from sight in the palm of her hand. She then drapes her arms around Marcotti's shoulders, and moves her head down beside his ear to whisper, "You obviously failed in miserable fashion." Margaret squeezes the trigger of her pistol, sending a .22 caliber bullet straight into Marcotti's heart. This is what her father wanted, but couldn't do himself. As much as she may have despised Darien, on so many levels, he didn't deserve to go out like that. After all, like her, he was a Callistone. With her actions against Marcotti carried out, she feels that she has offered some measure of justice for the act against her brother. "This so-called rebel vigilante should have never been a threat to my father, or Darien."

Carmine De Luca, one of Antonio Callistone's oldest and most trusted associates, becomes uneasy in his chair with Margaret's action. To him, it seems obvious that Margaret's distance from the family business has blinded her to Darien's true nature and lifestyle. Feeling the need to speak up, Carmine adjusts his old-fashioned coat, and prepares to address Ms. Callistone. At first glance, he resembles a character right off the celluloid strips of a fifties gangster movie, completing his pinstriped attire with slicked back hair and wingtip shoes. "Margaret, in Marcotti's defense, not that it really matters any more, your brother believed himself to be untouchable, and refused Marcotti's obligations. Darien ignored the warnings believing he was in charge of his own fate. He said the words to me personally, not two months ago." De Luca stares at Margaret expecting some kind of response, but it's only obvious that his explanation doesn't interest her in the least.

She sits down in her chair, never taking her eyes off of her father's number two man, as if reminding him that she still has a bullet left in her pistol. "My brother was nothing but a child who had found the keys to his father's gun cabinet," She watches as her Uncle Frank looks at Antonio. She sees the effect of her statement on her father's face, but dismisses his anger and continues with her little speech. "In light of Marcotti's forced resignation, I have offered to step in and handle the matter of this rebel vigilante personally, as a gift to my father and brother. In the mean time, while my father takes his time to mourn dear Darien, I will be stepping in to manage the business aspects of my father's corporation." Margaret opens her briefcase and retrieves a collection of organized files, and begins to pass them out to everyone. "I am well aware, that all of you know how I have made it a personal rule to stay away from my father's work…" Her statement is interrupted by Marcotti's large body rolling out of his chair, "…until now." Margaret opens her copy of the file and then looks around the table to prompt everyone else to do the same.

"What do you think you can do that any of us can't handle? This vigilante is just the type of guy I'm used to dealin' with." The gruff voice with the south side accent is that of Bruno Campano, who runs the Brooklyn district. His rough appearance and thick twisted nose, is testament to his earlier days, strong arming for Antonio's father.

"Dear sweet Uncle Bruno, I am a corporate CEO with resources at my disposal that would suffocate your Neolithic thought processes. If you'll try to follow along the best you can, I'll explain this outline of my plans real slow." Most of what is in this file, are the schedules that her father already had in play, which should add some credibility to her efforts. The rest is part of her agenda. "As I said, for my father's benefit, I will be taking charge of the legal aspects, with certain situations being my primary concern. I will not be stepping on any more toes while this takes place, unless I need to put my foot down again. My father deserves the right to mourn his son, and I will not tolerate anyone who doesn't tow the line during his absence. After all, it is my reputation that is being put at risk. First, we will continue to move forward with our relocation plans to Atlanta. The list of properties involved with the relocation is on the second page.

Frank Callistone, Uncle Frankie to Margaret, taps his knuckles against the marble table top. "Maggie, maybe you're jumpin' the gun with this, a little. The bad issue we already have in Atlanta has cost us a fortune. Shouldn't we be taking care of that problem first?"

Margaret gives her father's brother a loving smile, "Yes Uncle Frank, and as I said, that is a gift to my father. I am handling that issue personally, and already have my plan under way. As for the fair city of Atlanta, I have already entered into negotiations with Eric Chism, the son of the late Franklin Chism. Giving what was left of his father's organization new purpose, I have already doubled the fire power that we currently have in place. Gentlemen, I assure you that we will have no problems with the relocation. Soon, the rebel vigilante that runs the streets of that southern metropolis will be a thing of the past."

Bruno looks around the table before offering a hacking chuckle and asks, "Again, little girl, what can you do? What do you know about the mob?" He flips the ashes of his cigar into his wine glass and stares at the woman at the table who is almost half of his age.

Looking up from her papers, Margaret gives Mr. Campano an evil stare. "I own one of the nation's largest cable broadcasting companies. With a wave of my finger, I can send a thousand people to work on any project of my desire. With that kind of power, I can have any information I want, on anything, or anyone, with a snap of my fingers. As for mobsters; I deal with lawyers and Producers on a daily basis. In my opinion they're about the same. They are all about screw you, and money." Margaret thinks about picking up the derringer again, and pointing it at Bruno's thick skull. The one draw back is that she realizes she must maintain her composure to keep these men from seeing her true intentions. "First and foremost, I will not have my Corporation's name tarnished, in any way, because of someone's incompetence, on this end. I have not spent the past two years striving to achieve my latest endeavor to have it compromised now. Keep in mind, like Marcotti; you are all subject to replacement."

This is not what Carmine De Luca expected to hear, when this meeting was called earlier today. Antonio had informed his "Board of Directors" that there would be an announcement, but nothing like this was expected. How could Antonio make a decision like this be reached without first confiding in his bosses first? Not to mention the fact that Margaret has already made business decisions and plans before the change of command has been announced. De Luca looks around the table at his long time associates and sees nothing but passive expressions from a bunch of old men. Something has to be said, and Carmine sees that he is the only one who has the guts. He pushes his chair away from the table and stands up to voice his opinion. "Antonio, with all due respect I have to ask, why have we not discussed these decisions before now? I, of all people, have stood at your side since Tony Sr. handed the business over to you. Where has she been through all of this? I know she's family Antonio, but haven't I earned your trust and confidence with these matters?"

Margaret quickly stands up and faces off against De Luca, doing all that she can to keep her composure. The taking of Marcotti's life was exhilarating to say the least, but more than one mobster a day could be noticeable. "When my grandfather handed the business over to my father, you were nothing more than a two bit thug posing as a collections man that my father gave a chance to be more. All you have earned is the standing that you now possess. Do not ever question my father's decisions again."

"Margaret, that's enough!" Antonio stands and slaps his hands down on the granite table top, emphasizing his anger. His daughter assured him that he would not regret this decision. In less than ten minutes, she is already proving that wrong. "The reason I called this meeting was to announce my decision. You're all here to mourn the loss of my son," the saddened mobster looks around the room and waits for everyone to regain their composure, before he sits down as well. "Until I see fit, Margaret will serve as my voice in any meetings that will be held during my absence. She in turn will bring anything to me that may deserve my attention. The chain of command has not changed. You will all still report to Smithers, who will liaison between Margaret, and me. For now, I expect you to enjoy my hospitality and pay your respects to my son." Antonio stands, causing everyone around the table to stand as well, all except for Margaret. A nod of his head bids his men good day, before he turns to exit the room with Carlton and Uncle Anton following close behind.

With her father out of the room, Margaret calls on the attention of the syndicate heads one more time. "With the death of my brother being made public, our enemies may think they have an opportunity to strike. We can not and will not show any weakness during this time. We are going to surprise our competition by carrying on at an even faster pace, throwing everyone off guard. Those of you, who are associated with the relocation projects, expect daily conferences with me until the transition is complete. I must return to Boston tonight, but I will be returning to New York tomorrow, where I will take up residence here at the family home until this matter is resolved."

After gathering her paperwork, Margaret closes her briefcase and looks to her father's men once more. "This empire is as much yours, as it is my fathers, and I would expect all of you to defend it as such. You, gentlemen, have been the cornerstones of a world power for at least thirty years. My brother's death does not mark the beginning of the end for this empire, but the beginning of a new chapter in its history. Now, if you will excuse me, I must go to comfort my father." With no courtesy to the men who built the empire, Margaret stands and exits the room walking away from her father's associates. Her rude and abrupt exit leaves them grumbling amongst themselves, as she heads off through the lavish estate to keep in good graces with her father.

The first thing she needed to do is receive her father's blessing. She knows that her actions have irritated Antonio, but she couldn't help herself. Her path is taking Margaret across a perilous tightrope, but she also knows how to diffuse the situation as well. Walking up to the eight foot doors of the study brings back painful memories of her childhood, when she would seek her father's approval for her accomplishments. Sighing heavily, Margaret knocks twice on the solid mahogany doors. After waiting a few seconds for a response, she slides the doors open letting light into the darkened room. Upon entering, she closes the doors once more and searches the darkness of the room for her father. "This is no way to act, father dear." Even with her stormy past relationship, it still saddens her to see him grieving so. Darien was a worthless waste of flesh, but Antonio always held onto hope that one day the boy would turn his life around. Now, Antonio doesn't even have that. To her, it is solid proof that the world's most powerful man is but one loss from falling off his mountain.

Antonio's uncle moves from the shadows and steps in front of his great niece and stares at Margaret for a moment. Then, without warning, Anton reaches out and slaps her across the cheek, reminding her that he is the Patriarch of the family. "You have no right to treat the men like that, Margarite. They are not the meek board members you may be accustomed to dealing with. You may have some need to prove that you are capable, but remember, without them, there would be no organization to run." Without waiting for a response, Anton walks to the office doors. "Antonio, I shall let you know what I find out," he declares and then exits the room without saying another word.

Rubbing her cheek, Margaret walks over to her father's side where he stands at the window with the blinds partially closed. "Would you like me to open these for you?"

Antonio turns away from her and sits down at his desk. "If I wanted the shudders open, I would have done it myself. I like the darkness. It soothes my aching soul right now. For the moment, I want you to sit down and hear me out." Antonio motions at the chair in front of his desk, but Margaret ignores the gesture, until she sees fit to take a seat. "Don't go stepping all over the toes of my boys in there. I agreed to this because of your reputation in the business world, but more than that, I wanted you here to be a representative of the family, while I force myself through these troubled times. That still doesn't give you the right to disrespect my men." Antonio puts his elbows on the desk and props his head in his hands. "This isn't the way it's supposed to be. A man is not supposed to outlive his children."

"You told me that you didn't think you could handle this right now, and needed my experience. I said, fine. I'd sit in your chair as proxy to facilitate the relocation of The Cornerstone

Corporation. But, the one thing you have to remember is that your illegal and legitimate business ventures are in bed together. There is no way I am going to let anyone jeopardize my standing while this takes place. Fear not, Father, when the smoke clears, you will be where you belong, and I will have moved on to bigger and better things."

Antonio ignores her declaration and stares into the darkness across the room, pondering his thoughts of days gone by. Looking up at his daughter, Antonio grabs his glass and finishes his drink. Never taking his eyes off her, he stands up to walk over to the window, and pries the slats of the shutters open slightly to look outside. "I can still see you and Darien building snowmen out there in the back yard. It seems like only yesterday."

"Yeah, and I remember Deluca and Marcotti standing over us as protection in our own back yard." Margaret walks over to her father and drapes her arms around his shoulders. "It hurts me to see you in so much pain. Is there anything I can do to make you feel better?" God, how those words are sour in her mouth.

Antonio spins around to face his daughter, and then pushes her away. "You can bring me his head!" His tone is cold and dark. Never in his life has he felt so violated. Antonio Callistone is one of the biggest crime bosses in the world. He has connections in every dark alley around the globe. Who is this upstart vigilante that has taken Antonio's son from him? "Find this man, Margaret. Find him, find his family and anybody that knows his name, and kill them, kill them all. Then, bring me his head on a plate." Giving into his anger, Antonio throws his glass across the room and shatters it against the marble column. Now he is pissed, and doesn't have a drink. "Tell Carlita to bring me another Scotch. That one was watered down."

Margaret walks over to his side one more time. "Don't fret, Daddy dear, I'm taking care of everything. I promise to play nice with the boys as well." With the kiss as her goodbye, she strolls over to the door and turns to be excused by her father.

"Good, I want to know that I'm going to have some closure with this soon. I have a meeting with Cortez coming up in Miami that will give us a direct line into Florida for our narcotics, by bringing his group into the fold. I want the trade route through Atlanta to be open without any setbacks." Antonio sits back down and rests his head on his hands.

"Again, I have to protest this trip of yours. I don't think you've given yourself enough time. Besides, if you travel south, you're liable to mess up my plans. Give me a little more time, and then take your trip." Margaret turns away to open the door. "You know I want what's best for you, don't you?"

"One day, you will find that there are some matters that won't wait, because there is no time for it. Tell your Uncle Frankie that I am ready to see him now."

Margaret exits the study, wearing a smile across her face. She is actually quite pleased with the outcome of her visit with Antonio. After placing her father's drink order, she announces Frank's summons to the study before exiting the gathering for the closest restroom. Her cousin, Jonathan Callistone, follows his father Frank to the study, trying not to be to obvious watching Margaret's actions down the hall, as she makes her way frantically into the downstairs powder room. The door quickly slams closed behind her and it is locked just as fast. Looking into the mirror, she sees not her reflection, but the image of another woman. "Everything is progressing as you have foretold, Mother. Soon, there will be no one to stop us."

The reflection in the mirror shows a ghastly backdrop behind the woman's image, depicting painful suffering for the lost souls crawling about on the floors and walls. Demonic spirits dart about, tormenting the down trodden, but the mistress of the room is unbothered and ignores the activity. She seems to be forced to live in this existence, as if exiled to some cavern in the pits of hell, but in the same instance seems to be at home just as well. For whatever reason, Margaret seems like she can see none of this, or she's doing a hell of a good job ignoring it.

The woman in the mirror responds to Margaret's statement, but when she does, the sound of her voice comes from Margaret, with a different tone and dialect than her own. "You have done well, my child. The time is drawing near, but there is no need to rush. For the prophecy to transpire, everything must be given due time to unfold."

A knock at the door breaks Margaret's trance. Looking back at the mirror, all she sees now is her reflection staring back. This angers her to no end, but she did promise a few minutes ago to maintain some sort of civility. She snatches the door open, and then stares at her cousin with eyes that could kill. "What in the hell do you want, Johnny? The men's room is on the other side of the study. But for you, the little boy's room is upstairs in the nursery."

"Hello, cousin, I was actually more curious about who you were talking to in there?" Annoyingly, Johnny tries to look past his cousin just to see if there was another woman in the room.

To satisfy his perverted curiosity, Margaret swings the door open all the way to reveal the room void of another occupant. "Understand this, Johnny, if you ever question me again, I'll put a bullet in your skull, personally. I believe my brother Robert would condone my actions." Frustrated, Margaret then pushes her way past the male Callistone to exit his company as fast as possible. She needs to return to Boston as soon as possible. A slight measure of paranoia sets in on her, knowing that someone heard her conversation in the powder room. What compounds this is the fact that it was her cousin who was doing the eavesdropping. This could pose a problem later on should her plan be compromised before it is achieved.

"Easy cousin, I just wanted to give you fair warning. The word in the other room is that you stirred up a hornet's nest within the organization. If you're not careful, a true Callistone heir could take your place running the show." Johnny quickly enters the powder room and closes the door to avoid Margaret's response, when she stops dead in her tracks. There is no plot against her that he knows about, but in the same instance, if there is, he doesn't want to mess things up for anyone.

Chapter II

Present Day...

Is it possible that the weather and Billy Ray McBride's emotions are somehow connected? Arriving in Atlanta from Miami, the weather was as dreadful as Billy was feeling. Exiting the airport, he was broke with no means of transportation, and walked almost twenty miles in the rain to get to his truck at his apartment. His state of mind deemed it necessary for him to suffer that way. For what he's done, he doesn't deserve any better. Even so, part of him was glad that the Toyota was there, so he didn't have to walk all the way home.

The drive home was not much better. It was a long and lonely two hour drive that gave Billy plenty of time to think about the changes in his life. Not one thought offered him any sign of hope, or happiness. Billy walks up to the front door of his ranch house in Smiths Station Alabama, dreading the next few steps that he has to take. There is no happiness waiting for him on the other side of the door. Deep down inside his heart, he fears now that Taylor's gone for good, and there won't be any more happiness in his life. His trip to Miami was the proverbial straw that broke the camel's back. In some ways, it feels a little comforting to be home. Sometimes, the best place to work out your problems is when you go home. There, you feel safe from the outside world, so that you can sort out your troubles undisturbed. After taking a deep breath, Billy unlocks the door and pushes it open to enter the darkened house. "I'm home," he says, expecting no one to answer.

The house is dark, except for the lone light in the living room, adding to his gloom. He looks up the stairs in front of him with no rhyme or reason, and follows the banister that continues along the balcony leading to the master bedroom. The double doors to his room stand partially open revealing the cold dark emptiness that waits for him there. "Well, what did you expect?" He asks himself icily.

From his position at the front door, Billy looks around with hope of finding something that makes him feel good about being home. The living room laid out to his right is decorated with the furniture that Billy's grandmother picked out forty years ago. There is nothing there that brings him any joy. When he was a child, Billy wasn't even allowed in the living room, much less sit on the expensive furniture. The open formal dining room, or area, offers no sign of life being tucked away under the balcony adjacent to the kitchen. Even in the kitchen was nothing but Dark lonely despair.

His foster brother has gone off to Auburn to make a try at dorm life, wanting to be closer to school, or so he says. Billy could sure use Scotty's friendship now. He suspects that Scotty moved closer to school to make his earth first girlfriend happy by not contributing to auto pollution, by driving that beat up piece of shit truck of his back and forth to Auburn. Good for him, but that doesn't mean that Billy won't miss Scotty being around. There is a special place in his heart for the little crippled kid. Together, the two young men share the knowledge of a great and dark secret.

Isaiah, the ranch manager, has gone home for the day, and Taylor; well she's just gone. Everywhere he looks, he sees reminders of the red headed beauty that shared his life for a short while. The pain of it all starts to well up in him like a bad taste in his mouth, making Billy think that this might be harder than he first thought.

The flight from Miami gave him plenty of time to think about what has happened, what he's done, and what he's thrown away. He thought that he had it all worked out. He thought he was in control. The truth be known, Billy lost control when he let his selfish pride and inflated ego overwhelm his conscious reasoning. It was a madness that drove him to the point of no return and cost him everything dear in his life. Taylor said in her message that she left him because she couldn't take the lies and deceit, and who could blame her? She didn't deserve that kind of treatment, but that was how he repaid her love.

Then, there is the issue of his mother Sarah, ignoring his calls. Obviously, she has seen the footage of him and his activities in Miami, and has probably disowned Billy for lying to her again. Four months ago, Billy promised Sarah McBride that he and Taylor were through with their vigilante activities. Even after his vow proclaiming that it was over, and believing that he was right in his defense against Darien's death, Billy couldn't sway his mother's outlook. Sarah still blamed Billy, naming him as the reason Darien died. She told him on that day, that if he ever went out seeking vengeance again, her son would be dead to her, whether Billy still breathed or not. The death of Darien Callistone was supposed to be the end of it all. How was Billy to know that the dreams would return to haunt his sleep?

The biggest thing is that Billy betrayed the fact that he was a man of his word, a stand up guy. He broke all of that, forsaking everyone he loved. Never has he felt so alone. For the first time in his life, he truly understands the meaning of the term, a beaten man. Having no reason to keep standing there, Billy closes and locks the front door and walks upstairs to his room. Stopping at the bedroom door, Billy turns on the lights in the room to scare away the ghosts of the past. One spirit lingers as he sees a vision of Taylor lying in the bed, with nothing but the sheet hugging her bare curves. Then, that vision is gone as well, leaving Billy with only a saddened heart. Sitting down on the end of the bed, he stares out through the doorway wondering what he should do next. Looking over at the nightstand, he sees the light flashing on his answering machine. Billy wants to see it as a twinkling glimmer of hope. It could be a message from Taylor. After all, if she really did love him the way she professed, she could find it in her heart to forgive him, right? Yes, he did lie to her about what he was doing, but it isn't like he was cheating on her or something like that.

Using this line of thought as incentive, Billy musters up the strength to move over to the side of the bed and presses the play button on the answering machine. He isn't overjoyed when he hears the message. Could he really be this disappointed, or even surprised by the call? His anxiety increases when another part of his psyche laughs at his pathetic attempt at hope.

> "Kid, it's me, Rick. Listen, I really wanted to give you another chance, but when you flake out on me and don't return my calls, I have to believe that your wrestling career isn't as important to ya. Good luck, Billy, you really had potential."

The message ends with the effect only adding to Billy's depressed mood. One thing is for sure, there is no better reason to end a day, than taking another kick to the balls. Heading for the bathroom, Billy turns on the water, hoping that a long hot shower would wash away some of his misery. He knows that it won't, but Billy is the forever believer in hope. Most of all, he hopes that he can lay down without having any dreams tonight. Looking in the mirror, He thinks about what Taylor saw in him that she liked. It wasn't a scruffy four day beard, that's for sure. To appease what gods it may, he decides to shave for her.

The steam begins to fill the air as Billy stares at himself. The eyes, it's always been those deep blue eyes that caught the girls' attention. He's saddened that they seem to have lost their gleam. The eyes are the windows to the soul. Perhaps it's just the reflection of that. To keep from beating himself up too bad, he declares that it is the mirror fogging up that distorted the reflection. Looking back at the medicine cabinet, he can barely see his features clearly now, but he can make out the reflection of a dark haired woman standing behind him in the steam. Shocked, and surprised by the sight, he spins around to find that he is the only one occupying the room. Looking back at the mirror, he wipes away the condensation on the glass, but there is no evidence of anyone present to be seen. Is this all just part of the madness that he is suffering? Surely his mind is playing tricks on him. If he were to take the time think about it, nothing could be right with him after all of the punishment his body and mind endured in Florida, right?

Get in the shower. Forego the shave, because that can wait. His body will heal on its own, as it always has. To move forward, Billy has to get his mind straight, so that he can make a come back from this. The only way to clear his mind is a good night's rest. His body is exhausted, and his mind suffers because of it. His original thought is still sound. The time has come for him to call it a day. He stands there in the glass enclosure as the hot water pours down over the back of his neck, and relaxes his tense and sore muscles. If he was going to keep pursuing his vigilante lifestyle, he should consider utilizing the modified flack jacket he confiscated from his dad's assault gear. Lucky for him, there won't be anyone shooting at him here on the ranch.

Exiting the shower, he gets an uneasy feeling and looks around his bedroom. For a split second, he thinks that he saw someone standing at his bedroom doors, as he was putting on a pair of sweat pants. Defensive mechanisms kick in sending Billy stumbling towards the double doors, with one foot still stuck in his pants leg. Looking out of the room, he scans the darkened house for any signs of movement in the shadows.

His mind is still playing games with him. Who could have been in the house in the first place? "Get over yourself, McBride," he thinks, "You really do need some down time to regroup." Then he hears a sound down below in the dining room. Billy rushes up to the balcony railing and looks over into the living room to see if everything is everything. Was that a dining chair being slid across the hardwood floor? That's what it sounded like to Billy. He even holds his breath for a second, trying not to make a sound while straining his hearing for any noises coming from below. When he hears it, Billy reacts, as usual without thinking.

What he heard was the sound of someone bumping into the back of another dining chair, causing its legs to rise up and drop back to the floor before the rubber feet rub on the wood planking a little. His reaction is to leap over the railing to drop to the living room floor below. Of course, a cautious man always looks before he leaps. This time would have been good, if nothing else so that Billy could have avoided the sofa table that breaks his fall. Crashing to the floor amongst the splintered wood, he wonders if the impact with the antique table broke his ankle as well.

Jumping up, but favoring his right foot, Billy looks around the large dining room table but sees none of the chairs disturbed. Through the kitchen doorway, he sees the shadowy figure at the back door. As reckless as possible, Billy rushes around the table to enter the kitchen, only to find it empty. The sheer lace curtain on the door's window is moving slightly. The trespasser has made it outside. Billy rushes over and grabs the doorknob to snatch the door open, but pulls himself face first into the wall, and realizes that the dead bolt is locked. Still, he doesn't give up the pursuit just yet, fighting the door open to rush out into the rain.

The yard between the house and stables is empty. The light outside the barn lights up the grounds, and everything, or in this case nothing around it. There's no one moving about down there. Did he really see someone, or did he just want to? He's getting soaking wet, and his bare feet are now covered with mud and grass. Still, he continues to look around hoping to find some kind of explanation for what is going on. His ankle is throbbing, and he can see that it is starting to swell up, even in the dim light of the back porch light. There is nothing left to do now, except go back upstairs and lay back on his bed, and close his eyes. Of course, this is after he cleans up his dirty feet and gets a dry pair of pants. To hell with the rest of the world, Billy Ray McBride; tomorrow will take care of itself.

Chapter III

Antonio Callistone storms into the foyer of his palatial estate, and shoves his overcoat into the driver's already full arms. Ready to rip the head off the first person he sees, Antonio hopes that it is his daughter who is the recipient of his anger. "Margaret!" Seconds pass, and there is no response. Stubborn, he continues to stand at the front door, unwilling to move until his call is answered.

The house maid, Carlita, hurries out from the kitchen to humbly greet her employer. "Mr. Callistone, it is good to be home, yes?" The elderly woman takes Antonio's coat from the driver and dismisses him with a wave of her hand. Draping the garment over her arm, she faces Antonio again and explains, "Your daughter, Margaret, is lounging by the pool. How was your trip to Miami?"

How was his trip to Miami? His trip to Miami is the main reason he is so infuriated at the moment. His trip is the reason he spent yesterday in Atlanta, visiting his doctor that Margaret had already relocated in the south. He can't help but give her an angered stare as a response to her inquiry, knowing she is undeserving of the treatment. Carlita bows her head, as if ashamed for her actions. Of course, seeing her reaction to his abusive attitude quickly calms Callistone down. Carlita has worked for the Callistone estate, since Antonio and Frances were young boys. That kind of loyalty deserves better treatment than this, a more civil approach.

"How was my trip? Carlita my dear, you really don't want to know." Antonio turns away from the long term employee and head for the back yard. "I'm sorry for the rudeness, my dear. I do hope you can forgive me." Stomping through the house, he ignores all others as he seeks his destination being the vast landscaping of the back yard. To most, it resembles the grounds of a Roman spa, decorated with marble columns, and statues of Nude Gods and Goddesses stationed around the pool deck. Through the clouds of steam rising up from the warm waters of the pool, Antonio sees his daughter on the other side of the fountain pool. "Margaret, I want to see you in front of me, immediately." It's when she sits up to respond that he realizes that his daughter is topless. Turning his head, Antonio tries to hide the embarrassment of the situation while waving for her to stay where she was.

The eldest daughter of the mobster Callistone raises her sunglasses to get a better view of her father's embarrassment, loving the fact that it bothered him so. But then again, it doesn't quite balance out the anger that she is going to deal with in a few moments. After a deep sigh of regret, she drops her cigarette into her champagne glass and slips her camisole over her naked torso. She then stands and marches right over to her waiting father, "Yes, daddy dear, how was your trip?"

Without any warning, Antonio reaches out and introduces the back of his hand to her cheek. It is an action that Antonio regrets before it even happens, but at the moment, he isn't himself. "That sonofabitch almost had me in Miami! You really need to come up with a good excuse for why he isn't dead yet!"

Gritting her teeth to bear the sting of his attack, Margaret stares off to the side of the pool imagining how she would love to push over one of the statues on top of him right now. Trying to keep her cool, Margaret turns to face her father and replies, "I'll have you know, father dear, that everything was moving according to my schedule, until you took off to Florida. Correct me if I'm wrong, but wasn't it me who said that you needed to postpone your trip until I had this matter wrapped up, didn't I?" Margaret pauses for a moment to give her father a chance to reply. "You do remember the conversation, don't you? I told you that my team were ready to make their move, but needed more time. All of the pieces were in play, but if you came out of seclusion, it could jeopardize everything. I hate to say it, but obviously I was right. If you had just trusted me, your demon would already be at your disposal." Margaret shows her arrogance by turning away from her father to walk away. Grabbing Margaret's shoulder, Antonio stops his daughter from disrespecting him by walking away. Infuriated by his gesture, Margaret spins on her heels to face him again. "That's the second time you've touched me today in an aggressive manner. Don't do it, again!" This time she turns away and leads Antonio over to her lounge chair beside the pool. "You want answers? Okay, here we go. My boys had him pegged in Georgia. What we were unaware of was that you had already scheduled the first delivery to the new refinery in Atlanta. The next thing we know, the delivery boys rolled over on their boss, sending your demon to Florida, looking for you. You run the biggest crime syndicate in the world. If you make a move, people are going to find out. That's why we have a team of lawyers on the clock to keep the necessaries out of the public eye, remember? By the time we figured out where he had gone, it was too late to relocate the team, eliminating plan A. Don't worry though, father. There is a plan B, and it is already in action." Sitting back down, Margaret returns her sunglasses to the bridge of her nose and sits back down on the lounge chair. Margaret knows that she can push the limit with him, because of the guilt deep inside his heart for what he did to her mother. Even after thirty six years, she takes advantage of that fact. As long as she can get away with pushing the envelope, his little retaliations are inconsequential. "Oh, by the way, Dr. Romero called from Atlanta, and said that he had your test results?"

Antonio hangs his head, "Yes, well that's another thing I need to talk to you about. Evidently, this last little episode in Miami might have had an adverse effect on my heart. I want you to know about this, but no one else must know. As far as anyone is concerned, I am simply resuming my seclusion until the matter is resolved. For now, I just need you to humble me by telling me what you have planned."

"Sorry, father dear, but that isn't going to work on me. I don't want any of your men trying to earn a gold star and screw up another one of my plans. Soon, you will have your revenge for your son's murder, and be rid of this nuisance once and for all."

"Darien was just as much your brother, as he was my son." Antonio looks back at Margaret with a concerned expression.

"I know that. Believe me, Father; that is the only reason I am doing this for you." Once she shifts her position on the lounger, Margaret lays her head back so that she can ignore her father's doubtful appearance.

"Why are you doing this, Margaret?" Antonio looks around, shivering from the cold of the winter air. "Why don't you come inside where it's warmer?"

"Because, father dear, I am right at home in this cold weather. It soothes my cold heart that you created inside of me. Why I am doing this, is because it's my obligation to the family, representing the last in line. As far as the secret of your broken heart is concerned, it's safe with me. The last thing we need right now is an excuse for Uncle Frankie to try and slip Johnny in as the heir to the family name. Now go and relax like your doctor said."

Antonio leans over and gives Margaret a kiss on her forehead, "daddy's little girl." He turns away and heads for the warmth of his extravagant home while removing his cell phone from his inner coat pocket. All of this madness, this rebel vigilante, his son's death, coupled with the day to day stress of running the business is taking its toll on the aging mobster. Before entering the house, he pulls a small prescription bottle from his pocket and tosses one of the pills into his mouth. Times have changed, and the days of old lay by the wayside. His apprehension to change with the times could cost him more than his health. Margaret is the prime example of the next generation of leaders, but there now seems to be a darkness that shadows her personality. Perhaps it is all just part of some paranoia that has coupled with the anxiety of recent events. Standing at the bar, he dials a number on his phone, and then holds it up to his ear with one hand, while pouring him a drink with the other. "Carlton, where are you? I told you to meet me at the house first thing this morning."

Carlton Smithers sits back in his car seat and watches as the gates to the Callistone estate swing open for the arriving limousine. "As a matter of fact, we are pulling up in front of the house, as we speak. I'm sorry that we're running a little late this morning, but we had to find a new driver on short notice. I'll tell you what happened to the other driver, when you get in the car. We're at the front doors now." The line goes dead as Carlton watches the front door of the house open, and his employer walk out. Tossing his cell phone onto the seat beside him, Carlton opens his briefcase and retrieves a stack of papers to be ready for the barrage of questions he is about to face.

The car stops abruptly, as Callistone makes his way down the front stairs. The driver then jumps out and hurries around to open the door for his most important passenger. Antonio climbs into the car, but never looks over at Smithers. The door quickly closes behind Antonio, with the driver already running back around the car, before the door latches shut. Still without facing his right hand man, Antonio asks, "What happened to Rodney? I liked that kid."

Carlton lets a half smile cross his face. "Well, it came to our attention that Mr. Rodney Carson was actually Federal Agent Ronnie Bradford, who somehow infiltrated our ranks. With this new information coming to light, I felt it was necessary to terminate Mr. Carson's employment, and had your son's bodyguard, Mr. Jones, let him go. I believe Mr. Jones let go somewhere out over the Atlantic, about five hundred feet in the air. I'm afraid that there is more distressing news. Unfortunately, we missed an opportunity at Agent Justice, again." Carlton pulls out a phone log with certain numbers highlighted on the list, but Callistone simply waves away the evidence. I'm starting to believe that your daughter may be right. If we don't make this move soon, you could find your empire crumbling down around you, Caesar."

"You're right as usual, Carlton. Put in a call to Agent Justice's partner, and use this little revelation to apply some pressure. He should have warned us about the mole." Antonio finishes off his glass of scotch and sets the empty glass in the cup holder molded into the door panel of the limousine.

"Actually, he was the one who opened our eyes to the situation." Carlton looks down at his feet disapprovingly at the empty glass at his feet, and then asks, "Should you be drinking liquor in your condition?"

"Should you be questioning my actions?" Antonio looks out the window, "you need to let him know that I appreciate his loyalty to us. In fact, call him and thank him for me by giving him an extra twenty thousand for a job well done. Then tell him to stand clear and let Justice die where he stands. Margaret already has her people creating a paper trail that will sweep everyone off our backs once we finish the relocation. With Justice out of the way, our people on the inside can bury the case he has against us once and for all." Antonio finally turns to face Smithers. "Do you think I made a poor decision having Margaret sit in my stead, during these troubled times?" Callistone waves off the papers that Carlton suddenly was shuffling through again, "forget about that for now, and answer the question."

Carlton looks at his employer and friend with a concerned expression. "Antonio, I think you have gone through some pretty traumatic experiences as of late, and that it will take some time for your scars to heal. But, regardless to our personal needs the empire must remain in operation. Having Margaret at the helm is a necessary evil. She may be a wild bitch, but with the right bridle and reins, she can be governed."

Sitting back in the seat, Antonio looks out the window. "I'm sorry old friend, for putting you in that situation. Maybe I do need to remain distant for the time being." He turns to face his friend, "I want you to make sure my men are involved with her little plan, whether she likes it or not. She doesn't have to know, but she can never find out. Just because I'm stepping back, doesn't mean I'm willing to give up my power." Returning his focus from the scenery outside back to Carlton, Antonio asks, "What else is on the agenda?"

"Well, I found out why Crossfire hasn't been answering, or returning your calls. It seems that Margaret has already hired him for the job. I hope you're not angry, but I overheard her phone conversation."

Antonio laughs wholeheartedly. "Don't be absurd, Carlton. That's exactly what I want you to do, for me! I want you spying on the girl. Hell, if you need to, have her phones tapped, for Christ's sake. I don't care, as long as we are the ones staying on top of the situation."

Carlton pulls his glasses off and drops them into his briefcase. Facing his employer with a more business like attitude, he continues with the report. "So far, Margaret has transferred Fratelli and Maroni to Atlanta, to oversee the relocation of our assets there."

"That's all fine and dandy. They're both loyal men to me. But, I want our focus to be directed at our problem here also. My family has run parts of New York, if not most of it, since the prohibition. Jonathan Justice must be dealt with, permanently. We're not moving the entire organization; we're expanding. I can't run the organization from Atlanta, while worrying about what is happening up here in New York. You said yourself that my driver was a Federal snitch. Carlton, I know you are just trying to look out for me, the way you always do. God knows I wished Darien carried that trait. Just remember that as long as Special Agent Justice is alive, we will always be threatened by the Bureau. Take him out, and the interest they have in us, will die with him."

Chapter IV

Billy has spent the morning moping around the house unable to find anything to do that would fill the empty feeling inside. The rain outside, and Gods of fate, are determined to keep him trapped in this haunted house. What a boring life it would be to just hang out around here all day, every day, with nothing to do. Sooner or later he is gonna have to let go of this hope of Taylor coming back. Deep down inside, he knows that it isn't going to happen, and jumping at every sound is just tearing him up inside. Maybe it is a form of punishment for what he has done. To go back in time and change one thing would be impossible to do. If he could, it would be at his father's funeral. There he stood, standing next to Barbara Cox, where he made the decision to walk away from her. He could have turned to her and accepted her love to carry on with his life with her. At that very second, he made a decision to seek revenge for his father's murder. Had he taken the first choice, Barbara would still be alive, and he could've been happy with her. He would have never moved back to the ranch. He definitely wouldn't have met Taylor, and be so sad hearted. Of course, Taylor wouldn't be homeless, nor on the run from the local authorities of her hometown, had her path not crossed Billy's.

Too many have died, and too many have suffered, for this crusade for vengeance to continue. Today has to be the day for Billy to put his alter ego to rest. This will be his first step in recovering what life he has left. Tomorrow, he will go to Atlanta and make arrangements to liquidate his property there. His war against Callistone for the city is over. Detective Trey Simon gave Billy some good advice once. Billy plans to take it to heart, and start a new life. With what he has stashed away, and the money he can make off the sale of his condo, he should have enough money to support himself for a while, or at least until he figures out what to do. Who knows, maybe he'll just settle down at the ranch and help tend to the horses. Right about now, that sounds a hell of a lot better than getting beat on, whether in the wrestling ring, or streets of Atlanta.

Coming out of the daydream, he finds himself staring out the window and sees that the rain had stopped for now. Finally, he can get out of the house without getting soaking wet. Through the kitchen he goes, heading out the door and into the back yard. The breeze is crisp as it blows the storm clouds across the sky. There is supposed to be a chance of rain all day, but that patches of blue sky appearing lead Billy to believe that it isn't raining any more, any time soon. That's fine with him, as he stops to take a deep breath of clean fresh air. He's as fed up with the rain, as he is with the Callistone situation. After stretching, he wonders what he should do next. The snort and neigh of his horse catches his attention. Looking towards the end of the barn, he sees his faithful friend waiting for some attention. Billy seems to have neglected a lot of things lately, one of them being his horse, Midnight. He starts for the corral, stopping at the steps of the service doors to grab an apple, hoping to bribe the animal for some forgiveness. "Hey there, big guy, how are ya doin'?" Billy twists the stem off the apple, and then smashes the piece of fruit against the fence post. Offering the first half to the horse, Midnight shoves his head over the fence and devours the apple half, almost taking a couple of Billy's fingers with it. "Take it easy, boy. I need those fingers," Billy pauses for a second. "Well, I need 'em for whatever it is that I'm gonna do." Midnight bows his head and lays the bridge of his nose against Billy's forehead, looking Billy in the eyes. This gives him the opportunity to apply a good scratching behind Midnight's ears, followed by a couple of gentle pats to the side of the horse's neck. The magnificent beast shows its appreciation by stomping its foot, snorting, and huffing, as it pushes its head against Billy's hand. "Hear ya go, boy." Billy tosses the other half of the apple up into the air to let Midnight catch it. The horse gobbles the fruit down, and then gives Billy a snort, as if boasting about the catch. Then, as if Billy no longer mattered, Midnight trots off to the other side of the corral to be with the rest of the horses.

Right on cue, the elderly manager of the ranch, Isaiah, walks up beside Billy and props his foot up on the lower bar of the fencing, assuming the same stance as Billy. No one has ever spoken up to assign him the duty as the property' advisor, but Isaiah has served as such with three generations of McBride men. "So, what'cha been up to, Billy Ray?"

Billy jumps at the sound of Isaiah's voice. He was so focused on the antics of Midnight bullying the other horses that he didn't hear the ranch manager walk up beside him. Boy, you can tell Billy Ray McBride is really down and out when a sixty five year old man can get the drop on him like that. "Oh, hey Isaiah, I didn't hear you walk up." Billy calls for Midnight to come back over, hoping the horse would offer a diversion for any questions Isaiah might have. Unfortunately for Billy, when Midnight doesn't see another offering of fruit, he just trots away to go back to mingling with the other horses. With no other option, Billy decides to go ahead and get it over with, and now is as good a time as any. "So, how have you been, Isaiah? We haven't had much time to talk lately, have we?"

Isaiah looks around at the barn and then props himself up on the fencing. "Well, I'm a busy man, running this place for you. You, you're a busy man, doing whatever it is that you've been doing. Sometimes, busy men don't have much time to talk." One of the mares walks over interrupting the conversation. "Where's that redheaded beauty of yours? I was beginning to think that the two of you were connected at the hip."

Billy lets a half smile curl up the side of his face. He knew that someone was going to ask the question sooner or later. Billy actually likes the way Isaiah goes about it. "We, uh, kinda had a falling out." Billy hangs his head as the guilt and shame sets in. He has to be honest, as much as possible, if he is going to get through this. "To be honest, I screwed it up between me and her, Isaiah. I don't know where she is, or nothin'." He looks up at the sky as if looking for an easy way out of this. "Basically, I've come home to try and start over, straightening out my life, and my head, so that I can put some roots down." Billy glances over at Isaiah to try to get a read on how the old man would respond. "What wise words do you have for me today, old man?"

Again Isaiah looks around at the buildings as if his mind is occupied with something else. Shaking it off, he refocuses on the conversation, but never turns to face Billy. "Sometimes, a man ain't supposed to change who or what he is. Sometimes you have to stay your course and let things work out, on their own. This thing between you and Taylor will pass. She'll be back and the two of you will move on. You just have to want it enough to recognize the opportunity when it comes around." Isaiah finally turns and looks Billy in the eyes. "Have you talked to your Daddy about this?"

"My father is dead, old man." Billy doesn't mean to sound cross. This is the second topic of conversation that Billy wanted to avoid.

"I know that, but sometimes it's easier to talk everything out with a loved one, even if they don't give you a response." Isaiah steps away from the corral and starts for the barn, "Go see your daddy. I've gotta remember what I did with my apple."

"Ya know what I like about you Isaiah? Your manner is a lot like Morgan Freeman, in the way everything you say comes out sounding profound." Billy turns to acknowledge Isaiah's statement, but the ranch manager was already entering the barn through the side doors. Isaiah's right. He does need to go announce his decision at his father's grave, but first he has another funeral to attend. He feels like a major weight has been lifted from his shoulders. It isn't because of what Isaiah said to him, but more of Billy admitting that he was at fault that made him feel better about his situation. To perpetuate this, Billy declares to himself that the change in his life begins today.

Determined to push forward, Billy heads straight into the house and marches upstairs and into the master bedroom, through the room and into the master closet. Over to the side beneath a supply of unused winter coats, sits a cardboard box. Thrown inside the box in no organized manner, are the rest of Billy's vigilante costumes. Most are blood stained, ripped, and burned, displaying the pain and suffering that he has endured. For a second, he remembers the night when he picked these up from Barbara, at the wrestling school. Then, he is really hit with a slap to his face, when he sees Taylor's outfit at the bottom of the box. Billy pulls it out and looks it over, stopping to stare at the bullet hole and remembers when she was shot. He sees the blood spattered stains from the battle in Stone Mountain Park, serving as reminders of her suffering. So much pain, and so much lost, forever. The time has come to lay it all to rest.

Billy closes the lid and makes his way out of the closet with the box tucked under his arm. As he heads for the bedroom door, he sees the light flashing on his answering machine. He's already convinced that Taylor won't be calling the house any more, but he still goes over to check the message any way.

> "Yo Billy, it's me, Scotty. Hey listen, my roommate said that there were some guys asking about you at my dorm. I guess they were looking for me, but I was in class. Just checking to make sure you and Taylor are alright. Give me a call when you get this, okay? Talk to you later, bro."

It was good to hear Scotty's voice. At least it sounded friendly. He and Billy were close once. Hopefully, Billy's relationship with his foster brother is one that can be salvaged. Still he is slightly disappointed with the message enough to send him on his way without further consideration for what Scotty said in his message. Resuming his task, Billy picks up the box from the bed and walks back downstairs. Just as he exits the back door of the kitchen, the rain sets in again, hurrying his pace across the yard to the barn. The first thing he does is look around for any sign of Isaiah. The last thing Billy wants right now is a round of twenty questions about what's in the box. Without delay, Billy walks right up to the huge iron furnace stationed in the middle of the barn. He opens the heavy door, and with no conscious regret, tosses the box inside. With the door closed, his paranoia causes Billy to quickly look around to see if his actions had been seen. Now he needs to get rid of the evidence. A short trip around the fat belly of the dragon brings him to the furnace controls. After looking over the gauges and switches, Billy decides that it is probably better for him to leave the firing up of the furnace to Isaiah. Besides, he doesn't want to draw any unwanted attention to what he was doing. The old man will come along and light it, sooner or later, to warm up the stables after this rain storm so that the horses don't get damp and sick. That will solve Billy's problem for him, and no one else has to be the wiser. As far as he's concerned, the matter is officially closed for good.

What are you doing back out here, Billy boy?" Isaiah rounds the corner, still looking for his elusive apple, but is surprised to find Billy instead.

"Huh? Oh, I'm just looking the barn over. How is this old place, you know, structurally speaking?" That was quick thinking, Billy. Now you need a reason for asking the question.

Isaiah stares at Billy for a moment, wondering the same thing. "Why, do you plan on selling the ranch?" The concern for Billy's question is showing all over Isaiah's face, even though there is no cause for it, yet.

"Oh, No, no, it's nothing like that! I'm so sorry Isaiah! I surely didn't mean to scare you like that." Good stall tactics, now sound convincing with your alibi. "Actually, I was planning on going up to Atlanta and put my condo up for sale, and was wondering if I could store some of my stuff in this part of the barn."

Isaiah laughs at Billy, assuming the boy was asking him permission. "Hell, Billy, it's your barn. I guess you can do whatever you want with it, as long as it don't interfere with my work." Isaiah looks around Billy searching the shelves behind his employer for the elusive apple. "Hey by the way, did I tell you that my granddaughter was gonna come stay at the ranch for a little while? She needs some space from her mother and grandmother, while she works through her problems."

"No, in fact I don't even remember you asking me about that." This could be detrimental to Billy's plans.

Isaiah scoffs at Billy's comment and starts to walk away. "Like I said, Billy Ray; you don't have to ask me permission, so why should I have to ask you." Isaiah laughs at his response, especially when Billy doesn't see the humor. "Now, what in the hell did I do with that apple?"

Laughing off the old man's comment, Billy hurries back to the house to get out of the next rain shower that was beginning to fall. Okay, so it won't be completely horrible if Saphyre comes to stay at the ranch. Besides, what reflection would it have on his manners for him to turn the girl away? He stops just inside the kitchen door and grabs a coat and a ball cap from the small mud room's hooks, and turns around to leave again. It is then that he sees the stack of mail sitting on the corner of the kitchen cabinet. What caught his eye was a certain envelope bearing the crest of The University of Alabama. Has he really lost touch with everything that means anything to him? Stepping over to the end of the counter, he slips the envelope out of the stack, knowing what is inside. There is a football game this weekend, and he is holding two tickets. Why not? Why not go to the game? It could be a good distraction from the woes plaguing his life right now, and it is something he enjoys, or at least did at one time. It won't cost him anything except gas money. There's no one in his life to contradict his plan. Yes, it's settled. He is going to the football game, and will begin to resume his life with that. What better way could there be to get back into the swing of things, than with the atmosphere of college sports? He'll get a good night's rest, and head out early in the morning to make a day of it. Sunday, he can kick back and watch the Falcons on DirecTV, and wait for Monday to start a new week. Who knows, maybe having Saphyre around for a while will help add some life to the place? He thinks for a second, realizing that it's been six, maybe seven years since he's seen her. Then he remembers what a little bitch she was, at the time. Okay, if the house doesn't liven up, he can leave here and follow up with his plans in Atlanta. The real question should be, is this fate or destiny that is taking him down this path of decisions?

With his collar turned up, Billy sets out through the back door of the kitchen to take the long drive down the 280-bypass, to the Lakewood cemetery. It always seems to be raining when he comes here to see his father. For some reason, it doesn't seem to bother him as much this time. Ducks and geese take to the pond as the low, ominous growl of the Camaro's exhaust startles the water fowl. Billy laughs at the birds, knowing he could really wake the dead, pardon the pun, but he keeps the car at a gentle rumble, to respect the others visiting their lost loved ones. Reaching his father's grave, Billy pulls the car off to the side of the driveway to park, and then climbs out into the rain. On cue, a crack of thunder follows a flash of lightning across the sky. It seemed as if some unspeakable force was trying to awaken the sleeping monster inside of him. Not today, Billy is strong in his decision. He has seen the error of his ways, and hopes that his father will give him another chance to live again.

"Hey Dad, I had to come see you today to tell you that it's over. I can't do this anymore. The cost has become too much for me to bear." Tears begin to roll down his face mixing with the raindrops hitting him. "I tried Dad, really hard, but I can't afford to lose anyone or anything else. I know now that there is no way to beat Callistone. There, I did that for mom, what she said you could never do; I admitted the truth. Now, if she would only answer my phone calls, I would tell her so." Billy wipes the tears and rain from his face as another crack of thunder rolls across the sky. He looks around for a second, and then adjusts his ball cap before facing his father's grave again. "You're gone Dad, and nothing I do is going to bring you back. The only thing this quest for vengeance is going to get me is in a hole next to you. Sorry Dad, but I finally opened my eyes to see that there is still plenty for me to live for, right now. I want that chance to live. If you are listening, I hope you can understand."

Even though it is the right thing for him to do, Billy still feels deep down inside that he has let his father down. Trying to escape the pain of his decision, he spends the rest of the day driving out a tank of gas on the streets of Phenix City and Columbus. With nothing better to do, and plenty of time to kill, he figured that he should at least reacquaint himself with his new hometown area. To wrap up the day, Billy winds up down at the Chattahoochee River where he sits along the river's edge at the base of the old damn for the textile mills across the river in Georgia. He spends the time watching the men fishing out on the rocks for their evening meals, wondering if his life could ever be that simple again. Then he wonders if it ever was. Billy remembers back to when he was a kid, when the river's water level was twenty feet deeper where the men were fishing. Now days, the mighty Chattahoochee is but a trickle of its former self.

There are some things around here that will never change, and then there are some things that are constantly moving forward, as an example of life moving on. Across the river, the magnificent and old textile mills are being converted into living spaces consisting of lofts and condos, giving new life to the ancient buildings. There is a similar restructuring that must take place in Billy's life if he is to move forward. Like the old 14th Street bridge, Billy must close the past so he can move on with his future, but like the old bridge, it will remain as part of the landscape, to serve as a reminder of what was.

The sun drops below the horizon with the twilight setting in. Billy pulls himself up off the cold concrete and makes his way up to the river walk, a public parks path that runs the banks of the river. Once in the parking lot beside his car, Billy looks around still holding onto the feeling of being unsure about what his next move should be for his life. In the mean time, his empty stomach votes for food. With no reason to dispute his body's needs, Billy jumps into the car, and takes off for the 280-bypass. After two stops, one for a sack of Krystal cheeseburgers and the other at a convenience store for a two liter bottle of Mountain Dew, he heads for home with good intentions to restart his life and existence.

At first, the night started out alright. While eating his dinner, Billy tested his knowledge by watching Alex Trebek and Jeopardy, with the first six small burgers devoured. Then, he finished off the other six while laughing at Jon Stewart and Steven Colbert on Comedy Central. After that was when the night started to turn sour for Billy. All he wanted was some restful sleep, even though he couldn't force himself to sleep in his own bed. What he received instead was one nightmarish episode after the next, with a couple sending him rolling off the plush sofa of the family room. This continues until he awakes to find himself sitting up in the middle of the floor, soaking wet with sweat.

It's the middle of the night now, and his mind is a blur, trying to figure out what it all meant. The first thing he needs to do is get up and walk out the front door onto the porch for some cool air. Is this what's in store for him every night? The images of Taylor, Callistone, and all of the others crowd his mind and haunt his thoughts. How can he look to the future when the ghosts of his past cloud his vision? The strain of it all is too much for Billy to bear at the moment, so he does what any sane man would do. He breaks down and cries.

Chapter V

In New York, a few hours ago...

Alone man walks south through the lower west side, always staying to the shadows, trying to be as inconspicuous as possible. Finally, he has received valuable news and information that he has waited for almost fifteen years. His cloak and dagger actions are strictly for personal safety, after what has happened tonight. His name is Special Agent Jonathan Justice, of the Bureau's Organized Crime Task force.

Earlier tonight, he received a phone call from an informant, who said that he had breaking news about Agent Justice's "special case", and that they had to meet immediately to pass the information along. For Jonathan, this was too big for him to pass up, and agreed to make the meeting. There was no way that either man could have known that it was a set up. Jonathan passes the time blaming himself for Ronnie's death, while traversing the enemy territory. Of course, he has no way of knowing that Ronnie blew his own cover, snooping around the Callistone estate, while the mob boss was out of town. Still, the Bureau's loss did not occur without positive results, no matter how small or insignificant.

The information he delivered to Jonathan may help the FBI Agent end a vendetta that has been stored away in the back of Jonathan's mind, for all of this time.

Ronnie was tired of the undercover work and was beginning to suffer from paranoia that his cover had been compromised, and wanted out of his assignment. Knowing Jonathan as close as he did, Ronnie figured this information would be a good bargaining chip for Jonathan to pull some strings for him. Ronnie was right about the information. Unfortunately, Ronnie Bradford's death is just another secret that Jonathan Justice will have to learn to live with for the rest of his life.

The reason this meeting was set up on the spur of the moment tonight, was because Ronnie had been instructed to drive Sal Gambenni home from his meeting with Margaret Stanford. Ronnie saw this as the first opportunity away from Callistone's people that would allow him to meet with Jonathan with no one wise to his actions. Jonathan arrived at the designated meeting place, deep in the middle of Gambenni's territory. The information was exchanged without a hitch, with Justice more than happy with what he was given. As he climbed back into his car, he looked back at his friend just in time to see Ronnie being pulled from the limousine by a very large black man. Then, if that wasn't bad enough, the attacker's associates opened fire on Jonathan's car and sending him fleeing on foot. The last time anyone saw Ronnie Bradford, he was being shoved into the back of a black sedan, never to be seen again.

As for Jonathan, if he can safely maneuver his way out of this part of town, he can finally move forward with righting the wrong that changed his life so many years ago. But to do this, he will have to alienate himself from his job and his partner. The last thing he wants to do is jeopardize another partner's career. Walter McBride was lucky to only be transferred, the last time Jonathan's off the clock activities got him, and Walter, in hot water. Pete Del Gato has a promising career ahead of him, and doesn't deserve to be dragged down with Jonathan. Already, his personal crusade against Callistone has Del Gato asking too many questions. This personal matter is even further outside the box.

For thirteen years, he has lived with this deep down desire for this day to come. When no one else seemed to care enough, Jonathan carried the torch. Sure, he has moved on with his life, doing his best to raise his teen age daughter, on his own. What happened years ago would have pushed most people away from society, but Jonathan stayed with the Bureau and picked up the pieces. He had a job to do, upholding the law and protecting the innocent. But that doesn't mean that he didn't hold on to hope, that one day the betrayer of men would cross his path again. If and when that happened, Jonathan would be ready.

Suddenly, a car pulls up in front of Jonathan, startling him for a second. Relief comes quickly when he realizes that it's his partner. He may have decided to keep Del Gato clear of his special case, but that didn't mean that a rescue ride was out of the question. "Man, I am so glad to see you, Pete." Jonathan opens the passenger side car door and climbs into the warmth of the interior.

"What in the hell happened to you tonight?" Del Gato steps on the gas and heads the car towards Queens. "How many times have I told you that this personal vendetta against Callistone is going to get you killed?"

Relax, Pete, this wasn't about Callistone, tonight. But you're right. I have been pushing myself a little too hard lately, and I've decided to take the boss's suggestion and use some of my time I have built up. After tonight, I feel like I could use some alone time to clear my head." Jonathan sits back in the seat and tries to relax a little, finally realizing how lucky he really was tonight. He can't tell Pete about Ronnie's demise, and keeping something like that hidden is killing the veteran agent inside.

The rest of the ride into Queens is quiet between the two men until Del Gato pulls up in front of Jonathan's home. "I sure wish you would tell me what's going on. If something big is going down with Callistone, I deserve to know about it. I am your partner after all, God Damnit."

"Pete, you've got to believe me, when I say that this has nothing to do with Callistone." Jonathan starts to get out of the car, only to be stopped by his partner, who grabs Jonathan's arm. "Come on, Pete, don't do this right now. I'm cold, tired, and just want to go to bed, okay?"

"Don't give me that shit, Jon! You call me from the heart of Sal Gambenni's domain, begging for help, and then have the audacity to tell me that your sudden change of heart has nothing to do with Callistone's activities? You've got to give me more credit than that, Jon. After all, I am a detective by trade."

Jonathan hangs his head and sits back down in the seat before closing the car door. Turning to face his partner, Jon tries his best to be convincing. "Listen Pete, you have to believe me when I say that this is old history coming back around. If you want to help, check in on Kaitlyn for me, while I'm gone. I don't expect her home much, but keep an eye on her for me when you can." Jonathan looks over at Del Gato one more time as if he had something else to say, or confess. After a second or two, he just shakes his head and offers his partner a handshake, "Thanks Pete, for everything. Hopefully, when all of this is over, we can go back to tracking down ordinary criminals."

Chapter VI

The betrayer is introduced…

Billy Ray McBride?" Isaiah's granddaughter, Saphyre Colton, crunches through the frozen blades of grass in the front yard of the McBride home, surprised to find the man of the house sitting on the porch swing asleep. The air is crisp and clean from the rain, but the frosty chill that set in overnight left everything around the house covered in a crystalline glaze. "Man, you must have really tied one on last night, to pass out here on the front porch! Aren't you freezing?" She looks around and wonders how often this sort of thing happens.

Opening one eye, Billy sees the young woman of African American descent standing in front of him. Realizing that he's outside, and wearing only his boxers, Billy tries to sit up and find some measure of modesty and composure by covering his lap with one of the swing's pillows. In doing so, he knocks over an empty bottle of Patron, sending the container skipping across a couple of the porch floor planks. Needless to say, this only adds to his embarrassment for the situation. Most people tend to get a little rowdy when they drink too much tequila. For Billy, it's a case of where two negatives make a positive and calm him down. The downside is when he wakes up in the morning to deal with the aftereffects. He never gets drunk, but he always seems to have a hangover the next day. "Oh crap, I can't believe that it's morning already." Billy stands up and staggers a couple of steps before he gets his footing. "Well, come on in, there's no reason why the both of us should be out here freezing to death."

Into the house he wobbles, gently brushing his shoulder against the door jamb, altering his course towards the stairs. "Ignore the mess on the floor in there; I'll clean it up in a little while." How bad does this look for him? No one really knows what he's going through right now, so there is no justification for his actions to be offered. This makes him even more self conscious about being found on the front porch, by someone he barely knows. Before heading upstairs, Billy looks over his shoulder and says, "Do us a favor, and don't say anything to your grandpa about me being out there on the porch, okay? I just had a bad night, that's all. I don't want him to start worrying about me again." As Billy's head begins to clear, he looks back at Saphyre surprised at how much she has grown up. "How long has it been since I've seen you?"

"Too long, based on what I'm seeing." Saphyre is suddenly overwhelmed by the embarrassment of speaking the words out loud. "Uh, nine years; you pushed me out of the tree house and in to the pond below, scaring me to death. Grandpa was so mad at you!" The young lady begins to laugh recalling the incident.

To ease the tension between him and her, Billy heads on upstairs to put on some clothes. "I remember that," he replies through the open bedroom door. "As I recall, it was your first swimming lesson, and we spent the rest of the day climbing the tree and jumping back into the water." Exiting the bedroom, his attire is now more appropriate for the company of a young lady. Heading back downstairs, he finds

Saphyre in the family room, getting started on the clean up detail of Billy's last night's meal. Embarrassed to have someone cleaning up after him, Billy rushes over and grabs the empty bag to collect Saphyre's collection of burger boxes and napkins. "So, how long are you gonna be here?"

Saphyre looks at Billy, as if feeling that she was imposing on him. "I'm not putting you out, am I? Grandpa said that it would be alright. I hope he didn't overstep any boundaries, did he?"

"Oh God, no; you and your grandparents are as much a part of this place, and the family, as I am, if not more. Besides, what kind of guy would I be, to have all of this space and not offer you a room?" He rolls up the top of the full bag of trash and then tosses it into the kitchen.

"A jerk, that likes to push little girls out of trees." Saphyre reaches out and gives Billy a friendly punch to his shoulder, aggravating one of his many wounds he received in Miami. "So, what have you been up to, Billy Ray?" Giving his bicep a little squeeze, she's impressed by the muscle tone.

Billy slips away from Saphyre and starts for the stairs. "Listen; like I said a few minutes ago, I had a bad night last night. Make yourself at home, Saphyre. My home is your home as long as you need refuge from your grandmother. I'm gonna go take a shower and try to bring myself back to life. I've got a busy day today, so I'll talk to you later on, okay?"

Saphyre calls up to him as he reaches the top of the stairs, "Grandma said that you have a new girlfriend. Is there a chance that I'll get to meet her? Better yet, maybe I could steal her away one afternoon for some quality girl time." Right away, Saphyre sees the pain associated with her question all over Billy's face, as he turns around at the top of the stairs.

"Like I said, it was a bad night." Billy rolls his head from side to side, trying to realign his neck, before heading off to the master bathroom.

"Okay, but if you want to talk, I'll be around, okay?" She watches as Billy closes the master bedroom doors, wondering how and if she should take that as an answer. Trying to make the best of the situation, she heads back into the family room and turns on the TV.

The hot water running over his body slowly begins to melt away the numbing cold that set into his muscles overnight. Still, there was no way to wash away the memories of last night's dreams. This is going to be harder than he thought. Sooner or later, these memories will fade. The question in his mind now is whether or not he really wants to let go. Somehow, he will have to continue to move on the best way he knows how, until he can figure it all out.

With the hot water going cold, Billy shuts off the shower, and walks out into the bathroom without drying off. It's a shameful habit, but what does he care. There isn't anyone who can see him. Exiting the large bathroom, Billy is left feeling no different than when he entered, except for the fact that he was warmer now. What he needs is a hobby. Sitting down on the end of his bed, Billy wonders how one goes about selecting a hobby. What he needs is something to occupy his time, and his thoughts. Most hobbies are born from a personal love for something. Billy has dedicated time to two things in his young adult life; school to follow in his father's footsteps, and his quest for Callistone. His brief wrestling career was fun, but it wasn't a hobby.

The front door closes downstairs, causing Billy to jump up, hoping to see Taylor standing at the bottom of the stairs. Instead, it was Saphyre, who had gone out to gather her bags from the front porch, where she had left them. Why does he do this? He knows that Taylor is gone for good, so why does he continue to torture himself with this false hope that she is going to return? It's because that deep down inside he knows that he screwed up big time, and there is no way he can deny fault. Around and around it goes driving him insane.

Sitting back down on the bed, Billy decides to begin his self administered therapy. To do so, he needs to determine a beginning point for reference. Where did everything go terribly wrong? That one is easy for Billy to figure out. It was at his father's funeral when he made the stupid vow to exact his revenge against Antonio Callistone. The specific moment was when he turned away from Barbara. He could have taken her in his arms and accepted her love and companionship, and moved on with his life. Nick Landry told Billy about how a person has to move on after the loss of a loved one, or that person would die inside as well. Billy thought he could just put his life on hold while he took on this crusade, and then pick up the pieces when he was done. Had he accepted the first choice, he would've never had to watch Barbara lose her life when she was gunned down. Of course, he never would have met Taylor, if he was in a serious relationship with Bobby Sox, either. He laughs to himself remembering Barbara's ring name. The thought of never meeting Taylor is a disappointing one, but if he hadn't, she wouldn't be homeless right now, trying to sort out her life. Taking a few seconds out of his plans, Billy grabs his phone and calls his mother's number. But, like all the other two hundred thousand attempts, she doesn't answer. The last time she wouldn't talk to him like this, lasted for almost two weeks.

Too many have died, and too many have suffered, for Billy not to take this course of action. The decision is already made. Now he just has to move on with it. Suffer what you must, Billy Ray McBride. You owe that much to all of those who have suffered because of you. This doesn't mean that he shouldn't be entitled to a chance at starting over. Monday, he will begin his extraction from Atlanta. If Callistone wants it, he can have it. Detective Trey Simon gave Billy's alter ego some good advice, once. Billy is going to take it to heart. Today, he's going to the football game. Looking out the window, he's happy to see that the skies were clearing up. Wanting to be optimistic, he hopes that all of the skies in his world will clear up the same way. With his mind made up, Billy stands up off the bed and looks at his reflection in the dresser mirror. "You can do this, right?" A tilt of the brim of his hat answers the question. "Hopefully it will be a good game. The team needs to really show up today if they want to redeem their season," he says, talking to his reflection.

For a split second, Billy thinks he saw the faint reflection of a woman's face in the mirror. He shakes it off, chalking it up to one of the ghosts of the house, and then leaves the room, not wanting any of his mind games to deter his decision. As his therapist, Billy prescribes a road trip for the game, and it is to begin immediately, hoping the open road would clear his mind. He's bound to run into some of his old friends, from before the Taylor era, which would help keep his mind on track, and off his troubles.

Down the stairs and out the kitchen door he goes, before Saphyre even realizes that he has left his room. He wasn't trying to be rude. Billy was just wanted to avoid the uncomfortable position of not offering her the other ticket. No offense to Saphyre, but private company is not what Billy needs right now. Besides, she's almost four years younger than him. How much could they have in common? No, a solo run at this is what's best for him. If nothing else, he doesn't have to worry about having a breakdown in front of somebody.

Heading out to the first stable, where he parks his Camaro, he sees Isaiah out in the pasture, trying to flag Billy down. Ignoring the old man's call, Billy jumps into his car and drives the hot rod out nice and easy. As he pulls out onto the main road from his driveway, Billy begins his form of silent, positive, reinforcement, trying to psych himself out for the day's events. Deep down inside, he really wants this to work. Better yet, it has to work, if he is ever going to have some kind of future. So focused on his thoughts, Billy doesn't see the black SUV driving down the road from the opposite direction. Most people would be suspicious about its plain black paint job and pitch black windows, but Billy doesn't even know that it exists. By the time it reaches the driveway of Billy's ranch, he is already pulling out onto the 280-bypass, out of sight of the SUV, and vice versa. "Okay, here we go to have some fun," He says trying to convince himself that it's really going to happen. Deep down inside, Billy wishes that he could be a little more convincing.

Chapter VII

And so the power of a child shall be introduced to the fold…

Saturday afternoon in New York; there isn't much to do for a young ambitious girl on a chilly afternoon. Nothing for a girl to do that a teenager can do with a father who is attached to her hip, that is. "Ya know, Jonathan, you're a real buzz kill." In this duplex home of Federal Agent Jonathan Justice, there is always an overwhelming occupancy of stressful situations. As if tracking down dangerous criminals wasn't enough, Jonathan has the privilege of facing the struggles of being a single parent raising a teenage daughter. At the moment, his current issue is young Kaitlyn Justice sitting on the edge of her father's bed, trying to rekindle an ongoing debate. "What is it with you, Jonathan? When are you going to drop this chauvinistic attitude and face the fact that I can help you?"

When are you going to learn that no matter how hard you try to break me down, I'm never going to let you go with me? On a more personal note, why is it so hard for you to call me dad, or pops?" Jonathan slams the closet door out of frustration and turns around to face Kaitlyn. Startled by the slamming of the door, Kaitlyn leaps up to the ceiling where she seems to defy gravity. Of course, her father sees this as her displaying her immaturity, as usual. "Quit clowning around and get down here, now!" He walks over to his bedroom desk and grabs his coat, and a small notebook that he shoves into his coat pocket. Nonchalantly, Kaitlyn drops back down to the surface of the plush mattress. With a well positioned bounce, she lands on the floor to stand right in front of her father. "Listen to me, young lady, because I don't want to say this again. I promised your mother that I would make sure that you finished school and did something with your life. What I'm going to do is not what she had in mind."

"Wanna know what I think? I think both of you can kiss my white butt. Tell me something, Jonathan; is she controlling you from the grave, or has she just possessed your body? Ya know; you have been acting like a puss lately." Kaitlyn frames Jonathan inside her fingers trying to picture him wearing one of her mother's dresses. "Why won't you give me a chance? What if I called you dad? Would you let me go with you then?"

"No. I had to stand over your mother's grave because she felt some uncontrollable urge to put herself in harm's way, saving others. I won't stand over your grave for the same reasons." He turns to face his impetuous daughter, hoping she would be reasonable. "You have a chance to live a normal life, Kaitlyn. There is no law that says you have to put your life in jeopardy, just because you have abnormal abilities."

Stomping off to the kitchen, Kaitlyn grabs a can of soda from the fridge. "So tell me, father, are you going to keep me in the dark about where you are going, or will you at least give me an emergency number, in case I get scared at night?" She exits the kitchen just in time to see Jonathan standing at the front door.

"Oh, don't give me that crap. We both know that you are capable of taking care of yourself for a day or so. Besides, if you need anything, you can always give Pete a call." Jonathan grabs his bag and then sets it back down. "Hey, I know; when I get through with this, you and I can head upstate for a few days. Your mother loved it up there in the country," he adds, while heading towards the restroom.

This is the moment that she has waited for, just about all evening. Kaitlyn knew that her father wouldn't leave the house without making a pitstop first. With her cell phone in hand, Kaitlyn grabs her dad's notebook from his coat and begins to snap off photos of each page, as fast as she can. The sound of the toilet flushing warns her that time was up. With the notebook returned to its proper place, she moves back over across the room as Jonathan swings the bathroom door open. "Just in time, as usual," she thinks to herself, as he walks back into the room. Now she can resume her debate about wanting to help. "By the way, you and mom never took me to do anything like that. You were always off on one of your cases, while mommy dearest was wrapped up with those rocket boys at Darkside Command. I, on the other hand, spent many a miserable day with my loving sister, in upstate New York with dear ol' Aunt Syla and Uncle Jude. Were your parents as whacked out as those two are? Because I'm thinking that it might explain some of your little eccentricities."

"Alright, to be honest with you, I have a lead on the man that is responsible for your mother's death. If I'm right, there is no way I'm taking you with me." Jonathan grabs his things and looks back at Kaitlyn one more time.

Kaitlyn steps in front of the doorway, hoping to delay her father long enough to change his mind. "Come on, Dad, Daddy, Daddy-o, let me go with you. If this guy really is responsible for mom's death, then I should have some stake in this as well. I won't get in the way, I promise." To prove her point, Kaitlyn scurries up the wall and stops above the door, stating her case, and giving Jonathan a clear path out the door.

What was he thinking, when he told her about the man known as Crossfire coming to town? Obviously, he was thinking at that specific moment, about anything to get her off his back. "Kaitlyn, damn it now, I don't have time for this! Get off the wall and get off my back! That's my final word." He grabs his coat and stares at her for a second, before shaking his head and walking out the front door. Why can't you act like a normal teenager?"

"Yes, but is that your final answer?" Kaitlyn follows Jonathan out into the cold to continue the discussion on the front stoop. His response is just a look, but it's enough to tell her that her conversation is over. "Ya know what? You take the fun outta everything! So, I guess there's nothing else to do, but lay around and act like all of the other teenage girls, getting pregnant and strung out on dope. Would that be a little more normal for you? She tries to ignore the neighbors on the street, who disapproved of Kaitlyn's remark. Of course, the fact that she made the proclamation out in public, while wearing a t-shirt and boxers gives her no grounds for defense. "I was meant for more than this, Jonathan!" After watching Jonathan walk off down the street, she flips him the middle finger and walks back into the house. Her mind is already made up about what she was going to do, whether father dear likes it or not.

She believes, deep down inside, that she was meant for something bigger. In fact, it is that belief that has caused her so much grief in her life. It's the reason she has pushed her father to the breaking point time and time again, and it's the reason she is doing what she's doing now. Rushing into her room, multitasking, Kaitlyn emails the pictures to herself, and grabs her laptop computer and turns it on. While she waits for the system to boot, Kaitlyn uses the cell phone her father gave her, the one that has the hidden GPS sensor, and calls her best friend. She is disappointed that she gets Toby's voice mail, but knows that he's at home. He'll get the message long before she gets there, just like he always does. "Hey, Toby, call the gang and tell them to meet us at your place. I'll see you in a few minutes." She hangs up the phone and tosses it over onto her bed. That way if daddy dear checks on her whereabouts, he'll see her phone right there in her room.

The "you've got mail" announcer sounds off on her computer, alerting her that the photos had arrived on her email. Her next task, with a couple of entries and a click of the mouse, sends the photos to her printer, while she gathers her most important accessory; her costume. More than anything, she wants to wear the costume. With her mom holding her position with Darkside Command, and Kaitlyn's own abilities manifesting in her, wearing the costume is more important to her than preventing crime. Yes, she is a superhero nerd, and has been most of her life, which is why she has longed for the opportunity to be seen as more than a teenager. The only thing standing in her way is dear ol' dad, but what he doesn't know, won't hurt him. In fact, it could work out to where her efforts help him, or at least prove that she is capable of helping. Jonathan Justice only thinks that he is keeping secrets from her. Kaitlyn knows that whatever he's doing, it isn't under FBI jurisdiction. This gives her an edge for her defense, should anything go wrong, that her actions are technically no different from his own, and that she was simply following his lead. He can have his secrets, if he wants. Kaitlyn has her secrets as well, and if she sticks to her plan, Jonathan will never be the wiser. With the copies of her father's notes in hand, and dressed in grey and red spandex, she's ready to prove Jonathan and the rest of the world wrong about her.

Out her bedroom she goes, taking to the night air of the rooftops for her means of travel. Scurrying up the wall of her house, she finds her playground empty of watchful eyes. Without any worry or hesitation, Kaitlyn leaps to the roof of the tenement building across the street, a hundred feet away. This is her gift, her abnormality; the ability to defy gravity. It stems from her mother's side of the family; however, Kaitlyn's psychic ability is quite unique compared to her mother, and sister's, which is to heal the wounded. It was this "gift" that got Julie recruited into DSC's covert ops teams. Jonathan is the one who decided to hold Kaitlyn back, not allowing her to pursue her abilities the way her mother and sister did. It is Kaitlyn's ability to defy gravity that could make her a viable commodity to one government agency, or another. Thus, the ability to leap great distances and climb on walls, but untrained and ignorant about her true abilities, Kaitlyn simply believes her power to be an example of mind over matter. Sure, she is right in most aspects, but she is far more powerful than she realizes. Believing that he has somehow succeeded in his efforts, Jonathan's next worry to conquer is that he fears Kaitlyn's excessive use of her power, could manifest itself into something she can't handle.

Kaitlyn doesn't worry about none of that. She is head strong, fearless, and a teen who has everything under control. Step one of her glorious plan is to get over to Toby's house as fast as she can, and show him the information she stole from her dad. That way, they can plan their next move when Henry and Amanda show up. You see, one of Kaitlyn's secrets is her friendship with three other teens, who roam the rooftops with her. Together, the four young adults have formed an alliance, due to their mutual aspirations for notoriety and fame. They search the nights for any signs of trouble. Wanting to join the superhero ranks, they have already faced off against some of New York's more common riff raff, but nothing big time yet.

Every night, Kaitlyn prays for her big chance. You should be careful what you wish for.

The last step of her plan is to convince her friends that this is their big opportunity to make a name for themselves, without selling out to the likes of Darkside Command. She's no longer the little girl that Jonathan still sees, when he looks at her. The time has come for her to take the role as leader of this motley little team, and lead them into the spotlight. Toby shouldn't be too hard to win over. Locking him down with a yes vote first will better her odds in winning over Amanda and Henry. They may still be a little sore at Kaitlyn for the result of their last escapade, but Kaitlyn knows how to butter them up. They've all come too far together to back down now.

She stops and stands at the edge of the roof's parapet wall and takes in a deep breath of cool night air. Everything coming together like this gives her confidence. Soon, she will see herself on the news, just like her heroes and idols, saving the day. With her head full of fanciful thoughts, Kaitlyn takes off again on a path well traveled. A strong leap sends her high into the air above the street life, with her target being a billboard on the roof of the building across the street. Focused on her happy thoughts, she's suddenly caught off guard by the sudden attack from a flock of pigeons, exiting the framework of the sign.

Instead of landing on the catwalk of the billboard with the grace of a butterfly, Kaitlyn hits the corrugated metal like an Albatross, and then rolls right off the side. Confidence quickly turns to panic as she reaches out to grab the metal walkway before plummeting to the street below. This fear of falling stems from an episode a few years ago, when she missed a landing and fell twenty feet. Breaking both of her legs, an arm, and a hip, is something that stays with a person for a while. The sudden confusion, coupled with the fear of falling blocked her abilities to control her descent. It's the one thing that she hasn't mastered yet.

At the moment, it is the pain in her arm and shoulder, coupled with the panic and anxiety of the incident that prevents her from using her power. Looking down at the street below, Kaitlyn seriously doubts that she could survive the twelve story drop. Unable to focus enough, her only other choice is to try and climb up. Tears stream down her face as she struggles to get a good finger hold with her strong arm. One thing is for sure; she's happy that her outfit includes gloves, as she feels the squishing of bird droppings between her fingers. She looks up at the pitch black sky and asks the question, "really?" Making herself laugh at the situation breaks her panic mode, and with her weight supported by her good arm, Kaitlyn is able to regain her focus. After lifting herself back up onto the catwalk, she takes a minute to catch her breath while she stares at the building across the street. From her higher perch, she can't see any movement on the rooftop. "Well, they're either already here, or haven't made it yet."

After wiping the cold sweat from her brow, and a couple of deep cleansing breaths, she looks herself over to make sure everything is intact. Her shoulder is sore beyond belief, but there doesn't appear to be any serious damage. With one more deep breath, she launches herself across the street to the lower roof where she lands flawlessly, as if the previous incident never occurred. Across the roof deck she bounds, until she reaches Toby's sanctuary, a rooftop pigeon coop. "Toby, are you here yet?" She hurries in and out the oversized birdcage looking for her friend, and wondering why he's a no show.

"You're three minutes late," Toby declares, walking out of the shadows of the nearby air conditioning units. "Listen, if you're going to keep wasting my time like this, you're gonna have to add more minutes to my phone plan." The young man steps up in front of Kaitlyn and plucks a stray feather from her hair, "Tell me something, Cricket, why do you keep pushing this?"

Kaitlyn ignores the question and looks around expecting the other two of their foursome to walk up any second. "Toby, didn't you call Henry and Amanda?"

He stares at her for a second and then shakes his head with disgust. Walking into the pigeon coop, he reluctantly admits, "I sure do wish you would listen to me, every once in a while." He, like the others, is through with Kaitlyn's grand illusion. Toby finds the nerve, and then turns to face his friend again. "Amanda and Henry are gone, Kaitlyn. Did you really think that I was joking when I told you the court threw the book at them? It's all your fault, Cricket. You wouldn't listen to me, and then you took off leaving them behind to take the heat." His tone is angry towards her, and justifiably so, after years of friendly abuse. "It's over Kaitlyn. This little fantasy of yours has run its course. You'd know that if you listened to us for once."

Kaitlyn is shocked and overwhelmed by the tone of Toby's voice. How dare her best friend speak to her like that? She's the one who kept her stupid modeling career to fund their little expeditions. She's the one who got them their leads by rifling through her father's case files. "Now you hold on there a minute, Toby. The three of you were all too willing to jump onto the band wagon when it pulled out. Honestly, I don't know what everyone is getting all worked up over. If you really think about it, they owe me. If it wasn't for me, they would have never been discovered!"

"Don't you mean arrested?" Toby can't believe her obtuse outlook for the situation. "If you really think that Amanda and Henry owe you some kinda debt of gratitude, then you have lost your freakin' mind!" Unable to breathe, Toby pushes his way out of the coop to get outside for fresher air. "Because both of them lived on the streets, the courts gave them the option of serving with Darkside Command, or twenty years in the state pen. All because they wouldn't rat us out. Oh, by the way, the salaries that they should earn are being paid to the courts for their restitution. If anything, they owe your father for getting them the alternative to prison. Other than that, neither one of them wants to have anything to do with YOU, ever again." He leans up against an air conditioning unit and stares back at Kaitlyn with a concerned expression. "Cricket, no, I won't call you that any more. Kaitlyn, I've been your friend since the second grade, and I will continue to be from here on out. But, as far as us going out on any more of your cases, we're done."

Toby's played his hand, telling Kaitlyn where he stands. Where they go from here is obviously up to her. It's not exactly what she wanted to hear, but Kaitlyn hopes that she can turn it around one more time. "Come on, Toby, just one more time, for old time's sake? I've got some killer stuff from my dad, on a huge case he's working. This is all off the record, so we don't have to worry about the authorities, this time."

"That's the proof I needed! You have lost your ever lovin' mind!" Toby gives her a double take, wondering how she could possibly be so thick headed. "Kaitlyn, if you think I'm gonna risk any involvement with your dad, you're insane. No, Kaitlyn, I'm done. Do you get it? Go home, Kaitlyn; it's the best and smartest thing you can do." He starts for the roof access door, hating himself for the way he talked to her, but she needed to hear it.

"So, what, are you just going to walk off and leave me?"

"Let's just say that I'm not fond of stepping on your father's toes, fearing that he might try to kick one of those size twelves up my butt. You go through with this, Kaitlyn, and I'll retract my earlier statement, and cut our ties right here, for good." He opens the access door, and then looks back at her one more time, feeling like a total heel. Part of him wants to run back over to her and give it one last try, but this is how it has to be. The alternative is to make a silent exit and let her make the choice.

"I guess I am all alone," she admits, watching Toby enter the building. Well, she'll have to come up with a new plan. Pulling the papers from the waistband of her outfit, Kaitlyn thinks hard about her next move. She better make sure that she covers her ass, but good, because there won't be anyone to save it any more. She looks at the papers, and then rolls her shoulder to test its limits. Tomorrow, she'll rest her arm and come up with another plan, to give this one more try. One thing is for sure. This little revelation of Toby's changes everything.

Chapter VIII

As the fold grows, strength is added to the light over darkness…

Jefferson David Johnston is trying to get back into the swing of life. After the past few weeks of chaotic lunacy, he would give anything for a year of solitude. He honestly believes that it would take that long to completely comprehend everything that happened to him. First, he was kidnapped and taken half way around the world to be held for ransom. The person responsible for paying that ransom was JD's friend, and former martial arts instructor, Nickolas Landry. His friend came through, obviously, saving JD's life, by freeing him from the maniacal aggressors that held him captive. Nick's reward for this act of honor was implications of murderous deeds, and accusations of criminal conduct. JD followed Nick's command and moved on from Florida, to start his life in college. The last he heard, Nick had vanished, escaping from jail and was now on the run from the Federal and local authorities. His information source is the same people that are hunting for Nick. Since he arrived in Auburn Alabama six days ago, JD has already been visited by two sets of FBI agents, some bozos who claimed to represent

Darkside Command and several other officers from state and local authorities. At the moment, JD doesn't even know if his best friend is alive, or not. Nick said that when the time was right, they would see each other again.

At first, when JD was returned to Florida from Japan, he thought that all of the madness was over. Then, when word got out that Nick had escaped custody, everybody came running to JD for answers. This obviously put a strain on JD's relationship with his aunt and uncle, prompting him to leave for college a week early. He should have known that it wouldn't be as easy as he was lead to believe. His own father has recently forbid him from even contacting his mother. All of this adds up to enough to make JD consider disappearing, the same way Nick did. Everywhere he goes, there is that feeling following him around, as if someone is monitoring his every move. Still, even with the irritations being added to JD's life from outside influences, he's got to admit that he is better off than Nick. At least JD only has people watching him as he wanders through life, instead of hunting him down. Of course, the dream he had the other night still doesn't sit well with him. In a way, it was kind of spooky. JD was visited in this dream by his sensei's master, Hiro Masamoto. The spooky part is that Masamoto has been dead for over five years, and JD has never met the man. This vision of a stranger spoke to JD, as if he they had known each other his entire life. Masamoto said to JD in his humble tone, "Your destiny awaits you, student of Landry. Become the conscience of the one who will betray the world." It was enough to wake him up, right away. JD's only explanation for the dream was his thoughts being fixed on Nick so much that his mind created the images from his past. Still, there was that one time when Nick showed JD a moment back in time, when Masamoto bowed to the young man, who wasn't there. Could this be a connection? There's no need for JD to go off on some wild tangent again, about helping Nick with his crusade. JD has enough on his plate to worry about.

Focusing on the start of his new life in college hasn't been an easy thing to do, after all that he's been through. His arrival at Auburn was an event in itself. First, the worn out junker of a Volvo station wagon that his uncle gave him, broke down twice on the way from Miami, and then again in front of the Dean's office. Second, he was early arriving, and almost didn't have a place to stay, but a room opened up in his dorm, at the last minute. Sleeping in his car outside the Dean's office, he found it curious that he received the phone call about the dorm room; after two mysterious men exit the building wearing traditional government issued black suits. And to top it all off, for the past two days it seems like it has rained nonstop, which hampered his daily training and running time. Basically, not much has gone right for JD, but he can't deny that it could be worse. At least the skies seemed to have cleared up for the time being.

Today was kind of crazy around the dorm. JD had never experienced a rivalry like the one that exists between Auburn and the University of Alabama. His roommate had an extra ticket and offered it to JD, so that he could experience the full effect of the "Iron Bowl" game. The atmosphere around campus was buzzing this morning, and he really thought that going to the game would be a great way to acclimate himself to college life, and meet some new friends. Unfortunately, JD's roommate and friends were more of the party crowd than JD expected. It didn't take him long before he alienated himself away from the party crowd and watched the end of the game from the tunnel. By the time the game clock reached double zeroes, he was already in his car headed back to campus.

All in all, the game was great, but with Auburn winning, and JD wearing his school colors, he felt like a lone soldier trying to get out from behind enemy lines, as he drove through Tuscaloosa. The rest of his drive home was turning out to be even less enjoyable. This car of his has given him nothing but trouble, since the day he left Florida. He's already sank all of his money in it to keep it running, so he can't afford to buy another car. Of course, to keep with tradition, the Volvo decides to die, twenty miles from JD's dorm and school, out in the middle of nowhere. "No, no, no," he shouts as the car putts to a stop just over the rise of a hill. "Come on you piece of shit! Don't do this to me tonight!" JD pounds his fist against the dash to express his distaste for the situation, as the car's muffler exhales one last puff of grey smoke to state its own. This car is so worn out, that it wouldn't even roll further down the hill in front of him. Recognizing the danger of the situation, JD jumps out to try and push the car off the road. "Of course, why break down in town, when you can do it out here in the middle of God's country."

JD just stares out the windshield at the dark road in front of him. He sits there for a minute or two, and then tries to start the engine again. His effort is useless as the rest of the cars systems suddenly start to shut down one by one, until JD is left sitting in the dark. "Damn!" He climbs out of the car and walks around to the front and raises the hood. JD might not know what he is looking for, but he gives the engine compartment a thorough inspection any way. Basically, his diagnosis is that the car has died. "Well, someone take down the time of death and tag the body."

A glow of headlights coming over the rise in the road catches JD's attention. Looking over the hood of his car, he sees a truck load of rednecks rolling up over the hill. He figures that they are probably like him, returning from the game. The problem is that these aren't your typical good ol' boys that you'd see at the Piggly Wiggly, unless they're robbing it. No, these men are mean, ignorant, and always looking for some kind of trouble. Tonight they are in luck finding JD on the side of the road, and it doesn't matter to them who won or lost the football game. Seeing JD's skin tone gives them all the reason they need to stop for their version of fun.

As the truck rolls off the side of the road, six guys pile out of the bed of the pick up truck, making snide comments about JD's college attire. "Just when ya think it couldn't be worse, here ya go." He mumbles to himself, as the two ring leaders exit the cab, the chatter between the other men quickly quiets down. The driver of the truck walks back and stands on one side of JD, while the passenger takes the other side, corralling the young man between the two vehicles. This frustrates JD to no end, at the moment, believing that his inability to act in time has somehow dishonored Nick. Now he is pinned in between the men and the two vehicles, putting him in a very vulnerable situation. Nick tried to train JD to avoid situations like this, and the young man just isn't quite sure how he dropped the ball like this. Now, he knows that the only option he has at the moment, is to just see where this is heading, and wait for his first opening.

"Would you look at this, Claude? There's a poor Auburn fan boy broke down on the side of our road." Jackie's statement brings out a chuckle or two from a couple of his boys.

"Poor Auburn fan," Claude replies. "It's a damn shame for him to be broke down and out here all alone like this."

Jackie lets a smirk cross his face. "If it's a fifty dollar fine for an Alabama fan to be parked on the side of the road, how much is it for an Auburn fan?"

Before this goes any further, JD turns to face Claude. "Uh, hey guys, I think I'll have this thing up and running in no time at all. In fact, I've already called AAA, and they're on the way. So, it looks like I don't need to bother y'all for assistance."

"Who said we were here to help you, boy?" While JD was focused on Claude and the others, Jackie delivers a blow to JD's back, hitting him with an axe handle, as if swinging a baseball bat. The rest of the men watch the victim crumble to the ground, with JD caught completely off guard by Jackie's brutal attack. "Pick him up, boys," Jackie orders. "The poor guy seems to have fallen down." The rest of the backwoods thugs laugh at the patronizing remark, and JD's upcoming misfortune.

Following orders, Claude bends over and reaches down to grab JD. Before he could latch on to the young man, Claude is the first to realize that JD isn't as defenseless as they believed. Using everything that Nick taught, JD grabs Claude by the collar of his shirt and uses his opponent' own weight and momentum to drive Claude's face into the front of his Volvo. "Hey, look at that, a grill for a grill," JD retorts sarcastically.

The action happened so fast that the rest of the rednecks are dumbfounded by the result. Taking the advantage, JD leg sweeps two other men, sending them to the ground flat on their backs. With a path to open ground, JD sees the opportunity and takes it. "You want my money? Here, take it." JD flips his wallet up into the air, distracting Jackie by hitting him in the chest with it. Then, with one bound, JD back flips over the heads of the other men. Believing that he had a clear path, JD takes the opportunity to flee, but finds himself tripped up by one of the men lying on the ground. Down to the gravel strewn side of the road he goes uninjured, but the delay is enough to give Jackie's boys the chance to recover and grab JD.

Claude jumps up to display his nose laid open from the impact with the car's hood and bumper. He's enraged by the humiliation and has a strong need to retaliate. "Hey Jackie this little punk ass just called you a racist bastard!"

Not needing any more fuel for the fire, JD is quick to deny the accusation, "No I didn't!" He struggles to break free from the men holding him down, but at the moment his efforts are futile.

"Oh really," Jackie motions for Claude to do his worst, and asks, "He really didn't say that, did he?"

"No, I actually said it," Claude explains, shaking the feeling back into his hand. "But, you gotta admit that it sounded like something he would have said. If nothing else, it seemed to fit the occasion."

Jackie gives JD a disturbing look. For a split second, JD thinks he sees the color of Jackie's eyes turn a shade of red, as his body seems to jitter, or vibrate back and forth. "I promise you this, Mr. Auburn Fan; you'll never talk to anyone like that again, when we're through with you." Jackie draws back the axe handle and readies to hit a homerun against JD's chest. JD just closes his eyes and focuses. This causes Jackie to hesitate for a second and laugh at the situation. "Look at this boys, he don't wanna see it comin'!" Jackie resumes his attack and swings the axe handle with all of his might. At the last second, JD produces his force field, knocking all of his attackers to the ground. Three seconds head start; JD takes off running for the nearby pasture. Right on his heels, Jackie jumps up and takes chase after his prey, humiliated by what this boy did to him and his buddies. The distance between the two runners was quickly growing; leaving no doubt that Jackie couldn't catch the young man. As a last ditch effort, he draws back the piece of hickory wood and lets it fly at the fleeing JD. The axe handle evens the odds, hitting JD right in the back of the knees, to send him to the ground once more. "I got him! Did you guys see that? Come on, boys we've got ourselves a runner!"

Claude and a couple of the other guys head back to the truck to retrieve their weapons, while the rest of the boys take chase after JD and their leader. In the cab of their truck, Claude grabs a mason jar of moonshine and takes a big drink to fuel his courage. Then he steps away from the truck and tosses the jar of alcohol through the window of JD's car. To finish off the act, he tosses his lit cigarette onto the front seat igniting the moonshine.

JD's left leg is injured from the assault of the axe handle, but only enough to slow him down. His pursuers are closing in fast, and there's nothing JD can do about it. This will force him to make a decision, sooner or later. Should he turn to fight, or continue his flight, as long as he can? At the moment, his head is throbbing from using his defense mechanism, making it hard to see where he's going, and what's in front of him. Why is he running? These guys are nothing compared to what he and Nick faced in Japan, or are they? If JD saw what he thinks he saw, they could be some of Doomsayer's agents, trying to find Nick. If that's the case, this could get a whole lot worse. The little voice in the back of his head tells him that Nick would be disappointed in JD's actions. He stops and turns around just in time to see two of the guys run passed him, each holding onto an end of a rope. JD drops to the ground just in time to see the rope fly over his face. It's time to man up, JD. He tried to avoid the confrontation, but these guys don't seem to wanna give up. So, it is time for him to initiate his number one rule. When forced, JD will defend himself, violently if necessary. "You trashed my car, roughed me up, and I was willing to let it go. But no, you're too stupid to know when to walk away." This is his new code. "You have no idea who you're messin' with."

Chapter IX

Billy's drive home is about as uplifting as the social atmosphere of the football game's finale. He really did try to have a good time, but just couldn't find a way to fill the emptiness inside. Last night only compounded the negativity of his emotional state. While passed out in his drunken stupor, Billy suffered a nightmarish image of Taylor screaming his name for help. Dream analysis has never been his forte, if you take into consideration his recent activities, based on previous dreams. But this one was different in too many ways. How could his mind develop such an agonizing image of the woman he loved, and believed her to be too strong to suffer like that? Still, to picture her suffering like that tears at Billy's heart. For now, he can only write it off as part of his punishment. He knows that it will take time for these wounds to heal. Billy hopes that it will be brief.

As his car comes to a rise in the road, he fails to notice the faint glow on the horizon, being wrapped up in his thoughts. By the time JD's burning car comes into view, Billy barely has time to avoid a collision with the Volvo and truck partially blocking the road. At first, Billy has to assume that the situation was being handled. Then, he sees how the situation is being handled, in the nearby field. What he sees is eight men standing around one lone opponent. If it wasn't for the flashes of red energy around the single man, Billy wouldn't have noticed them at all. The little voice in the back of Billy's mind screams, "let me out!" Before he realizes what he's doing, Billy stomps on the brakes and jumps out of the car. This is the perfect opportunity for him to vent a little, without it having anything to do with Antonio Callistone. His actions are easy for him to justify. No one deserves to stand against odds like this, no matter what they've done. The attackers don't appear to be interested in apprehending the guy, judging by the way they're swinging axe handles and baseball bats at the victim. No one would ever expect any less from Billy Ray McBride. He isn't trying to be a hero. He's just going to make them see the error of their ways. If he can't convince them to back down, then he will show them the error of their ways. Oh how he hopes they won't see the light. It's how he met Taylor, and it's what she would want him to do. She wanted Billy to be the hero, so that's what he's going to be, Damnit.

Without any hesitation in his stride, Billy takes off running towards the conflict. The closer he gets, the better he can see what was really happening. To his surprise, the flashes of red energy seemed to be the result of the attackers' weapons deflecting off of some kind of energy field protecting their victim. The guy seems to be holding his own for the moment, picking and choosing his shots before ducking back under the safety of his force field, but who knows how long he could hold them off? The upside to this is all too clear. So focused on getting at their victim, the attackers are completely unaware of Billy's rapid approach.

Claude draws back his baseball bat to take another swing at JD but never gets the chance. Billy charges in and hits the man in his open ribs, and takes him to the ground, some ten feet away, and taking two more thugs with them in the process. In an instant, the odds even up a little for the young man from Miami. Claude, on the other hand, isn't as happy with the turn of events, raking the dirt and mud from his face to prove it. Looking up, the backwoods racist can't believe the luck of it all, "You? You're the one who took our Taylor away from us!"

How is this possible? Billy recognizes the crazy redneck by the scars that criss cross his face. These are the result of Taylor's punch, when Billy first met her, and these clowns, at the bowling alley in Alexander City. What is so perplexing is the fact that Taylor's punch was so destructive, Billy thought the guy was down for good. How could anyone survive a devastating blow like that, much less be able to speak clearly again. The monster inside sees this second encounter as a personal challenge, for Billy to take this cretin out for good. He acknowledges Claude's statement by delivering a devastating punch to Claude's face. Then, with both hands charged with energy, Billy leaps up from the ground and hits Jackie and another man with the blasts of energy. JD takes the cue and drops three others using his martial arts skills, taught to him by Nick. The other two men, who were knocked down by Billy's collision with Claude, quickly stand to resume the fight. As soon as they realize that they're the only ones standing against Billy and JD, Claude's buddies take off scampering into the pasture.

"Your car up there is toast. If you want a ride somewhere, we need to leave now, okay?" With no one to stand against him, Billy calms down a little allowing rational thought to return to his mind. The last thing he could want right now is to be caught here by the law enforcement, investigating the burning car. "Otherwise, you can hang out here and wait for your new friends to wake up." Billy doesn't wait for an answer. If JD did want a ride, he seemed like a smart enough guy to follow Billy's lead. As expected, JD falls in behind

Billy having no desire to waste any more time waiting around for anyone or anything. Stopping at the front of the car, JD reaches out to Billy, "hey, wait a minute." He follows the request with an offering of a handshake. "Listen, I just wanted to say thanks for stopping."

Billy looks around, displaying his anxiety growing from the situation. "No problem, but do you think we could save the introductions until we're further down the road?" Continuing on over to the driver's door, Billy leaps up and slides inside through the open window, as if he'd done it a thousand times or more. JD's impressed, but still opts to open the door to get in. Once inside, Billy turns the key and presses the electric starter button that brings the monster under the hood to life.

Out in the pasture, Jackie stands up and watches the taillights of Billy's Camaro disappear down the road, while dialing a number on his cell phone. "Yes sir, it's me, only I have some distressing news. Our attempt on the Guardian's student was interrupted by outside interference. No sir, we will not fail in our attempts again."

North, in the Appalachian Mountains, a lone figure stands at the mouth of an abandoned coal mine, forgotten by man, over a hundred years ago. "If I need to send more troops to aid you, or replace you, I will. The time is drawing near, but the Guardian's protégé must be removed from the equation, at all costs. Do you understand me? Kill the witnesses. I want this finished tonight! Then, go to join the rest of your troop and wait for further instructions." The man turns and walks deep into the mountain allowing it to end his transmission.

Hanging up his phone, Jackie turns to face Claude who was finishing off one of his buddies. "We need to take this up a notch. Do we know where to find Landry's student?" Claude walks over, wiping the blood from his mouth, and slaps Jackie on his chest, pinning JD's wallet under his hand.

This gives the two men reason to smile, while their eyes flash the color of red.

"Hope you don't mind driving fast." Billy stomps on the gas sending the vintage Camaro rocketing down the two lane highway. With twenty miles behind them in a matter of minutes, Billy relaxes enough to resume their previous conversation. "The name's Billy, Billy Ray McBride." Not forgetting his southern hospitality, he offers JD a handshake along with his introduction. "You look okay, but it never hurts to ask. Are you okay? If you need me to drop you off at a hospital, just say the word."

JD sits quietly staring at Billy. He shakes his head no as a response to Billy, but for whatever reason, can't say a word. Billy, on the other hand, isn't quite sure what to think about his travel companion. He can't tell if the kid is in shock, or what? Unintentional or not, JD's silence is starting to bother Billy just under his skin. "Listen, Bud, where I come from, it's rude not to take the hand of the man who offered to help. Weren't you the one who started this back there, in front of the car? If you want out, all you have to do is say the word, okay?"

As he starts to drop his hand, JD reaches out and grabs it to shake vigorously. "Dude, I am so sorry about sitting here with my tongue hanging out. To be honest, I can't believe that I'm actually sitting in the car with you. My name is JD, Jefferson David Johnston. Man, am I glad to meet you!"

Staring at JD with disbelief, Billy can't believe what he just heard. "How could you possibly know who I am?"

"Let's just say that if I'm right, and I believe I am, you are responsible for coming to my aid twice now, Billy Ray McBride. Tell me; have you been to Miami recently?"

Billy's reaction is not what JD expected to receive. His hospitable demeanor quickly changes from curious to anger. Stomping on the brakes, Billy sends the hot rod into a tire squealing halt off the side of the road. Looking at JD, Billy's eyes light up with energy to state the severity of the situation. "Who are you?"

JD presses himself back against the passenger door trying to put as much distance between him and Billy as possible. "Easy, bro, the last thing I want between me and you is a misunderstanding." As a natural defensive measure, JD raises his force field just to be on the safe side, so to speak. "All I'm asking for is a chance to explain before this gets out of control."

"You've got thirty seconds."

JD relaxes a little, lowering his force field. "One name; do you know a guy by the name of Nickolas Landry?" Seeing the tension easing in Billy's expression, JD relaxes a little more, pulling away from the Camaro's door panel. "He was my sensei, my martial arts instructor. He's the one who told me about the alliance between the two of you, and how you helped him get the talisman back. Without that taking place, he could've never made it to Japan to save me. Ya know, he told me that the world was too small, and that I'd probably run into you sooner or later."

"Sounds like Nick don't know when to keep his mouth shut." Billy puts the car in gear and points it towards the black top one more time. "So, where do you want, or need to go? I owe a friend of Nickolas Landry that much."

JD exhales a sigh of relief and replies, "To be honest, I would love to you if we could stop and get a bite to eat. I didn't want to pay those high dollar food prices at the game, so right about now, I'm starving like you wouldn't believe. Afterwards, you can drop me off at my dorm." Removing his arm braced against the dashboard, JD turns in his seat to face forward, realizing how fast they were actually going. Nick mentioned how good Billy's driving skills were. Sitting in the passenger seat gives JD a whole new perspective. This

Billy Ray McBride is definitely the two sided coin Nick described.

Food sounds good to Billy too. He didn't eat at the game, simply because he wasn't in the mood. All around them is nothing but forests on either side of the road, so they'll have to wait for an opportunity to show itself. In the mean time, Billy feels that he should at least try to break up the ice even more between JD and himself. After all, their mutual acquaintances with Nick prevent them from being complete strangers. "So you're staying on campus, huh? Is this your first year at Auburn?"

JD looks over at Billy and laughs at the question, but quickly regains his composure not wanting to give off the wrong impression. "Hell; technically, I haven't even started my first semester yet!"

Billy looks over at JD to give him a cordial smile, and then grabs his Alabama baseball cap off the dashboard. "I've got a foster brother who just started at Auburn. It's not all that bad though. Not everyone can get into the U of A. Besides, Auburn is the next best thing. Billy laughs at his remark, and then lets it die off when he realizes that JD is unfamiliar with the rivalry. "Man, you've got a lot to learn about the Heart of Dixie." Noticing a road sign, Billy starts to tap his finger against the windshield to point it out. "Hey, check it out. There's a Waffle House just before we get into Auburn. Do you feel like getting something to eat there?" JD gives Billy an enthusiastic nod, and then leans his head against the cool window glass hoping it would help ease his headache.

The rest of the drive is quiet, while the two occupants of the car process the information about their chance encounter. Billy glances over at JD from time to time, trying not to be too noticeable. He can't help but wonder how much JD really knows about Billy, and his alter ego. This changes things a little for Mr. McBride. He's supposed to be leaving that part of his past behind. He never considered someone coming along to open the doors Billy is trying to close.

Across the Georgia state line, a certain black SUV races up the I-85 towards the outskirts of Atlanta. The occupants of the vehicle have completed phase two of their plan, and are heading to prepare for phase three. "Yes ma'am, the message has been delivered. Yes, after a brief stop in Atlanta, we are heading to New York, and should be there by morning. Yes ma'am, Ms. Stanford, I look forward to seeing you as well."

"Call my father. He deserves better from you."

With that, the phone goes dead in Simon Ryker's hand. Before he can drop it into his coat pocket, the phone rings again with the sound of the death march echoing through the vehicle. He holds up a finger to quiet the chuckles and then answers with a serious tone, "Hello?"

"Do you know who this is?"

Ryker gives his men a big smile, "Of course I do. In fact, I was just having a lovely conversation with your daughter, Margaret, and was telling her how busy I was as of late, and couldn't return your calls."

Antonio activates the speaker phone setting and places the cell phone on the table. "Cut the shit, Ryker. I know that you're working on a project for her. I want to make sure we're clear about this! I don't care what she's paying you; I'm willing to pay your original price on top of hers, to make sure this goes the way I want." Antonio clutches his chest, while raising his other trembling hand to pop a pill into his mouth. "This guy had better be delivered to me alive. I want him beaten, bloodied and bruised! Then right before he takes his last breath, I want him to watch everyone he knows die before he bleeds out in front of me. This is what will happen.

I will have my satisfaction." Antonio hangs up the phone and throws it across the room.

"Yes sir, Mr. Callistone." Ryker hangs up the phone and smiles confidently at his associates. "Boys, I think Christmas is going to come early this year!"

In upper Manhattan, Margaret Stanford hangs up her phone, and drags her naked body over her lover's to crawl out of bed. "Why do you do that to me?" He asks, as he watches her nude form slink across the bedroom. She looks like some sort of predator in the moonlight searching for unsuspecting prey. "Why are you doing any of this, Margaret? All that you have is a very elaborate plan that has plenty of weak spots. If you're not careful, it could all blow up in your face."

"There is one thing that you should know about me, lover. I succeed at all costs. I do what I want, when I want, and always make sure that there is no room for failure. My father taught me that. No matter how elaborate the plan may be, it will be a success. If my father wants his revenge, then he will have what he deserves. I, on the other hand, simply want the power." After donning a sheer robe, Margaret looks back at the man in her bed. "Go back to sleep. I want to be alone for a little while." She enters the master bath and closes the door. Sitting down at the vanity, she looks into the mirror as she starts to brush her long black hair. The reflection she sees is not her own. "Everything is transpiring just as you said, Mother. Only, I worry that this plan of yours may be too much for me to handle all alone."

"Do not fear, child. I have people in place to support you with this endeavor. They must remain hidden, even from you, but when the time comes, they will reveal themselves as allies to our cause. The man in the other room, does he please you, my daughter? You must not lose focus on the task I have laid out for you."

Margaret tosses her brush onto the vanity and stares into the mirror. "As you have said, Mother, he is but the means to an end. What does it matter if I reap the benefits of carnal pleasure along the way."

"You must remain focused!" The woman's image grows angry, and the calms just as quick. "My child, you have taken but the first steps of many. For you to achieve the power I promised you, nothing can be neglected, and no one can stand in our way."

"Margaret," her newly acquired love toy stands at the bathroom door, curious about what was taking place on the other side. "Are you alright in there?"

Margaret looks back at the mirror and only sees her reflection. Enraged by the intrusion, she jumps up from the chair and snatches the door open. "If you ever invade my personal space again, I'll make sure I never see you again!" She walks back into the bedroom and gestures to him that she will be spending the rest of the night alone.

Meanwhile in Atlanta, a woman sits in a black Mercedes staring at the lavish home of Richie Frattelli. As the mobster exits his home, the woman watches as a lone man comes into view. At first, the mobster's bodyguards are apprehensive about the man's mysterious appearance, but Frattelli waves the man over. After a brief conversation, the mobster reaches into his pocket and gives the man some money. With nothing else said, Frattelli retrieves his cell phone and dials a number, before he climbs into his car to leave for his appointment.

The woman in the Mercedes waits until Frattelli's car is well out of sight, before she starts up the engine of her car. Suddenly, the man who met with Frattelli appears at the side window of the Mercedes, motioning for the woman inside to open the door. As if expecting his arrival, she rolls the window down and then leans over to look him in the eye. To his surprise, he bends down and looks right into the silencer of the woman's pistol. A quick pull of the trigger administers payment for a job well done. She dials a number and activates her Bluetooth. "The message has been delivered," she states in a thick Middle Eastern accent. Ending the phone call, she pulls away from the curb, allowing the dead man's body to fall into the gutter.

A few blocks away, a man in a gas station convenience store hangs up his phone and replaces the magazine he was looking at back on the rack. Walking up to the counter, he grabs a hand full of small rebel flag souvenirs and a lollipop. Paying for the items with a hundred dollar bill, he gathers his purchase and graciously leaves the change behind. As he exits the store, the same woman in the same Mercedes pulls up in front of the store. As if planned, he opens the passenger door and gets in, before she speeds off around the corner. A few blocks away, she pulls the Mercedes into a vacant lot and shuts off the engine. Looking over at her passenger, she can't help but ask, "What are the trinkets for?"

"Party favors," the man replies, getting out of the car. As the two walk back to the side of the street, a black SUV pulls up in front of them. "Haven't you done your homework, Den mother?" Once inside the vehicle, the Mercedes in the field erupts in a destructive explosion, eliminating any possible trace of evidence.

Chapter X

"Here we go, Mr. JD Johnston; one Waffle House complete with late night truckers, and waitresses to match." Billy pulls the Camaro into a parking space and quickly exits the car to stretch his legs. He looks across the roof of the car wondering what was taking JD so long. When JD looks over, Billy shrugs his shoulders. "Dude, what could possibly be wrong now?"

Giving Billy a look as if the world is against him, JD slumps his shoulders and hangs his head. "Man, we're gonna need to call this off. I don't have my wallet," he explains, remembering his little ploy to get away from Jackie and the others.

"JD, don't sweat it, man, I can cover this with no problem." Feeling good about the situation, Billy walks around the car and puts his arm around JD's shoulder. "One thing you need to learn is that southern hospitality is still alive and well. Come on, that little scuffle while ago really worked up an appetite that's starting to eat at me, from the inside out."

The two men enter the eating establishment and are quickly pointed to an empty booth in the corner, by an elderly waitress standing at the cash register. Billy climbs into the circular booth and claims his side, and then waits for JD to sit down before he starts his interrogation. There is an overwhelming desire that has come over him, needing to know if the information JD possesses is a liability or not.

"Hey kids; my name is Barbara," the waitress declares, arriving at the table with a couple of menus and two place settings. The woman's name sends a small dagger into Billy's heart, but he does his best to hide the uncomfortable pain. "Y'all look over the choices, and I'll be back with some waters in a minute," she suggests, as she hurries to lay out the table settings.

Billy gives her a cordial smile and waves her off. He then focuses on JD who was looking over the menu. "So, Jefferson, what did Nick tell you about me?" There ya go, short, sweet, and to the point, just the way Billy likes it.

JD glances over the top of his menu to see Billy waiting impatiently for an answer. After staring back at Billy for a second, JD smiles back and replies, "So, you want to know how much I know, to determine whether or not I can keep your secret, right?"

"Is it that obvious?" Billy lays his hands on the table and laces his fingers together as if stating that he still awaits the answer. "Good, I've never been one to beat around the bush."

JD lays the menu down, and then sends Billy over the edge by motioning for the waitress to come over and take their orders. Billy starts to object, but JD holds up a finger as if asking for a temporary delay. Barbara walks up and sets the two glasses of water down on the table and then pulls her pen and notepad, out of her apron pocket. "I'll have the country fried steak and eggs, scrambled, with sweet tea."

"And, what will you have, darlin'?"

Billy looks up to be polite and requests, "Let me have a double order of biscuits and gravy, with a side of grits, and two sides of bacon." He closes the menu and hands it back to her with a wink and a smile.

"What will you have to drink with that, handsome?"

"Do y'all have Mountain Dew, by chance?" Billy takes her silence and single raised eyebrow as a no. "Okay, then I'll have a glass of sweet tea as well," he answers chuckling at her expression. Do me a favor though, and change his order to the T-bone steak and eggs. I have a feeling my friend here would rather have some real meat. I know I would if I were him."

JD sits up in his seat, almost embarrassed by Billy's offer. "Come on, man, that really isn't necessary, Billy. I'm okay with the country fried steak, and I don't want to impose." He then looks at Barbara and says, "Medium, with just a little pink in the middle.

Billy chuckles again, "that will be all, Ms. Barbara, and thank you very much." He sits back as the waitress nods to her customers before heading off to place their orders. Focusing on JD, Billy tilts his head to the side slightly, and takes on a serious but friendly personality. "Since you seem to know more about me, why don't you give me the 4-1-1 on Jeff Johnston, including what and how you know about me? Oh, and don't leave out the part about your little trick you do, either."

Lifting his water glass, JD inspects the contents thoroughly before taking a drink, and setting it back down on the table real slow. Obviously, he was stalling but Billy couldn't figure out why. JD was simple arranging his thoughts for the conversation. He's got a pretty good read about people, and can already tell that Billy could be skeptical about a lot of things JD has to offer. "Okay, for a steak dinner, or breakfast in this case, that's fair enough. I was born in Atlanta Georgia. My father is a minister there, and my mother is the organist for the church. Because of my father's firm belief abhorring violence, I was constantly picked on because I wasn't allowed to defend myself. When it got real bad, and I mean real bad, I was shipped off to Miami to live with my aunt and uncle. That's when and where I met Nick. As for my little trick, as you called it, he believes that it stems from the fact that my mind was trying to compensate for my inability to protect myself. Since then, he has shown me that defending myself, is my God given right."

"That would explain all of that karate stuff."

"Yeah, but most of all, he taught me that I don't have to live with fear any more." JD takes another drink of water, and then eagerly continues, "As for you, here's what all I know, according to Nick's assumptions and facts. You, on the night when you met Nick, had followed a group of criminals to the benefit concert, supposedly to foil their robbery attempt. In the chaos of what was happening, Nick was separated from the talisman, and Sonny was shot. The two of you took chase and rained havoc on the streets of Miami. In the end, Nick got the talisman back, but you missed your opportunity at your primary target." After checking the restaurant to make sure no one was eavesdropping, JD looks back to Billy, carrying on the conversation in a quieter tone. "Ya see; it was that involvement with Nick, helping him to regain the talisman that saved me the first time. By doing so, it gave him the opportunity to travel to Japan where I was being held hostage, and rescue me from the bad guys, by offering the talisman as a ransom. Then, the second time is tonight, when you showed up to help me deal with those lunatics earlier. Maybe I could have taken those guys, maybe not. The thing is that your assistance assured me the opportunity to walk away from both events." As a sign of appreciation, JD raises his water glass to Billy as a toast. "You are a hero, Billy." To his surprise, Barbara walks over, thinking JD wanted more, and fills his glass to the top.

Billy sits across from JD, stunned by his new friend's statements. If he'd heard a story like that from anyone else, Billy would have to claim that the tale was bullshit. If he ever was suspicious about JD, the young man seems to have put Billy's worries to rest. What he is dealing with now, is the little voice in the back of his head, serving as the defense lawyer for the monster that dwells within, "Not all of your actions have ended with pain and suffering. Don't forget, the man sitting across from you believes he owes you a debt of gratitude, times two." Billy shakes his head and dismisses the thought. Looking back at JD, he asks, "Japan?"

JD leans forward and speaks in an even softer tone. "Did Nick ever mention to you anything about his destiny?"

"Yeah, he said something about that chunk of gold, and keeping the world out of darkness."

"Dude, you would not believe some of the shit I seen." He looks around the dining area real quick, and then back at Billy, "What he possesses is just one piece of something that is a far greater danger. When all of the pieces are assembled, they construct a key that will unlock a portal to the Devastator's realm. When Nick first told me about this destiny of his, I honestly thought he was jerkin' my chain. You've got to admit that some of that hocus pocus stuff seemed a little far fetched."

"Huh? Uh, oh yeah," Billy answers, feeling that some of this story that he's hearing right now is a little far fetched.

"Well, trust me, I've seen a chick that sprouted wings out her back and turn into some kind of dragon lady. As for the people who were holding me in Japan, it was their head honcho who wanted Nick to return the talisman to them in Japan. That guy was way out there. Let's just say that ripping the skin off his face to reveal his true identity was just the low end of the freak scale, I'm here to tell ya." JD suddenly sits back when he realizes that Barbara was standing beside the table with their orders of food.

Barbara places their plates in front of Billy and JD, swapping their plates while never taking her eyes off JD. Unsure where his story his was coming from, or going to, she opts to just make a silent withdrawal, as quickly as possible to avoid hearing the rest. Once the waitress is on her way, Billy laughs at her and JD's uncomfortable encounter and then resumes the conversation. "So, what happened to Nick's friend, the girl who was shot at the nightclub?" In a hurry, Billy stuffs the first bite of his meal into his mouth, savoring the home style cooking as he looks to JD for a response.

"She was the one who turned into the dragon lady! That crazy bitch went on a killing spree that the cops want to pin on Nick. The crazy part of it all was that it was supposed to happen. It's just another example of destinies being intertwined." JD cuts into the steak, with his mouth watering when the juices start to flow freely onto the plate.

"Yeah, well, I have a hard time buying into that destiny stuff. Everything that happens in a man's life is the direct result of the choices he makes, or made."

"Oh yeah, Well what if I told you that we were destined to meet?"

Billy wipes his mouth and drinks some of his sweet tea, "I'd have to say that you've spent too much time with your buddy Nick." He stuffs another large bite of gravy soaked biscuit into his mouth.

JD watches curiously, wondering how long it's been since Billy has eaten. "No, really, think about it for a minute. The events that have taken place in each other's lives can be lined up to bring us to this point in time where our paths cross. If we weren't supposed to meet for something bigger than the both of us, then what are the odds of us meeting by coincidence, when our paths have run in parallel lines?"

"Probably as good as the Panthers winning next year's Superbowl." Billy finishes off his glass of sweet tea and motions for a refill. "You can believe what you want, JD, and I won't fault you in any way. Me, I'm more of the realistic type, needing facts and physical proof to convince me of anything. You come up with some of that, and then I'll listen to the long version of your theory. Here's what I do know. When I get up in the morning, everything that happens tomorrow will be an action, or reaction, to each and every thought, movement, or decision I make. There is no grand force of the cosmos laying out my path. If there are they oughtta stop, because they have been screwing it up ever since the beginning." Giving the waitress a nod of appreciation for her quick service, Billy looks back at JD and asks, "how is your buddy Nick, any way?"

It's easy to see that JD doesn't need to push this destiny issue with Billy any more. For now, he'll keep his theories about the dream he had to himself. With Billy changing the topic, it makes it easier for JD to make the transition to keep the conversation going. No matter what, there is still that measure of sadness that accompanies thoughts of Nick's current situation. "To be honest, Billy, I really don't know. I guess the investigation is still going on. God knows that I'm being harassed enough by the authorities, trying to figure out where Nick might be. No offense to my friend, or nothing, but all I want to do now is move on with my life. I'm happy to wish Nick the best of luck, and Sonny good riddance." He cuts off a bite of his steak and shoves it in his mouth. Then, he points his fork at Billy and asks, "This guy that you followed to Florida, what did he do to you?" JD quickly sees the signs of how his question changes Billy's demeanor. "Whoa, hey man, I see I hit a nerve with that one, so I understand if you don't want to talk about it."

Billy lays his fork on the empty plate in front of him, and pushes it to the edge of the table. He knows that JD meant no harm, and he isn't insulted or angered the slightest. There's no way for JD to know the specifics that have happened in Billy's life, since leaving Florida. "No, it's alright, JD. I guess it's just part of the rehab, that's all. Sooner or later, I have to accept what happened for what it is; my fault." Now he's the one stalling to gather his thoughts by taking a drink of sweet tea and starts to work on his order of bacon, shoving a slice into his mouth. After swallowing hard, Billy begins his tragic tale of his tilt against Antonio Callistone. He can't explain why he feels the urge to be so open, but he chooses to follow the course all the same. What starts out as a brief explanation, winds up being a lengthy discussion about Billy's tales of woe. What a difference it makes to be able to lay it all out like this. It's truly like a major weight has been lifted from his life. Billy's not too sure, but he thinks that he might know how Catholics feel, after they go to confession.

Now JD is the one who is dumbfounded by the conversation. "Wow, man, you've had it pretty rough, and yet you still had it in you to stop and help Nick, and now me. JD looks at his watch, and then realizes it must have been broken during the conflict on the side of the road. "Crap; have you got the time?"

"Yeah, um," Billy pulls his cell phone out and looks at the screen, "It's a quarter 'til two."

JD jumps up and looks around, "aw man, listen, you've got less than fifteen minutes to get me over to my dorm before I'm locked out. I don't have my keys, and without my ID, security won't let me in."

Even though he finds humor in the situation, Billy can understand the urgency that JD is feeling. He pulls a twenty and a ten from his wallet, and leads the way towards the cash register. "Here ya go, Barbara. The service was great, so you go ahead and keep the change." Out the door and to the car they run, racing against the clock like two teenagers trying to get home before curfew. "Ya know, worst case scenario would be that you have to hang out with me another day." He starts up the engine and steps on the gas, sending the Camaro rocketing out of the Waffle House parking lot. "Okay, point the way, Jefferson."

"Do me a favor and don't call me Jefferson, okay? My father is the only one who calls me that, and I hate it." JD looks around to get his bearings, and then realizes where he's at. "Okay, up ahead at the next light, you're gonna want to take a left, and then your third left and a right."

"You got it, Jeff." Billy thinks about what he just said for a second. "Naw, Jeff sounds like the guy from west Hollywood who can decorate the hell out of your house." Billy sends the hot rod racing past the volunteer fire department, surprised to see and hear the alarms going off. Wanting to avoid a delay brought on by the departing emergency vehicles, Billy stomps on the gas to send the car on passed the fire station. Through the college town they race, crossing their fingers that they won't run into any late night police officers set up for a speed trap. To be stopped for a speeding ticket would certainly doom JD's chances of making it home, just about as much as them doing the speed limit. The closer Billy drives them towards JD's dorm, the brighter the night sky seemed to glow. Billy recognizes the similarity to what he saw on the road, with JD's car a raging inferno. "That's a fire, a big fire." As they turn on the next street, both of them see the cause of the glow in the night.

"Oh shit, Billy, that's my dorm that's on fire!" JD exclaims as the building comes into view. A security guard waves Billy off from pulling into the parking lot, but that doesn't stop JD from jumping out of the car. Without any regard to the guard's warning, he sprints across the lot and right up to the front of the building. Everything he has to his name, is inside the building, and he isn't about to lose it, if there's still a chance of saving any of it. Seeing a newly acquired friend from the building he stops to ask, "Jeremy, what happened?"

College classmates run from the building, screaming with fear that adds to the chaos taking place, and distracting JD's friend. "I-I don't know," Jeremy finally responds. "All I heard was that there was some prowlers spotted snooping around the building before the fire started." Jeremy continues to become more and more worried as he scans the gathering crowds. "You haven't seen Tina, have you? We got separated when we came out of my room. I don't know if she's made it out of the building yet!"

"Don't worry, Jeremy. I'll bring her out if she's still in there." JD turns and rushes right up the front steps of the building with no worry about his own safety. At first he was only worried about his personal belongings, but knowing that there might be a young lady in there who is pregnant, changes his line of thought completely. He'll still make a play for his things, but only after he's sure that Tina and her baby will survive this criminal act.

Billy runs up to the front entrance of the building where the crowd was gathered. He can't help but wonder what could be so important to send JD running right inside like that. Seeing the kid that JD was talking to, Billy grabs Jeremy and spins him around. "Hey pal, JD Johnston just ran into that building. Before he did, he talked to you. What did he say?"

Jeremy never looks at Billy, not wanting to miss any sign of Tina rushing out of the growing inferno. "Yeah, he did," Jeremy answers, borderline hysterical from worrying about his pregnant girlfriend. "I told him that my Tina hadn't come out yet. Do you think he has a chance to find her?"

Billy kicks something as he steps away from Jeremy. Looking down, he sees a wallet lying on the sidewalk, and thinks that some poor shmuck dropped it while fleeing the building. Carelessness is no excuse not to give it back to the owner. When Billy looks inside to check for an ID, he realizes the severity of the situation. "Where's JD's room at inside the building?"

Once inside, JD rushes upstairs where he finds the fire didn't seem to be spreading as fast as downstairs. The smoke from the first floor however was filtering up through the stairwells reducing his visibility. The one thing that is slowing him down at the moment is the wall of fire blocking the hallway. Trying to remain calm, he deploys his force field and steps through the flames, trying something new. Once on the other side unharmed, he can hear the cries of Jeremy's girlfriend huddled over in the corner nook of the hallway. Now his needs have been outweighed by the needs of another. To ignore her pleas for help would be dishonorable to JD, Nick, and Masamoto as well. "Tina, I'm here to get you out." He looks around taking notice to how the fire was now starting to move faster through the second floor. His time is running out.

"JD, is that you? Oh God, please help me get out of here! I don't want me and my baby to die this way."

With all of the determination he could muster, JD scoops the girl up in his arms, and looks into her tear soaked eyes. "Do you trust me?" Tina frantically nods her head, willing to trust anyone just to get out of this hell. "Good, then close your eyes and hold on tight." With a good grip on her, JD deploys his force field and marches right through the fire and downstairs as fast as he can. He knows that he is rough and forceful with his flight but hopes that Tina can see the necessity of it all.

Stopping at the bottom of the stairs, he takes a deep breath and rushes towards the flames blocking the front doors. At the last minute, he drops his force field and shoves Tina through to safety. Jeremy rushes up to collect his Tina, but there is no JD to be seen. "Hey mister, JD must have gone back inside." Jeremy looks around but there is no sign of Billy now either.

With no time to spare, JD rushes back upstairs to his room and opens the door, never realizing that it was unlocked. The room was filling with smoke from the room next door, but the fires hadn't come through the wall yet. It's definitely a bonus for him, so he takes advantage of the time he's given to gather his property. It may not seem like much to risk your life for, but it's all that he has. Grabbing his tote bag, he begins to stuff anything and everything into it that would fit.

The sound of an old fashioned alarm clock rings out behind him, catching his attention. "I don't have an alarm clock!" JD looks into the mirror on his dresser, to see the clock, which was actually some kind of timer that was wired to several sticks of dynamite taped above his door. In that split second, he sees the graffiti painted on the walls and door that said, "Not so smart after all, are you college boy?" Entering the room must have somehow activated the timer.

His actions are instinctive, sending him sidestepping over in front of the window and tensing up every muscle in his body, as the dynamite explodes. The race was on to determine what would envelope him first; his force field or the force of the explosion. The debate is answered when the explosion drives JD and his force field through the exterior wall of the dorm building with no problem. The problem created is the mental strain he suffers, causing JD to drop his energy shield, which leaves him vulnerable for the impact with the ground outside. At the last second, as he tumbles through the air towards the ground, he gives it one last try, able to get his force field under him to absorb some of the agony, as he hits the ground and rolls to a stop.

JD looks around, realizing, and fearing, that he was no longer in Auburn Alabama. If he didn't know any better, he would think that he is dead, but that's one thing JD is sure a person would know or not. "Okay, somebody answer the question for me. Am I dead, or not?" He sits up in the middle of an ancient temple, and is shocked to see the image of Hiro Masamoto standing in front of him. This troubles JD even more. "You're Master Masamoto, right? If that's the case, then I probably am dead, right? Well, this sucks, then, if that's the case."

"There is no need to call me master. I have not earned the honor to be your teacher, nor have you earned the reward of what I teach. Your destiny is at hand, student of Landry. The focus is now on you, and what your true contribution will be. This is very taxing for me, bringing you here like this. I may not have another opportunity, Jefferson. Believe what you see, and follow your heart's guidance, warrior of light." With that, Masamoto's image vanishes, leaving JD in a very dark and spooky strange place. Hoping for positive results, JD closes his eyes with the theory that he could leave, the same way he arrived.

Slowly, JD opens his eyes to see that Billy is crouching beside him, some twenty feet away from the building. "Dude, are you gonna live? Listen, no one knows you're over here yet. If you don't need medical assistance, and you don't want to be discovered over here, then I suggest we get our butts outta here, before you're discovered." Billy looks to the front of the building to see a group of firefighters coming there way to investigate the explosion. For now, Billy and JD are in a darkened area of the common grounds, but they're still out in the open. This can be classified as another situation that Billy would prefer not to be connected to, or with. If JD wants to stay behind and face the music; it's his choice to make. Billy, on the other hand, is taking his taxi service straight out of town. His new found friend nods with agreement, and then reaches up for assistance to get up off the ground.

As JD stands up, Billy looks around, and then pulls JD over into the shadows of a large oak tree. After verifying that they weren't seen by the arriving firemen, Billy checks on his new friend to make sure he was ready for travel, or not. "Okay, bud, are you rolling with me, or taking a different course of travel? There are way too many cops around here for my taste." Too many people saw JD run into the building, so Billy is sure that there will be plenty of questions to be asked. How can so much happen so fast? A debate is raging inside Billy's mind right now, with JD being the topic of interest. Part of him believes that he should just cut his losses right now. With all of the red flags waving around in front of Billy's eyes, it's not hard to see that they are connected to JD, and Billy's destined meeting with him. Billy's defense is strong in that with all of the stuff taking place in his life right now, he really doesn't have enough to give to another hard luck case. On the other hand, there is something about JD that Billy can't turn away. That little bit about destiny has dug deep into Billy's mind like a tick on a hound. No matter how much Billy wants to deny the aspects of fate and destiny, it's come up in conversation with two separate people, in two separate states, with all of the participants somehow knowing each other, for God's sake.

With his senses slowly returning, JD sits down in the car, and then remembers why he entered the building in the first place. "Aw man, my bag was the whole reason why I went in there."

"No sweat, bud. I've got it right here," Billy explains. He jumps into the driver's seat and starts up the car, and looks over at JD, "You're good to go like this, right?"

"Yeah, go, get us outta here." Right now, JD just needs some time to ease his migraine headache, so that he can think straight. Once he is able to get some rest, he'll be able to figure all of this out, and which move he should make next. As Nick would say, "tomorrow will work itself out.

On the other side of the building, Jackie smiles at the result of his handy work. Being the only one standing after the explosion occurred, he starts to walk through the group of onlookers squatted, or lying on the ground, as he dials a number on his cell phone. "Yes sir, Landry's student has been expelled from the equation. Yes sir, we both witnessed him running into the building," he explains, as he casually walks through the college students sprawled out across the lawn. "There was no way out for him with all of the other exits compromised." He hangs up the phone and looks over at a young college student motioning for him to get down. To show her that he has nothing to worry about, Jackie lets the true color of his eyes show, sending the young woman cowering back to the ground instead.

Billy puts the car in gear, and tries to be as nonchalant as possible while leaving the crime scene. "Hey, by the way, what you did for that girl back there was top notch, pal. You were the hero tonight." Reaching into his coat pocket, Billy pulls out JD's wallet to hand to him. "This was lying at the top of the stairs, in front of your dorm. I think it's enough evidence to tell us who was responsible for the fire. You said that the goon squad from earlier had this, right?"

JD eases back in his seat and closes his eyes. Everything that has happened tonight has been too much for him to process. Leaning against the window, JD drifts off to sleep to avoid the morality of it all.

Seeing that his conversation partner was out cold, Billy turns on the radio to see if anything was being broadcast about the fire. "…I'm Susan Ruth, and we're here tonight on the campus of Auburn University. Tonight, we stand outside what is left of over a hundred students' lives. The pile of glowing embers behind me was once a full co-ed dorm, until tonight. Here comes Fire Chief Howard Kunkle. I'm going to see if I can get us the latest update about what happened." The reporter pauses while she hurries over to the Volunteer Fire Department's leader. "Excuse me, Chief Kunkle, could we have a word or two with you sir? The reporter shoves the microphone in front of the man's face, before he has a chance to deny her request.

"Yeah, sure, I guess that'll be alright," he replies, forced to stop and talk to her.

"Thank you, sir; I guess my first question is, do you know how the fire started?"

The Fire Chief removes his volunteer ball cap and gives his scalp a good work over with his finger nails. "Well, I'm not sure what I can say, but the arson boys believe that they have found some evidence that might link this to some sort of hate crime." Hating the limelight, the chief tries to end the interview with his one answer and starts to walk away. "Chief would you answer just one more question?" Susan takes chase trying to match the old man's fast pace. "What about the reports of a student who went into the building and rescued a young lady. Witnesses say that no one ever saw him come out. Has he been listed as a casualty of this hate crime, and have any other bodies been found in the debris?"

Chief Kunkle stops dead in his tracks and spins around to face the lady reporter. "If I'm not mistaken, that was about three or four question, just then. Which one did you want answered?" Kunkle looks around, "Hey, where's your camera crew?"

"Sorry to disappoint ya, Chief, this is radio," she replies, following him over to his pickup truck.

"Oh well, that changes everything then, doesn't it?" Relieved that he wasn't on TV, Kunkle pushes his ball cap up onto his head, revealing more of his face. "All we have right now is a few eye witnesses that said they saw him go into the building, but the young lady you mentioned was the only one seen coming out. As far as I know, there hasn't been any bodies found, but the guys inside had to pull out, and we can't risk going back in at this time. Until we know more, all names of any victims or witnesses will be withheld until the investigation is completed." Kunkle starts to open the door to his truck, when screams of panic sound out from the scene of the fire. "Get outta there!! The rest of the building is coming down!" The elderly man takes off towards the destroyed building, waving onlookers away from the clouds of hot ash rising from the collapsing structure.

"Well, Phil, there you have it. Our hearts go out to that missing hero of tonight. Back to you at the station…"

Billy switches off the radio and looks over at JD. "There, now do you believe me? I told you that was some heroic shit you pulled off," Billy's declaration falls on sleeping ears, and Billy knows that. His passenger didn't hear a word said. Billy can't help but wonder what will become of his newfound associate. One thing is for sure; the drive should be quiet all the way to Billy's house.

Chapter XI

Pulling up to the turn off that leads to his home's driveway, Billy stares at a post light, shining alone on the corner of his property in the darkness. Billy's seen this post and light a thousand times, but in his life of almost twenty two years, he's never seen the thing shine. It was originally installed by Billy's grandfather and father, when Walter was a little boy. After all of these years, Billy simply assumed that the light didn't work.

If it does, and it's on right now, then something must be wrong at the house. Billy's mind is quickly consumed by a cyclone of questions and theories about what it could be.

What ever it is, there is no need to delay the inevitable any longer.

Slowly, cautiously, he starts the drive up to the house, constantly scanning the grounds for any signs of trouble. Reaching over, he nudges JD, "hey bud, I don't think now is the time to be sleeping." When he turns the car up the driveway, the headlights illuminate the condition of the house. "Aw, come on, can't I get a break just once in a while?"

"Huh? What, what's going on?" JD Sits up in his seat, first taking notice of the fact that his headache had gone away. Then he looks around to see the size of Billy's ranch. "This is your house? Why are all of the windows open?"

Billy pulls the Camaro up across the grass in front of the house, right up to the steps of the front porch. He looks over at JD and replies, "I don't know, but we're going in there to find out, understand? Are you with me?" He doesn't wait for an answer, climbing out of the car with JD following suit. The alarms in Billy's head are going off, because when he left for the football game, the only ones at the house were Isaiah and his granddaughter. As Billy walks up onto the front porch, he takes notice to how all of the front windows were broken in, instead of out, judging by the minimal amounts of glass on the porch. "Whoever did this may still be in there."

Then I say we go escort their asses out of there!" JD peers in through the open front door, hoping not to see anyone looking back at him. There are no noises coming from the interior, except for the sound of the light breeze blowing through the house. Still, JD isn't interested in taking any more chances at the moment. Being blown out of one building should fill his quota of dangerous events for one day. God knows, his excursion to Japan should have been enough. After a careful inspection, JD motions for Billy to follow him inside. Even though he's impressed by JD's cautious tactics, Billy is more than happy to lead the way. The burning question in his mind is, "who did this?" He knows that it wasn't the Police or Feds. If they raided the house, there would still be agents stationed out in the yard, and the house would be tied up in a bow with crime tape.

JD walks through the living room surveying the damage. The losses appear to be minimal, but everything was moved and turned upside down. "Billy, somebody was here looking for something, and they seriously wanted whatever it was, real bad."

Doing everything he can to maintain his composure, Billy walks in, slowly turning to examine the entire living room. "Do me a favor, JD, and don't move any further." As he suspected, the windows were blown in from the outside. Over to his right, after further examination, Billy sees a small metallic object lying on the floor. Stepping over, he squats down and picks it up and examines it. "Ingenious, isn't it?" About the size of a golf ball cut in half, the miniature explosives package was designed to adhere to the glass with just enough explosives contained inside to shatter the glass. What he finds interesting is how the delivery package was designed with a small port nozzle built into the back, to exhaust some of the explosive force to push the barrier inside. Standing up, he walks over to the next window and sees how the glass is dispersed onto the floor differently, without a similar object among the shards. Looking over by the table a few feet away, he sees the missing explosives package leaning against the table leg. A nod of his head means nothing to JD as Billy mumbles to himself and moves about the room.

The last window on the front of the house resembles the one by the front door, complete with the little metallic object lying in the middle of the broken glass. "Someone stepped in through the middle window. You can tell by the way everything is kicked around." When Billy focuses on the window of the living room's south wall, he sees something new. Walking over to investigate, he realizes that there are fifteen to twenty ammunition casings lying amongst the broken glass. "I've never seen bullet casings like this." Standing in front of the glass, Billy faces the room and then pivots his body in a slow sweeping motion from left to right. "The perp's target first showed itself there at the entry to the family room." He determines all of this by the pattern of the casings on the floor. With his arms held in front of him, like he was holding a gun, Billy continues his slow sweep across the room, until he determines when the gunman quit shooting. Looking up, he sees JD standing right in front of him. Looking above JD, Billy sees the evidence of penetrations in the wall at the top of the stairs. "He hit his target up there, at the top of the stairway."

Walking over to JD, Billy offers an explanation. "This is what I was going to school for." Feeling obligated to share his findings Billy puts his arm around JD and turns him around. "Here's what I've got so far. Three perps entered through the living room, one at the door, one at the middle window, and one at the south side window. It was the windows being blown in buy these charges that brought their target from the family room to the living room." Handing JD the small explosives evidence, Billy continues, "Somehow, their target was coerced into moving from one room to the other. It's possible that someone else was already in the house, or could be seen on the outside of the north side of the house through the windows."

JD offers a puzzled look and asks, "Who were they after, Billy?"

"The only person here that I know of was the ranch manager's granddaughter, so we should assume that it was her. Her name's Saphyre, great girl, your type, and about your age as well." Billy takes to the stairs and climbs them two at a time all the way to the top. Stopping at the top of the banister, Billy turns and looks down at JD. So this could go two ways. First, she could have seen someone outside while she was in the family room watching TV. Or, someone could've come in through the back door and forced her to exit the family room through the doorway at the bottom of the stairs. The second theory is that the sound of the shattering glass could have lured her out to the living room, but I don't see Saphyre as the type to be inquisitive about loud crashing noises, when she's staying in a big, strange, house, all alone.

She stops her flight when man number one kicks open the front door. The windows are blown and men two, and three, enter the room. Man number three is the first to have a clear sight on her and opens fire."

JD stands there dumbfounded by Billy's analysis. "Two things man; how could you possibly know all of this, and who is Saphyre?"

Billy turns around and faces the wall that separates the living room from the family room. After following and examining the marks on the wall, he pulls out his pocket knife to dig out what he thinks is a bullet. "To make a long story short, it's what I was going to school for. You know, follow in the old man's footsteps. I figured that if I couldn't have him in my world, then maybe he could have me in his." Looking around on the floor, he sees two small drops of blood, in two separate locations. "As for Saphyre, she was hit, probably twice, but they weren't meant to be kill shots," Billy explains, as JD joins him on the stairs. Handing JD the small knock out dart, Billy uses the upstairs balcony to walk to the other side of the house, where he can look down into the family room. The hallway behind him shows evidence of another entry through the sitting area's second floor patio door. "Four," he counts. Looking down into the family room, Billy sees all three windows blown in, and the evidence of two more intruders coming into the room. "These are the guys who scared her into the living room."

"What was that?" JD asks, as he hurries over to try and keep up with Billy's line of thought.

"Oh, nothing really, I was just thinking out loud. It's easier for me to keep everything in order if I hear myself say it." He knows that Saphyre didn't stand a chance against an assault force like this. What he doesn't know is what would they want with Saphyre? His calm, cool, demeanor is quickly fading. Billy is trying to do all that he can to keep the monster inside him at bay, but he knows that this is an attack on him. Someone has come looking for trouble, and innocent Saphyre has been put in harm's way. The monster inside him cries out for retribution. "Do me a favor and help me pick up some of this mess. I need to think about this for a little bit. I think there's a roll of plastic sheeting out in the barn that we can use to cover the windows. Hopefully we can find something that will tell us who's responsible for this.

"What will we do, if we find that something?"

Billy turns around to face JD. The energy highlighting his eyes and angered expression emphasizes his present mood. "We go to their house and do the same thing!" The two young men proceed to pick up the living room and family room, while working in silence. JD can tell by Billy's actions and mannerisms that he was deep in thought about what has happened here, and right he is. Billy's mind is overcrowded with thoughts about who was behind this attack. The equipment used, judging by the armaments used to disrupt the windows, is pretty hi-tech. That rules out the jerk offs who attacked JD. Those clowns couldn't afford that kind of hardware, much less figure out how to use it. Why did they take Saphyre? Was it simply because she was there? It's apparent that the invaders' plan was to take someone hostage. Otherwise, they would have been using live rounds. What a stupid term. Why call something live, when it can kill you? "I hate guns.

Hearing Billy's mumbled statement; JD looks over for clarification but Billy just waves him off. Each and every time his deductions and theories come back to one name, Antonio Callistone. Oh, Billy is sure that the old man didn't come to Alabama and knock on Billy's door, personally. But, the assault team that invaded Billy's home is well financed, and Callistone is the only enemy Billy has that can afford this kind of service. The problem with this line of thought is that it opens up a completely different box of questions. Mainly, if Callistone knows who Billy is, how much more does he know? Suddenly, a cold chill runs down the center of Billy's back.

"Um, hey Billy, did you know that you have a DVD in your player?" JD points to the flashing light on the entertainment system beside the TV. Billy hasn't watched any movies lately, and it would've been hard for Saphyre to, as well, since Billy's movie collection is in Atlanta. "Don't touch it! It might be booby trapped." There's a fine line between caution and paranoia. Billy may not be sure what side of the line he's standing on at the moment, but either way, he isn't taking any chances.

"No, you go ahead and play that disc," Isaiah commands, hobbling into the family room, carrying a box. At first glance, the old man looked like he had gone twelve rounds with a heavyweight contender. After further inspection, the estimate rises to three heavyweights. "Everything you need to know is on that disc," he explains, sitting the box down on the sofa.

Billy rushes over to help this old family friend down onto the cushions. The sight of this kind old man's condition sends the monster inside of Billy charging at the bars of its cage, trying to break free. To violate a man's home is one thing, but to attack an innocent defenseless man like this is enough to set Billy off. Still, he forces himself to maintain his cool. Walking into what he found, he kept a clear head and figured out what happened. He can continue this and remain calm cool and collected, until he is pointed in the right direction. Billy knows that this is what has to happen. The injury count has already doubled, and he fears that the number is about to climb even higher. "Do you know who did this?"

"Just tell your friend over there to press the play button and turn on the TV." Isaiah motions for JD to do as he's told, and then eases back on the sofa trying not to aggravate any of his injuries.

JD turns around and faces the television and DVD player and stares at them for a second. After a few seconds to figure out the controls, JD deploys his force field before carrying out the request. After Billy's warning a minute ago, he isn't ready to take any chances yet. With the TV turned on, he prepares for the worst, closes his eyes, and presses the play button. When nothing blows up, JD relaxes and backs away from in front of the picture screen.

An image appears of a mystery man standing in the middle of a dimly lit industrial building. "Good evening, Mr. McBride, or good morning, depending on when you find this. Actually, you're probably thinking that it's not so good after all, now is it? Let me get straight to the point. You, William, have pissed off the wrong people, forcing them to hire me and my team. Ya see, the service I offer is to kill people, and the price on your head finally reached my interest level. The arrangement is simple; you come to New York, and I kill you. Now, I know that this little proposal doesn't sound like there is much incentive in it for you, so let me explain the necessity of you coming north of the infamous Mason Dixon Line. If you aren't in Central Park by Wednesday night, they all die," images of Taylor, Billy's mom, Scotty, and others, flash across the screen. "If you try to save one, the rest will die. If you involve the authorities, they will all die. Oh, wait a minute, if you go to the authorities, they'll arrest you for your vigilante activities. Looks like it'll be just me and you, Billy boy."

The TV goes black, giving Billy reason to sit back on the sofa and bury his face in his hands. This proves that his worst nightmare has come to life. The one reason he was giving up this selfish crusade, the reason he chose to wear a mask in the first place, was to protect his family and friends. Only now can he accept the true punishment for his crimes against those he loves. Anger starts to grow deep inside him, but he chooses to hold it back. Turning to face Isaiah, he says, "Tell me everything you know, old man."

Isaiah reaches over and hands Billy the box. "I know that you'll need these. The men, who did this to me, said that they have your mother, her assistant from her work, Miss Taylor, Scotty, and they took my grandbaby. The man in charge said it was incentive for me to get the message right." A tear rolls down the weathered cheek of Isaiah's face. The last time Billy saw that happen, was at Walter's funeral.

Staring at his long time family friend, Billy is impressed by the strength the old man demonstrates. When he opens the box, he remembers what the contents are, and where the box came from. One would think that Billy would show some measure of discomfort for the situation, but instead he just shrugs his shoulders and asks, "What do you expect me to do, Isaiah? You know that they're all gonna die, whether I show up in New York, or not. Wearing these won't change that. And, walking up to him just to let him gun me down, will only satisfy him, not set mom and Taylor free."

"Boy, I don't expect you to lay down for nobody! I expect you to go save our family. I know it's hard for Billy Ray McBride to do it. But, the man in that box right there doesn't have to obey the rules and laws like you do." Isaiah and Billy stare at each other for a few seconds, until the old man knows that Billy understands what he's saying. "Billy boy, you took on this mantle to crusade for your father, because you believed it to be the right thing to do. Right now, I need you to do the right thing and hear me out. I never stuck my nose into your business when you became this crusading vigilante. And, when you decided to give it all up, I never voiced my opinion about what you should do. But now that my granddaughter is involved, I feel that I have to speak my mind. In all my years, I have never needed anyone to stand up for me, but if I ever needed to make that call, it would be to you. I'm making that call now, William. I believe with all of my heart that you are the only one who can bring Saphyre back to me. Go William, and bring our family back to us. Then, my only expectation of you is to hand that mobster his ass for ever thinking about coming down here to mess with us."

Billy never takes his eyes off of the old man. He studies every word that Isaiah said, mapping every blemish on the ranch manager's face as he made his speech. When he's through memorizing Isaiah's spill, and is one hundred percent sure that he understands completely what was said to him, Billy hangs his head for a second, partly out of shame, but mostly out of regret for what he must do. "How long have you known?"

Isaiah chuckles at the question. "Since the very beginning, Billy boy, and I'm talking about since you were three. When you see your mother, tell her that I said it was time for her to have that talk with you." Isaiah struggles to stand up and then pats Billy on the shoulder. "I've got a mare out in the stables that ain't doin' so good. I told Millie that I was going stay the night here at the ranch to sit with the horse, and nurse her through the night. By tomorrow, these welts on my face and head should be gone." Hobbling over to the kitchen doorway, Isaiah turns around to face Billy one more time. "This is gonna take everything you've got, Billy Ray. For the first time in your life; look before you leap, son. By the way, I told Saphyre's grandma that the girl was going on a road trip with you and your friends, to keep the child outta my hair. When you see my baby girl, make sure she calls her grandmother to let her know that everything is alright. Good luck, Billy, and y'all hurry home."

"Billy," JD walks over to his new friend, "What are you going to do?" Even with everything that JD's been through lately, he still doesn't know how and if he could handle the situation, if he was in Billy's shoes.

"Isn't it obvious? I'm going to New York to save my family." Billy's sarcastic remark deserves a "duh" at the end. "Weren't you paying attention when me and Isaiah were talking?" Billy walks away from JD needing a few seconds of alone time. When JD starts to follow, Billy just shakes his head quickly, and waves him away. Standing at the window, Billy stares out at the tree line along the edge of the north pasture. "You know you can do this, right? Yeah, I know I can do this. What's hard to swallow is the fact that one way or another, this has to end, for good, right?" His conversation with himself gives JD reason to wonder about Billy's welfare at the moment. He can't help but worry that Billy might be having a mental breakdown, or at least some kind of collapse brought on by the apparent trauma of the situation.

Billy is completely unaware of JD's eavesdropping, being off in his own little world for a minute. "First and foremost, we have to be concerned with the welfare of mom and Taylor, and the others. Whatever happens to me after that will be what it'll be, right?" If there was a window pane left intact in the window, he would probably look at his reflection, or something corny like that. Instead, he turns around and looks at JD, but instead of saying anything, Billy simply turns away and walks over to the home entertainment system beside the TV.

"I have to tell ya, Billy Ray, you've got me really curious. What is your plan?" JD walks over to Billy's side, hoping to get some kind of explanation. If JD knew what Billy was planning, JD could make his own set of plans. "Do you think there are some clues on there that could help you out?"

"For a split second, there was a frame of a city map tucked between a couple of photos of my mother and Taylor. This mystery man has a game in store for me, and he's left clues for me to follow." Billy fast forwards through the video until he thinks he's close to the spot on the video. Then with remote in hand, he sits down on the coffee table and sets the DVD player to frame by frame motion. He was right, to JD's surprise. There, between camera shots, was a single frame that consisted of a city map of New York and the surrounding areas. On this map are seven addresses circled, supposedly marking places of interest.

Not wanting to seem to obtuse, JD mimics Billy's actions and studies the map, having no idea what he was looking at. "Do you think they have a hostage at each location?"

Billy shakes his head no but still answers the question, "No, it's more than likely a twisted game of Russian roulette. This guy knows that I'm on my own with this. He's right about the cops. I can't go to them for assistance without turning myself in. So, since I can't check out all of the locations at once, he's going to have me guessing to which one I check first. Chances are that they're not at any of the locations marked on the map. I'll bet ya this, though. There's probably more muscle than I can handle at each spot, waiting to take me apart. I guess the best description is of me running a gauntlet. This of course, is based on the theory that he assumes I will be a thick headed, stubborn mule, and fight my way in and out of each place, until I can't any more. From there, I would be escorted to where my family and friends are being held, so that I can watch them die. At that point, Antonio will be given the honors of ending my life once and for all. So, to answer your question, I'm going to New York to check each and every one of these locations out, so that I can rescue my mother and the others." Billy faces JD and sees the confusion on his face. "Don't you see? There is going to be someone, at least one person at one of these spots that will know where they are. This guy thinks that I will try to save my family. He's already underestimated me."

JD gives Billy a double take, even more confused and curious. "But, isn't that what you said you were going to do?"

"Yeah, and that's where he's underestimated me, duh!" Billy turns away, and then glances back at JD out of the corner of his eye. Now he is the one who is wondering about JD's credibility. How did he survive everything he said him and Nick went through, and then reminds himself that JD is the newcomer to this game and doesn't know how it's played, yet? He doesn't know how Billy works. "There's one thing that you should know about me, JD. If you want me to do something that I normally wouldn't do, all you have to do is dare me. The problem with that is you never really know what I can't do, just because it's something I don't normally do. If I came across as a twit just a minute ago, I'm sorry. To be honest, I'm not sure how I'm going to do it yet, but I'm going to New York, to rescue my family and friends. If I'm successful, and can still walk, then I'll set my sights on the root of my problems and try to end this once and for all. Only then will I worry about the outcome."

"You need help," JD replies.

Not to be rude or anything, but Billy laughs at JD's statement. "Take a good long look around, Jefferson! Any and everybody involved with my life, or what I did, has or is suffering because of it. Do yourself a favor and forget about whatever it is that you're thinking. You've got enough problems of your own to worry about, instead of getting mixed up with me. Go clean up your own life, JD. I'll worry about my own. Billy starts to turn away, causing JD to reach out and grab Billy's arm. Billy stops, but he doesn't turn around to look at JD. "You really don't want to do this."

JD lets go of Billy's arm, but he doesn't back off. "Just hear me out for a second, alright? Sometimes in our lives, we have to know when to take the hand that is offered to us. Nick taught me that. He also said that we should always know when to offer a hand as well." JD stares at the back of Billy's head, hoping that he would turn around to give JD a positive response. "Come on, Man! I saw some of the other clues on the DVD too. Like, when the guy first started talking on the video, I saw the silhouettes of the other players in the background. In fact the background scenery changed five different times while he talked. Be realistic, Billy. It's only obvious that you'll be outnumbered." None of this sways Billy's demeanor, or decision. He's only got one ace left up his sleeve. "OH, come on, man, if nothing else I owe you!"

Finally, Billy responds, but it isn't quite exactly what JD wanted to hear. "Chances are that a lot of this is going to go terribly wrong, for everybody involved. If you can't see that, then you're either blind or a fool. Either way, you expect me to believe that you are willing to walk into this den of death, risking your life for a bunch of strangers?" Billy isn't sure if his question is meant to call JD's bluff, or test the young man's sincerity.

"Why is that so hard for you to believe?" JD looks around the room hoping to find the reason why Billy is so pigheaded. "Let me see if I've got this straight. You've done it twice now, that I know of, and are willing to rush off to do it again for a bunch of other people. What, do ya think you've cornered the market on helping and saving people?" With nothing else, JD offers Billy a hand, as a sign of unity.

Standing there silent, Billy stares into JD's eyes, hoping to see something that would sway Billy the other way. Finally, he reaches out and takes JD's hand, and then looks him in the eyes one more time. "Okay, here's how this is going down. It'll be sun up pretty soon. You find a bedroom and get some sleep. I want to head into Atlanta this afternoon and do a little snooping around, before we head north."

"Can I ask you something? Do you really think that they're still alive?"

Billy smiles and shakes his head. "Yeah, until I see them alive one last time. That's why you have to be my trump card. They don't know about you or expect your participation. You have to be that unknown variable that tilts the odds in my favor. Since they won't be expecting you, I'll draw their fire away, while you get my family to safety."

JD looks at his new friend with concern. "You make it sound like you're not expecting to make it back with the rest of us."

Billy turns away from JD and then spins back around to face JD one more time. "I know one thing that is certain. All of this has to end with this trip, or the people we are going to try and save will never be safe. It's my fault they've been brought into this mess. I have to be the one who sees to it that they're never threatened again. Whatever happens to make that a reality is what it is." Billy walks away, "Get some rest, JD. I'm gonna need you at your best on this one." Stopping at the foot of the stairs in the living room, he tries to let JD know how he feels, without turning around to face him. "Listen, I just want to let you know that I feel better about this, having someone in my corner. This doesn't come easy for me, but thanks. If it helps, I want to be around to bring everyone back with ya."

Chapter XII

The field truck of the McBride ranch races up the I-185 heading towards Atlanta. JD fell asleep two minutes after he laid down early this morning, and slept most of the day while Billy plotted and planned. "So, you haven't said, or asked, anything about this little road trip since we got up this morning. You're still up for this, right?" Billy glances over at his passenger hoping to draw out some kind of a response. The last thing Billy needs right now is JD getting cold feet. What worries him the most is that if JD gets cold feet, then it might undermine Billy's own confidence for the scenario?

Before this all started yesterday, Billy was already under the impression that he had already lost everything worth losing. That was enough reason for him to give up his crusading stand against Callistone. If for nothing else, so that he can hang onto what's left. If doubt settles in on him, it could undermine everything he has planned. Not to mention the fact that it could bring about a terrible end for everyone involved. He was never given any kind of guarantee that something like this wouldn't happen. That's why he tried to alienate himself away from everyone in his life to avoid this. They just wouldn't stay away. He isn't redirecting blame in any way. Billy just hoped it would have never come to this.

Now, Callistone has pushed his hand forcing this conflict. As Nick would say, "be careful what you wish for." If Callistone wants Billy Ray McBride, he's going to get what he wants.

Finally, JD breaks his silence and turns his focus from looking out the windshield to staring at Billy. "I've just been wrestling around with a few thoughts, that's all. Here's the thing; Nick told me once that in most situations like this, the hostages are usually killed before any kind of rescue plan can even be made. I know, what you said about Callistone's revenge and all, but I just gotta know that you really believe that they're alive." JD looks away for a second, a little embarrassed to be questioning Billy at this point. "Don't get me wrong, Billy, because I'm committed to this. I gave you my word, and did so without any doubts about what I was getting into. I guess I just need a little reassurance that we're not just driving up there to be added to the body count."

Billy hits the brakes and pulls the truck across three lanes of traffic to get to the side of the road. Leaving the motor running, he turns and faces JD, hoping to put both of their minds at ease. "Listen, if there is one thing that I'm sure of, it's that Callistone will have them all lined up for me to see. Then he'll have them killed, before I'm to be gunned down. That's why they were taken instead of simply murdered in the street." Billy turns his body and rests his arm on the back of his seat to get more comfortable. "See, here's my theory, so far. Callistone thinks he can use my stubbornness and desire to rescue them, against me. During my attacks against him in Atlanta, I gave him every reason to believe that I am an arrogant, egotistical, pit bull, that didn't know when to stop. This was mostly because I was all of that and a little selfish, self centered, and careless, can be added to that list as well. The upside is that this is who he expects to show up in New York. I'm sure he'll have plenty of firepower to face me. God knows I've given him reason to feel that necessity, so I'm positive the odds will be stacked against me. But, I have an edge. First, there is you, in the fact that there is no way for them to compensate for the unknown. Then, there is the fact that his people won't be facing the same Billy Ray McBride, this time."

JD has to stop Billy right there, for a little clarification. For whatever reason, he's always had this nagging feeling in the back of his mind that Billy wasn't telling him everything. "Do me a favor, and elaborate on that for a minute, please. It's not that I don't trust you. You've given me every reason why I should. I'm just trying to build the clearest picture of where we stand." He looks out the window at the traffic passing by, hoping he didn't just screw up in any way, by questioning Billy's integrity.

Before offering a response, Billy waits for JD to get up the nerve to look at him again. In a way, JD's question has boosted Billy's confidence about taking JD on this trip, simply because he seems like he's not the type of person to be lead into a situation blind. "That's fair enough," Billy replies, when JD does turn to face him. "When all of this started, I was hell bent for one thing, and I didn't care who stood in my way. My motives were always singular in design, and always straight forward, always direct. I had only one purpose, and that was getting my hands on Antonio Callistone. Now he's changed the perimeters, but he will expect me to stay the same. Rule number one; never underestimate your opponent. So, do you want to keep going, or do you want to stay behind? I've got a condo in Atlanta where you can hang out. It needs to be cleaned up, before I can sell it any way."

"What about you, Billy? Are you underestimating the opponent?"

"Not by a long shot, pal. Believe me; I've done my homework on this subject. By the time we get to New York, I'll have every scenario laid out and a plan in place. All I need from you is to watch my back, and get my family out of there as fast as possible. We make it through that part, and I'll take on the next step on my own, while you take Taylor and the others home. Should I come out on top with phase two, I'll move on to step three, where I will return home to live out the rest of my life in peace. That part I'm sure I can handle on my own. So, I hope you can see that in contemplating a happy ending, I don't plan on this being some kind of Kamikaze mission."

"Did you sleep any last night?"

Billy nonchalantly laughs the question, "I don't sleep much any more. So, are you with me?"

"What's OUR next move?" JD asks, hoping to reassure Billy of his intentions. "Listen, I hope I didn't offend you, or anything. I guess I just needed to hear your stand on this, one more time, that's all."

"No problem, brother man. To be honest with ya, it's good to know that you're not a lamb being lead to slaughter. As for our next move, I thought we'd make a quick stop in Atlanta for the night. It'll give us a chance to gather the information I have in my condo, to see if there is anything that might be useful." After putting the truck in gear, Billy focuses on the interstate and avoids the oncoming traffic as he pulls back into the driving lanes. Up in the distance, he can see the southern metropolis coming into view. Right about now, he is overcome by a feeling that hits him on every trip into Atlanta. It's a sensation that is brought on by the premature adrenaline rush, for what he was about to do. Even though this trip is different in nature, the adrenaline rush washes over him just the same.

Once into Atlanta, he sends the truck up the freeway off ramp and weaves the Toyota Pickup through traffic taking to the city streets. Slowing down, at the last minute, he drives into a parking garage, adjoined to a downtown condominium building. A quick right, and then a left, sends the truck straight into Billy's assigned parking space. He looks over at JD, who seems a little surprised at their location, "Come on, let's go upstairs and relax a little. I'm dying of thirst and have to pee like a race horse." Billy climbs out of the vehicle and looks around, feeling a little paranoid at the moment. He scans the level of the parking garage looking for anything or anyone that might appear to be out of place. Should he be expecting some kind of attack? It doesn't really make sense, but he feels that he shouldn't rule anything out, just to be on the safe side.

He waves JD on and heads for the parking garage elevator. With a press of the button, Billy calls for the elevator and impatiently waits as usual. By the time JD catches up, Billy is already entering the elevator car, and presses the button for the sixteenth floor. As the doors close, Billy looks over at JD and says, "Check this out. You're gonna love this." As the elevator car exits the parking structure, it continues up the side of the main building, giving JD a bird's eye view of the Atlanta skyline. Awestruck, JD looks back at Billy to see him acting unimpressed. After seeing the sight as many times as Billy has, it isn't that big of a deal any more.

As appointed, the car stops at the sixteenth floor, where JD stands there gazing out at the city. When the doors open, Billy is surprised to see an elderly couple waiting to go downstairs. Realizing who they are, he quickly throws on the charm to cover his paranoia. "How many times have I got to tell the two of you, to quit sneaking around here?" Billy quickly shoves his hand out to greet the elderly gentleman with a handshake. "How are you doing tonight, Mr. Davidson? Mrs. Davidson, it's always a pleasure to see you, Ma'am."

The woman, a neighbor of Billy's, and wife to the owner of the building, steps forward to be introduced to Billy's friend. "I'm fine, William. How is that dear woman, your mother doing these days? It's been a while since she's been by to visit you. In fact, now that I think about it, it's been a while since we've seen you around. So, are you going to introduce this fine young man to us?" The woman looks to JD, "I am Gloria Davidson, and this is my husband Peter. Are you another one of Billy's wrestling friends?" Then she quickly turns back to Billy, "oh, dear, I heard about that sweet Barbara, on the news. What a shame to have that poor girl taken from us, over a stupid car. She could have held the women's championship belt for a long time."

Her statement cuts deep into Billy's heart. No matter how hard he's tried to move on, Billy still can't seem to shake the guilt he feels about Booby Sox's death. To cover up the pain, he quickly changes the subject by introducing JD. "Yes ma'am, that was a shame, but let me introduce you to my new friend, JD. He's got the potential to be the next big superstar. In fact, we're heading out to the west coast for a string of matches, so we've got to be moving on. Y'all have a good evening now, ya hear?" Billy grabs JD by the arm and pulls him on down the hall.

Waving goodbye, Mr. Davidson looks to his wife for clarification. "When he said new friend, did he mean that the fellow was a replacement for Miss Barbara?"

"Oh, don't you worry, dear. I'm sure William is still interested in girls." Gloria looks back at the two young men and waves one more time.

"Hey, I like girls too." JD responds before he turns to face Billy for some answers. "What the hell was that all about?" Looking back down the hall towards the elevator, JD adds, "Those two were kind of weird, like Stepford Wives weird."

"Yeah, well I slipped up one day and brought Barbara over here for the night. When she blabbed to the Davidson's that we were Professional wrestlers, the old folks became my

biggest fans, always talking about the glory days of the sport."
After unlocking the door, he gestures to let JD enter first.

JD enters the condo, and begins to gawk at the interior design. "So, this Barbara, you and her were a couple?" He surprised at the condition of the condo. To be honest, the style and décor didn't seem like Billy's taste. Of course, keeping it clean didn't seem to be his thing either. "Wow, what an interesting odor you have working here."

"Yeah, make yourself at home. You can open a window, or five, if you want. I'm gonna be a while, going through my dad's stuff."

"What about this Barbara? What was she like?" JD opens the balcony sliding door and walks outside."

"I really don't want to talk about it, right now, Jefferson."

"Fair enough," JD replies, knowing when not to step on any toes. "Okay, let me ask you something else? Why would you buy a place like this? I mean, you've got that cool ass place in Alabama. Why would you need this, especially if you have an apartment up here too?" JD turns around, only to be surprised to find Billy standing right behind him. "Jeez man, I hated that shit when Nick would sneak up behind me like that! Now I have to worry about you doing the same thing?"

Billy just smiles and steps passed JD to make his way over to a telescope mounted to the balcony railing. "Making friends with the Davidsons was a blessing in some ways," he explains as he focuses the telescope. "For instance, they allowed me to attach this to the handrail. Here, take a look." Curious, JD follows Billy's gesture, and leans into the eye piece. "Do you see that desk chair?"

"Yeah," JD responds. He turns around, only to find Billy walking back to the door.

"That is the personal office chair of Antonio Callistone; the CEO of the Cornerstone Corporation. That building is meant to be the new corporate office of the Callistone Empire. Sure, it's a legitimate business. But the truth be known, it's nothing but a larger version of the two bit front companies that cover his dirty work. Well, at least until I stepped in and turned over the apple cart." Billy walks over to a small filing cabinet and sits down on the floor in front of it. Starting with the top drawer, he begins to rifle through the files and paperwork, leaving JD to entertain himself with the telescope.

Seeing a couple through an open window, having a romantic interlude, quickly ceases JD's night time sightseeing and sends him towards the balcony door. "Dude, I have to say that it seems pretty extreme to spend this kind of money just to spy on someone." JD shakes off the chill and walks back inside to join Billy at the filing cabinet. "Is there anything I can do to help?" Before Billy has a chance to answer, JD walks away admiring the photo collection of Mafioso business men that filled the living room walls. Apparently, Billy ran out of room for his classifications, and began to string twine from wall to wall, to hang photos from as well. This guy Callistone had all of these guys working under him. There was a separate classification for Antonio's family, in and out of the mob. There was a grouping for the men in Atlanta, with a much larger but similar group from the north. And then there was Billy's favorite classifications; the losses of men and properties suffered by Billy's hands.

"Wow, you were really serious about this at one time."

"You have no idea." Billy directs his attention to the stacks of papers and files pulled from the cabinet. "You can go ahead and watch some TV if you want. There's an Xbox 360 in the entertainment center. I'm gonna kill some time and go through this stuff, and then we'll head out." The rest of the afternoon is spent comparing notes in his father's files, to the locations on the map. Surprisingly enough, there are a couple of the addresses from twenty years ago, or more, that match, but there is nothing recently updated about the locations, since Billy's transfer to Atlanta. When Billy realizes that JD had fallen asleep, he moves his operation to the dining table and slows his pace a little.

After spending the next two hours going over the mountain of paperwork, Billy is surprised by JD's sudden appearance at the table. "Man, you're still at it, huh?" JD walks over to Billy's side, impressed by his friend's diligence. Like the photos on the walls, there were stacks of papers on the table, sorting and organizing all of Billy's information. "I'm surprised I fell asleep again like that." He's more surprised at Billy's change of clothes, now wearing a cowboy hat and long trench coat.

"Yeah, did you know that you snore really loud when you're lying on your back?" Billy shuffles a couple of stacks of papers together, and then hands them to JD. "Do me a favor and toss these into the trash bag over there."

JD examines some of the files, and then looks back at Billy, "aren't you a little bit nervous about someone finding this in the trash?" He pauses, holding the paperwork over the open bag, waiting to give Billy the chance to change his mind.

"When you get right down to it, what do I care? It's all dirt about scum bags that should be locked up any way. Besides, after our little trip north, none of this is going to matter one way or another. I say goodbye and good riddance." Billy gathers up the papers that he deemed necessary and stands up to face JD. "Are ya well rested and ready to go?"

"Sure man, but if you don't mind me asking, where are we off to now?"

Billy gathers up the trash bag and ties it off. "I wanna stop by my mom's clinic to see if he left any clues there. Isaiah said that this guy had mom, and her assistant, Greg. That in itself was a clue, or at least that's what I'm hoping. We'll do a little driving around just to see what's happening on the home front, and then I'd like to make my peace with those that I need to, before we take off tomorrow. Somewhere in there, we can grab something to eat."

"Ya know, I can't help but feel a little freaked out. It's like you're not planning on coming back here. The way you're tearing everything down and trashing the evidence; oh and then there's that little bit about making your peace and all. Like I said, you're a hard one to read, Billy Ray."

"Billy shakes his head with frustration wondering why they keep getting onto this merry-go-round topic of conversation again. "Look, JD, all you have to do is remember that I'm the kind of man who tries to cover all of the bases, in every aspect of my life, in everything that I do. If you feel that there is a need to question something I say or do, ask yourself if it would apply to that principle of covering my bases. Nine times out of ten, you'll reassure yourself that it has to be that, and you'd be right. But, if you must know, I feel that this place of residence has been compromised. I'm getting rid of the evidence before we leave, in case the cops are tipped off to what I was doing. Remember, when this is all said and done, I'd like to try and settle down, instead of dealing with the Feds or Police. I'm counting on you, JD. I know that there is a good chance that something could go terribly wrong, and if it does, it's nice to know that I've got you backing me up. But, if you want me to pretend that this isn't dangerous, or the mortality rate is lower than it is, then maybe you should just hang out here." On the other hand, if you're on board with me, and you just need to make your own peace, then I understand, and will take you wherever you want to go."

"No, no, you're right. I guess I'm probably just suffering from a case of butterflies. I suppose it's different when you charge into something, rather than trying to charge out." JD recognizes the confused look on Billy's face, about JD's statement. "You know; when I had to fight my way out of Japan, it was for a matter of survival. My freedom was taken away from me and I wanted it back. Now, it's like I'm giving up that freedom, only to fight for it back." He thinks he got the point across, but decides to change the subject any way, "but, now that you mention it, I would like to try and see my mom, if we're going to be making rounds."

"Yeah, well that's why I try not to think about it too much. After a while, you sorta get use to it." Billy heads for the door with the trash in tow. He stops for a moment and turns to look around the condo one more time. No matter how the next few days work out, he'll probably never see this place again. "Come on; let's go grab something to eat. Maybe it'll help put your mind at rest. Then I'll give you the guided tour of Callistone properties."

After a lengthy debate over Varsity hot dogs or burgers, Billy and JD spend the evening driving through Atlanta touring Callistone's business portfolio while eating the world famous hotdogs. During the brief interludes of Billy shoving food into his mouth, he gave JD the low down on everything he knew about each property and the person or persons connected to it and Callistone. To say JD was impressed with Billy's knowledge about the mobster's operation, and how well Billy could pull it up from memory would be an understatement. By the time the story was finished, JD had been told everything from Billy's first night out, to coming home from Miami. "…and that pretty much leads us up to where you and I met, which you know the rest from there."

Without making a sound, JD stares out the windshield as his mind continues to process the seemingly endless stream of information that has been given to him. One thing is for certain; JD was wrong about Billy. Even though Billy's escapades seemed to be carried out with a fly by the seat of your pants attitude, JD now understands that Billy had everything under control. Unorthodox or not, he could see that Billy had the base roots of a leader. This gives JD a little more comfort and security in following Billy's lead. "Obviously you've got it planned out, so what do we do now?"

"This is my mom's clinic, right here," Billy pulls over to the curb in front of the medical clinic. "I want to go in and take a look around real quick. I've got that strong feeling that we'll find something that was left behind for us to discover." He reaches into the car's console and retrieves a set of keys, and then climbs out of the car.

JD can't help but ask when he reaches the door, "What is it that makes you think he left a clue for you to find?" He checks the street to see if anyone views their actions as notorious. "What more could he tell you that wasn't already on the DVD?"

"I guess you could call it more of a test, than a clue." Billy pushes the door open and hurries over to disarm the alarm system, but isn't surprised to find it already shut down. "Ya see, our opponent is trying to figure me out. The first clue was the DVD, itself. The message was for me to face him in Central Park."

"Yeah, so why go through all of the trouble to leave you these other clues that you're looking for, that will tell you to go or do something other than going to Central Park?"

"If ya think about it, it's quite simple, and really clever." Walking back over to the front door, Billy gives JD a couple of gentle slaps to his chest, as if it was a sign of reassurance. "If I show up in Central Park as he requested, then he knows that my actions and thoughts are one dimensional, and his contingency plan is already in place. But, if I'm good, I would have caught the frame on the DVD…"

"Which you did," JD adds.

"…and would follow the new trail of clues." Billy escorts JD to the back room of the clinic and turns on the lights. "So to take it one step further, he wanted to test my intelligence and my loyalties to the hostages. While you were asleep last night, I went through the entire house, to see if anything else was left behind for me to find. That's when I found an address written on Taylor's vanity mirror, in eyeliner pencil. After googling the address on the internet, I found that the address was inside one of the circles on the map. Other than that, there was nothing else, but if I'm right about this, there should be something pertaining to another hostage location here at mom's place. Whoever it was that assaulted Isaiah at the house, told him who the abductees were, leaving another clue." Heading into his mother's office, Billy turns on the lights and takes a look around. The first and only thing he notices out of place is that the computer was left on, but the screen was dark. With a push of the mouse, the computer screen comes to life, alerting the user that there is a file waiting in the print queue.

From the other room, JD calls out, "Hey Billy, I think I found something." He tears the top sheet off of a prescription pad and heads into Sarah's office. "Is this what we're looking for?"

"I'm not sure," Billy replies, "I seem to have found something as well." With a click of the mouse, he prints out the file waiting.

The task is quick as the printer shoots out a single sheet of paper with one line printed on it. As Billy expected, it's another address, different from the one he found at the house, on Taylor's vanity. Staring at the paper, he takes a second to think about the red headed beauty that he thought was gone forever. This turn of events has changed his perception of the situation a little. Taking Isaiah's words of wisdom to heart, he can't help but hold onto hope that there is still a chance for him and Taylor to patch things up. Feeling the emotional monster inside him trying to intervene, Billy quickly takes control of his thoughts and refocuses on the present. Pulling the slip of paper from JD's hands, Billy sees that JD's clue isn't an address; it's a Business name, "J&J Seafood Transportation."

JD stands patiently waiting for Billy to give him some kind of explanation, being that he is the expert on the subject. After three or four seconds of Billy just staring at the paper, JD is forced to ask the question, "Come on, man, why did they write and address on one clue, and the name of a seafood company on another? Do you think they're both one in the same?"

"No," Billy shakes his head, "my best guess is that it's his sadistic way of toying with me. It's kinda like what he's doing to you right now. If you throw a monkey wrench into the works while it's running full speed, something is bound to jam up and halt production. This is a basic procedure to make me start second guessing myself. Besides, it doesn't matter any way. All of the hostages are being held in one place, where he can concentrate the most fire power. The problem is that we will have to visually verify each location on the map and determine it plausible value to this equation. Once we have done that, then we'll get together and brainstorm over what we've learned. Only then will we plan our assault to free the hostages. Don't try to be a hero; don't try anything on your own. If you come across anything, 9-1-1 me on my phone and I'll be there as quick as I can."

Hoping to appear confident, JD asks, "Okay, so what do we do now?"

Billy gives JD a disgruntled look with one eye brow raised, "Man, you sure do ask a lot of questions. Billy shuts off the lights and waves JD on to the front door. Once outside, he locks up the building and heads for the car. He remembers when his mother opened this clinic. At the moment, he wonders if she will ever see it again.

Chapter XIII

"To answer your question, I thought we would do a little investigative work, while we're in town." Climbing into the car, Billy quickly continues his explanation before JD could start asking questions again. "I noticed a lot of action taking place at Franklin Chism's old estate, and noticed one of Callistone's boys walking into Frankie's son, Eric's main hangout. I thought we'd go back and pay Eric a visit, to see if he's rolling over and crawling into bed with the competition.

"Dude, I have to say it now; I was wrong about you, completely wrong. Let me see if I've got this straight. While you were driving me around Atlanta, giving me your life's history in dealing with this guy, you were mapping activities and taking a roll call of who was present? How in the hell did you manage to keep your story straight?"

Billy ignores the question and looks over into the back seat. "Since you brought a bag with us, I presume you have some kind of ninja warrior uniform in it, resembling Nick's, right? Your buddy's outfit seemed a little too pretentious for me. The main thing is that you need to conceal your identity, but what I want you to do the most is just hang out in the shadows and be my point man while I do the leg work." He points the truck towards the Chism estate and begins to build his plan. For this, his biggest concern is not to lose control. He convinces himself that this is nothing but and information collection act, and can't afford to take it any further. At one time, Billy considered Franklin and Eric Chism as necessary evils. It was kind of like the old saying, "the enemy of my enemy is my ally. Billy never stepped on their toes, and their men never worried about a confrontation with the rebel vigilante. Billy's fight was against Callistone, not organized crime, as a whole. If Billy is right, then maybe this little visit could be used to persuade Eric to rethink his decisions. Siding with Antonio Callistone is not a healthy choice for anyone, as far as Billy is concerned. If Billy is victorious in his actions, there won't be a syndicate left to join.

"Not to question your decisions, oh fearless leader, but do we have time for this?"

"Like I said, they won't be harmed until I get there to see it happen. That's why we need to do this now. The more information we have, the better I can plan our strategy, the better chances they have of getting out alive." He turns the truck into a ritzy neighborhood on the northwest side of Atlanta and slows down as he tours streets. "Okay, this is it." Billy slows down slightly as he passes the house, surveying the grounds for any signs of life. Most of the house is dark, except for the lights in the front room. There's two cars parked along the side of the front drive. Billy recognizes one as being Eric's personal vehicle. The other one parked behind it is a new comer as far as Billy is concerned. The one thing missing is the Chism limousine that is always parked at the front door. "Come on; let's go get a closer look," he suggests, driving the truck passed the house again. As he parks the truck around the corner, a couple of blocks down the street, he glances over at JD to see his friend wearing his uniform given to him by

Nick. "How the hell did you change your clothes like that without me seeing it?"

"You were looking out the window; I was getting dressed." His reply is accompanied by pride, in knowing that he pulled off the little feat unnoticed. It may be nothing much to most people, but to JD it's sort of a step forward with Nick's training. To him, it's obvious that JD honors his teacher with his actions, which means more to him than anything else.

"Yeah, well I hope you can do that ninja shit like your buddy, or you'll play hell walking through an Atlanta suburb neighborhood dressed like that."

"I've got this," JD responds feeling a need to prove him and his abilities a little more. He jumps out of the car and tries to be as inconspicuous as possible while waiting for Billy. When Billy exits the car, he slings a nap sack over his shoulder. JD can't help but ask, seeing no need for accessories for what they're doing, "So what's in the bag?"

From his vantage point, Billy can see the entire street, including one certain oak tree at the corner of the estate's perimeter wall. "You'll see. Come on, there's no traffic. Our goal is that oak tree." Billy crosses the street and makes his way to the neighbor's front gate, where he stops in the shadow of a large stone pillar. He looks back to check on JD, but the young man is nowhere in sight. Quickly he scans the neighboring yards to see if there is any sight of JD. When Billy's line of sight falls on the oak tree, there stands JD leaning against the perimeter wall of the Chism estate wall, in the shadow of the tree's canopy. He's not sure how JD pulled it off, but Billy is impressed none the less. Walking over to join his friend, Billy looks over JD's attire one more time. The sleeveless shirt and pants are jet black. His head is covered with a matching black hood and red mask that covers his mouth and nose, and wraps around his face to tie in the back. His sashes around his waist and calves are as blood red as his mask, and there are quilted pads on his forearms and thighs made from white linen and trimmed in gold. "Yeah, I do like your suit better than Landry's.

"Thanks," JD replies. "Nick's serves a higher purpose than this one does. But, since he gave it to me, I'm wearing it to honor him. Especially after what happened on the road last night," he adds, remembering what he saw in Jackie's eyes. But before Billy could question the remark, JD quickly tries to change the subject, by leaping up and pulling himself up to the top of the wall. "Dude, I think I saw someone standing at the back corner of the house," JD drops back down to the sidewalk.

"Let me ask you this, ninja turtle, did the mask come with it?" Billy checks the street for any activity. "If so, what did he have in mind when he gave it to ya?" Billy leaps into the air and grabs the overhanging tree limbs to pull himself up to the top of the wall. Not completely disregarding JD's statement, Billy looks around the lawn to see if he can see anything. When JD joins him up in the tree, Billy asks, "Where was it that you think you saw someone?" JD answers by pointing towards the back corner of the house. Billy nods, knowing that the back of the house is where he would expect to see anyone standing guard, because of the driveway wrapping around to access the rear entrance to the home. Not to mention, there's a guest house and pool cabana accompanying the detached garage. Just because the main house is empty, doesn't mean that there isn't someone home. "Okay, I'm just gonna go take a look around and see what I see. All I want you to do is be my eyes and let me know if trouble comes my way. I know that this is crossing the line a little, so I don't want you to get your hands dirty with this, unless I need you to."

"What about an alarm system? Aren't you worried about setting one off?"

"Really? This guy's father was the mob in Atlanta before Antonio moved in. Do you really think he would be worried about ADT responding to a call, here? This ain't the movies pal. These guys are dirty, so dirty that they can't be associated with the law in any way, without being recognized for what they are. Their idea of a security system is enough automatic weapons to cover every side of the building. Shoot first, and then ask for ID." Before he drops down to the yard below, Billy looks back at JD to acknowledge his abilities. "By the way, that little trick you did getting from the truck to here, without me seeing you; that was impressive. Keep up the good work and we'll do just fine." With that, Billy drops to the grass below shaded from view by the oak canopy overhead. Still, he hunches over trying to conceal his presence as much as possible, as he starts out across the large front lawn. At the corner of the house, there appeared to be marks on the ground, as if something had been drug away across the first floor patio. Above him is a balcony, probably off the master bedroom, with the double French doors standing open to the night air. It's not the easiest method of entry, but it is the path of least resistance. He jumps up and grabs the concrete railing of the balcony and climbs up to the opened second floor. Immediately his senses alert him to possible danger, picking up the heavy smells of cleaning solutions. Looking into the darkness, he could see all of the furniture had been moved to the center of the room, and the lingering odor of fresh paint drifts in the air. This is all wrong. "Somebody is sweeping something under the rug." With his curiosity getting the best of him, Billy slips into the room and cautiously makes his way to the hallway door.

JD watches Billy enter the upstairs room, and then makes his way over to the house. He chose this new position at the corner of the detached garage, after losing sight of Billy when he went around the corner of the house. He figured that if

Billy objected in any way, JD could defend his actions by the fact that Billy himself instructed JD to watch his back. There was no way he could do that from the large oak tree, in the front yard. Nor would he have been able to see the two men exiting the garage to head towards the house. From his position, there's no way he could get to the house before Billy. Another side door opening behind him forces JD to make his move. Fortunately the door opening swings out, and towards JD, giving him a few added seconds of time to move before being seen. Around the corner, the other door that the two men exited first was still open, but slowly closing automatically. Since it was the only option, JD takes it, not wanting to be the one who is spotted by the bad guys.

Once inside the garage, JD stops at the door and prevents it from closing long enough for him to make sure that he had the all clear. After hearing one man tell the other to stay outside and stand guard, JD realizes that his choice of cover may have just prevented him from reaching Billy with any kind of warning. Suddenly a pair of clasped hands hit him softly in the middle of his back. Startled beyond belief, JD reacts without thinking deploying his force field that sends a young woman flying back against one of the many cars in the garage. Realizing what he had done, JD rushes over to her side, quickly noticing that her hands and feet were bound with duct tape. "Hey, are you okay? Come on, lady, I didn't mean to do that, honest."

"He said that I should get out of here, before they wake up," she mumbles before passing out.

JD lays her down gently, and then looks around. "Get outta here, before who wakes up?" In front of the Bentley are the shapes of three bodies rolled up in plastic. "Are you talking about them? Shoot, I thought you were talking about some dogs or something. Sister, these guys aren't waking up any time soon." His conscience is eating at him right now about inflicting pain and damage to the young lady. Being on his own, so to speak, JD makes a decision to end this little adventure right now. Seeing the outline of a cell phone in one of the dead man's pockets, JD decides to use it to make the call. "Sorry bro, I hope you don't mind, but you're not going to need this any more," he says, shifting the plastic wrapping aside to get to the phone. JD turns away from the body and quickly dials 9-1-1. He doesn't here the plastic being ripped away from the body. In fact, JD is unaware that Eric Chism's body was now sitting up in the middle of the garage floor.

"This is 9-1-1; please state the nature of your emergency."

Before JD could utter a word, Eric Chism grabs him from behind and pulls him close. "Actually, I do mind," he declares, ready to sink his teeth into JD's vulnerable neck. JD isn't sure what's going on, but this is the second time that someone has slipped up behind him in the past five minutes. This time he deploys his force field intentionally, driving Eric back against the wall. An impact like that took the girl out with no problem, but JD can now see that Eric Chism is no longer Eric Chism. Not wanting to relive the past, JD ups the ante on this deal and decides to end this his way, whether Billy approves or not. Igniting his energy shield again, JD sends the Bentley flying across the garage to meet Chism half way. The car takes the gangster's son and pins him against the wall of the garage, and ends the threat for the moment. Now aware of the present danger, JD hears the other two bodies sitting up to escape from their plastic cocoons "Aw man, screw this!" How did this go so wrong, so quick? All JD had to do is watch Billy's back while he did all of the hard work. Now he's dealing with these clowns and trying to save the girl, all while hiding in the garage of a known mobster. Let's not forget the fact that he has already placed a call to the authorities, and the cops are probably on their way. It's one of those days that you never expect to have when you get up in the morning.

The other two dead men rise from the concrete floor and move with animalistic tendencies, sniffing the air and ready to feed. It doesn't take long for them to set their sights on JD. He prepares to grapple with the two men and does not disappoint, when he stops the first attacker dead in his tracks with a kick to the face. Then without any wasted motion, JD back flips the second man into the side of the Bentley, leaving a recognizable impression of the man's head and back in the car's fender. Either blow should have taken both men out for the count, but they just stand up slowly and shake off the effects. It's during this second or two, when JD is able to notice the gunshot wounds to the men's chests, as he watches for their next move. Recognizing the puncture wounds beside their throats, he is only able to assume the worst, that they have been changed to serve the darkness. He's seen this before in the junkyard in Miami, but how it's taking place again in Atlanta Georgia is the riddle he'll need to solve later.

Inside the house, Billy has just about seen every room in the, all bearing the same fresh coat of paint and smell of cleaning supplies. The one thing he can't seem to locate is a living soul somewhere, anywhere, in the house. Judging by how thorough the cleaners were, you'd never believe that the Chism family has spent three generations in the estate. Nothing belonging to Eric, his father Franklin, or anyone else for that matter was left behind. It really shouldn't be too surprising, if Billy could be realistic about it for a moment. A lot could happen in the time Billy has been away from the big city. Still, there is something gnawing at his gut trying to warn him that something isn't right with this. With nothing left to investigate, literally, Billy's only option is to leave the premises and move on with his plans. "Well, it was worth a shot."

Heading for the back door, Billy suddenly senses a presence in the dining room with him. Unwilling to let JD get the drop on him again, Billy spins on his heels, but finds no one behind him. After surveying the darkened room for a little while longer, he resumes his trek to exit the house. When he turns around, Billy comes face to face with the three men that JD watched enter the house. Before Billy has a chance to offer any kind of defense, the leader of the trio reaches out and traps Billy in a crushing bear hug. "Where do you think you're going, meal ticket?" The man's eyes turn blood red in color, as if announcing his alliance to the enemy.

"That's neat; I can do it too." To prove his point, Billy allows the energy stored inside his body to illuminate his eyes, before he blows the man away at point blank range. Billy expected the man to be finished, but he is surprised to see a wisp of grayish green smoke rise up out of the body. Dismissing the event quickly, Billy focuses on the other two and the threat that they pose. One is no longer a worry, due to the tray of a nearby tea set being lodged into the man's chest when Billy's energy blast impacted everything around him. The last man standing earns Billy's attention. Without warning, Billy charges the man and drives him right through the back door of the house and out onto the driveway. The impact with the door, and then the ground is enough to separate the two combatants, but not enough to take the guy out completely. Before his opponent has a chance to make the move, Billy jumps over on top of the man and prepares to deliver a crushing blow to the man's face and head.

Inside the garage, JD has had his fill of this sparring match. With a headache already coming on from moving the Bentley with his force field, he's not sure about using it again. But, now with fatigue from battle setting in, he sees that his options are running out. Showing his weakened state, JD lures the two men in, and then deploys his force field one more time to send them flying away between the other cars, before the vehicles are pushed in around the men, sandwiching them in between. Believing the conflict to be over, JD relaxes a little and remembers the phone call he had placed. Surely the cops had been notified and were on their way to investigate the call. If so, he and Billy need to be leaving as soon as possible. But before he can make the retreat, JD has to check on the young lady who he injured with his force field. After all, he is the one responsible for her condition, so the least he could do is see if she's going to make it until help arrives. "Hey, are you still with me?" JD reaches down and brushes the hair away from her face. It is then that he sees the two puncture wounds on the top of her left shoulder. Immediately, the girl flips over onto her back, and then lunges up at JD, with her eyes glowing blood red.

"This can't be happening, can it?" JD falls back to the cold concrete floor with the girl landing on top of him, swatting at JD with clawed hands and gnashing her protruding, pointed, teeth. Before his momentum stops, JD kicks his legs up monkey flipping the girl away. Rising and turning to face his opponent, JD barely has time to duck as she picks up a motorcycle and heaves it at JD's head. Now he is certain about whom he is up against, and hits the girl with his force field as she lunges at him one more time.

Billy's opponent blocks the punch intended for his head, and gains the upper hand by flipping Billy over. Rising up to strike at Billy in the same fashion, the man is suddenly interrupted by the motorcycle flying through the garage door that takes the man right off of Billy's chest, and carries him deep into the house through the back wall. Rolling over to see who was responsible, he sees JD standing inside the garage, tired and out of breath. "Look out, JD!" He warns, but Billy can't make out who, or what, it is that is leaping at JD from behind. All Billy knows is that the person is a threat to his friend. Without any hesitation, Billy unloads on the girl with an energy blast that sends her back into the shadows of the garage. "What in the hell were you doing in there?"

Anxiety for the situation is showing all over JD's face. Ready to leave this place, he exits the garage through the hole in the roll up door and grabs Billy by the arm, "Billy, we need to get out of here as quick as possible!"

"Whoa, whoa, whoa, slow down there a minute and tell me what's going on." For whatever reason, JD was really uptight about the situation and Billy needed to know why. After a deep breath and a heavy sigh, JD begins to explain the series of events that brought him from the oak tree out front to the garage. However, when he reaches a certain part about calling the police, Billy has to stop him for clarification. "I'm sorry, but you did what!?" Billy looks at JD with total disbelief, "Have you lost your ever lovin' mind? I can't believe you were stupid enough to call the cops! You never, never, ever, call the cops; no matter what happens!" Turning away, Billy sees the house guests that were staring at them through the hole in the kitchen. Billy isn't quite sure who is more surprised to see who, but he takes the advantage as quick as possible, and sends an energy blast right into the middle of the group, and then takes off running around the house.

"Oh, no he didn't just call me stupid!" Not to be left behind, JD quickly catches up with Billy and follows his lead up into the oak tree, ready to continue their heated discussion about intelligence, but first they needed to get away from the gun toting thugs who had crashed Billy's little investigation. Up into the canopy, JD sees Billy retrieving the nap sack he had left in the tree, handing JD a grey sweat suit, before pulling one set out for himself.

"Here, put this on, quick, and let's move out of here." Billy commands, pulling the oversized sweat pants over his boots and pants.

"JD accepts the clothes, recognizing the fact that Billy is seriously pissed about JD's contribution to the necessary retreat. That doesn't mean that he feels the need to squelch his defense any. "Look, I only did what I thought was the right thing to do at the moment," he explains, pulling the sweat shirt over his head.

"I'm sorry, but we really don't have time to talk about it right now." Billy's response is cold and disconnected exactly the way he wanted it to come across. Dropping down on the other side of the wall, Billy stuffs his trench coat into the bag, and then takes off jogging down the street as JD hurries to catch up once more. To Billy's surprise and pleasure, a threesome of joggers turn onto the street just ahead of Billy and JD, making the two house invaders blend into the scenery even more. No sooner are they mixed in with the other joggers, two cars pull out of the Chism estate searching for the trespassers. Billy recognizes one of the cars to be owned by one of Callistone's head men. Once the two cars pass, Billy signals for JD to break away from the other joggers and head for the truck. Inside the confines of the Toyota, Billy unloads on JD for what happened at the house. "Mister, I don't know who you are accustomed to dealing with, but if you ever pull any shit like that again, I swear to God I'll leave you behind to answer all of the hows and whys. Now they have your cell phone number, connecting you to the crime. Damn, JD, you really have to be smarter than that!"

Okay, since the gloves are off about this, JD is ready to join in. "Well, before you get too comfortable on your high horse, let me tell you how I roll so that you have it to store in that great memory bank of yours! You said for me to be your look out and watch for trouble. Well, I couldn't watch your back from the front yard, after you took off to the back. So, I decided that I would set up at the garage, in case you needed me. From there, I watched three men exit the garage and enter the house. I was going to alert you to their presence, when the young lady that you blew back into the back of the garage surprised me. Unfortunately, I did something similar to what you did to her, with my force field. But that's when I saw the three other bodies wrapped in plastic. When it comes to murder, I believe the cops are the ones who should handle it. The young woman needed assistance, after being introduced to my force field, so I felt that I was responsible for seeing to her aid by calling 9-1-1." JD pauses as he watches two police cars and an ambulance race past Billy's truck on the street in front of them. "As for the phone, I took it off one of the dead bodies, and made the call. You really should have a little more faith in the people you hang out with, pal. As for the girl, and the other three, we'll talk some time about what happened in Japan. Oh, and just so that I don't have to kick your ass next time, don't ever call me stupid again!"

Billy has to ask, "Which other three are you talking about?"

"The three I had to fight in there, before the girl got involved," JD explains, wanting to drop the subject.

"The three wrapped in plastic? I thought you said they were dead," Billy clarifies.

"Whatever, let's just get out of here," JD replies, with disappointment in his heart.

Billy looks over at JD, and is somewhat humbled, and somewhat impressed, with JD's bravado. He stood his ground with Billy, and that impresses this rebel vigilante more than anything. "Ya know; that girl didn't seem to need too much medical attention, the way she was coming after you."

"Yeah, well after this is all over, you and I need to talk about the similarities I've seen from my experiences with Nick, and what I've seen since I've met you."

"JD, my friend, if there is one thing I know; it's that Atlanta Georgia is not located in the country of Japan. Trust me, brother, your spooks and goblins haven't tracked you down and set up shop here in the south, just to get under your skin." Billy isn't sure if he is trying to convince JD, or himself. He saw the red glowing eyes of his three opponents that confronted him in the house, but never even dreamed of making any kind of connection to them and JD's stories, until JD brought it up.

There's no time for this right now. Billy has to stay focused on his journey to New York, and everything else will have to wait its turn, if he makes it back. "Just for the record, I hope that next time never comes, for the both of our sakes." Billy starts up the truck and pulls up to the corner to see Callistone's cars being harassed by the police in front of the Chism estate. Just as he is about to pull out, a fire truck races by, responding to the call as well, "Okay, now it is our turn."

"That was pretty gutsy," JD thinks, examining his rebuttal to Billy's condescending tone and remarks. There was a time in his life when JD would have folded under such an attack, and would have responded with a simple, "okay." Perhaps a change has taken place inside JD. God knows, that he's gone through enough in the past few weeks to initiate something, good or bad. Hell, the events of the past thirty six hours should be enough to drive any man to his boiling point. Looking over at Billy, he realizes that good, bad, or otherwise, Mr. McBride has been the common denominator in the equation of JD's life, recently speaking. Weighing the pros and cons, and taking into consideration that the two of them somehow managed to escape with their lives, JD thinks that this might just work out after all. "Ya know, speaking of gutsy…"

"Who's speaking of gutsy?" Billy inquires, feeling the statement was out of left field.

"I am, so stop interrupting me." JD faces Billy, slightly embarrassed about thinking out loud. "You, your actions, your 'by the seat of your pants' attitude, is all pretty damn gutsy. You do know that you're bleeding, right? Does the desire to live hold any weight when you approach a situation? Ya know; Superman even approaches things with a little more caution than you do, and he's bullet proof."

Smirking at JD's remark, Billy looks over at JD and replies, "You need to keep in mind that there are two different kinds of work involved, in your comparison. He's in it for the long haul, so he can pace himself. I, on the other hand, don't have that luxury." Billy rolls his right shoulder forward to inspect the wound JD mentioned. "As for this, I must have done it coming out the back door."

"Okay, I see your point, but check this out." JD turns in his seat to face Billy, "you think that you don't want to be the hero, but in actuality you've been forced into this role to save your family and friends. You could have walked away, but the hero inside you accepted the challenge, putting the needs of others before your own.

"The only problem with your hypothesis is that I don't want to be a hero. Hell, I don't even want to be who I was. Unfortunately for me, I've been pulled back into this mess, along with all of the other victims. So, if they want me, that's exactly what they're gonna get, a whole lotta me!"

"Yeah, well I think you're meant for more than just some street thug with no conscience, looking to settle a score," JD replies.

"Street thug? Come on, man, it's a little more complicated than that." Billy isn't sure if he should be mad, or sad, at JD's comment. "I'll tell you what JD, since we're like a two man team, how about you be the conscience, and I'll take care of the rest." Billy points the truck towards Atlanta and looks over at JD. "So, we're taking you to see your mom, right? Do you have a way to get in touch with her?"

JD looks at the clock on the car stereo and replies, "yeah, now would be a good time. She's got one of those prepay phones that she keeps with her to talk to me. Right about now, Mom should be cleaning up the house so she can get ready to go to bed, while my dad goes over today's sermon to prepare for next week's."

Chapter XIV

On the south side of Brooklyn, is a small family owned Italian restaurant decorated as if it was brought over from the mother land. It has served as the meeting place for Carmine De Luca and his men, ever since Carmine earned his position with Antonio's organization. Carmine's right hand man has served De Luca for almost as long. "Come on, boss, what'cha got us sittin' around in the dark for?" Danny Boselli sits back in his chair to show his respect, as Mama De Luca enters the room with warm bread and wine.

Sitting at the end of the table, Carmine's attention seems to be fascinated with the flickering candle's flame that struggles to illuminate the shadow filled room. "Something," Carmine pauses as he gives his mother a kiss to her cheek, "bothers me, boys." Carmine waits for his mother to leave before continuing, " I don't like the way things are going. Mr. Callistone is in a bad way, right now, with the loss of his son, Darien. I expect you boys to make sure no one gets outta line, or tries to muscle their way in on our domain. Why he brought Margaret into the fold makes no sense to me, but it's not my place to question Antonio's actions. This doesn't mean that I can turn a blind eye, either. You boys have been with me since the beginning, and I know that everyone of you is loyal to me, and Mr. Callistone. All I ask of you now is nothing more than what's been asked of you all along." Carmine tears off a piece of the bread and dips it into his wine.

"Boss, I heard that Frattelli passed on a message that the crazy bastard in Atlanta that murdered Darien, is making his way north to finish the job with the rest of Antonio's men." Danny motions towards the bread as if asking permission to partake, and then tears off his own piece. "Is there any truth to this?"

"Yeah," a voice replies, from the darkness of the back corner of the room. "And, Johnny boy says that you should all be worried." Before guns could be drawn and aimed, the mystery man opens fire with his automatic pistol, spraying the mobsters with a rain of hot lead. The slide on the pistol rocks back and forth, with a musical repetition that serenades the gangsters as they fall to the floor. Seconds pass like minutes as the lone gunman empties his weapon into every last man in the room. Stepping from the shadows, he walks over to Bobby Moreno, who was dying, and yet still willing to try and pull his pistol from its holster, but not sure if he could even raise it. The mystery man loads a fresh clip into his weapon and pulls the trigger one more time, removing the threat one more time to Bobby's misery once and for all.

A woman dressed in black wanders into the room and admires the carnage that has taken place. Finding Carmine DeLuca still breathing, she bends over and sinks her teeth into his neck to finish him off. The gunman looks back at the woman's action, but pays it no mind, as if he's seen her do it plenty of times. Before leaving, the man pulls a small rebel flag from his coat pocket and lays it across Bobby's eyes.

"Outside the restaurant, Tony Gidducci pulls up to the curb, just in time to see the terrified patrons running out into the street. Climbing out of the car to investigate, he hears the final gunshot, explaining the peoples' haste. "Tommy, get on the phone with Mr. Vellecio and tell him we have a problem at Mama De Luca's restaurant. Then, you meet me inside, got it?" Tony draws his gun and rushes through the front door like a salmon trying to swim upstream through the last of the people to exit the building. When Carmine's mother exits the restaurant Tony stops her, hoping to get some kind of answer. "Mama, what happened in there?" Immediately, the old woman begins an explanation of what happened, all in a rapid gibberish of her homeland dialect. All Tony can do is wave his hands in front of her face, to try and slow her down. "Mama, Mama, you have to tell me in English. I can't understand you."

"Someone came in there, and killed my Carmine and his boys!" It's all that she could say, before she returns to her hysterical fit, but it was enough to tell Tony what he needed to know. With his pistol in hand, he enters the restaurant, where he immediately scared a lone waitress even more, causing her to scream out before running for the open front door. The young woman screams out again as she runs into Tommy and the other guys making their way inside.

"Tony, Mama said that it all happened in the back room. Oh, and Mr. Vellecio wants a full report as soon as possible." Tommy motions for Tony to lead the way not wanting to be the next victim of the mystery man's massacre. Besides, if Tony gets iced, Tommy will move up in rank.

Turning down the back hallway, Tony can see the kitchen's entry door standing open, revealing the gunman's escape route. Stopping at the door of Carmine's private dining room, Tony kicks the door open revealing the horrific scene inside the room. Inside the room, every man was laid out where they fell, except for Bobby Moreno. Curious, Tony walks over to Bobby, puzzled by the small piece of cloth placed over the dead man's eyes. When he reaches down to retrieve it for a closer inspection, Bobby surprises Tony, when the older man suddenly opens his eyes and gasps for air. "Tony Gidducci, you have to tell them…tell them that… that the gunman fingered Johnny C." With that, the mobster dies, taking the rest of his secrets with him.

Tony picks up the piece of cloth, recognizing it as a small Confederate flag. After a few seconds of deliberation, he pulls his phone out of his coat and dials a number. "Yeah, Mr. Vellecio, this is Tony. I've got some bad news, Sir."

Chapter XV

In college Park, Georgia, just south of Atlanta...

Madeline Johnston is as predictable as her daily schedule. With the dinner dishes washed, dried, and put away, she readies to sweep the kitchen floor before turning in for the night. As she reaches for the broom, a buzzing sound begins to emanate from her apron pocket. At first, it startles her, and then her heart beats with joy knowing that her baby boy is calling. She has been worried half to death about JD since she received the reports about his dormitory at college, and his sudden disappearance. Looking at the screen of the phone, Madeline sees the text message that reads, "Pulling up out front, in a few minutes. Would like to see you if you can come out."

Without any hesitation, Madeline drops the phone into her pocket and walks over to the trash can. The bag hardly has anything in it, but she grabs it just the same for a reason to go outside. Sticking her head out into the hallway, she looks towards her husband's study and says, "Isaac dear, I'm gonna take the trash out to the street." As fast as she can, Madeline hurries around the corner of the house and heads for the front yard.

Billy's truck rolls slowly through the neighborhood, trying not to draw any unwanted attention to their presence. JD sits up in the passenger seat as his parents' house comes into view, "there, Billy, the blue house with the white trim. Look, there she is standing beside the house!" He knows that he is taking a risk by coming here to see her, but it is a risk that JD has to take. If Billy's realistic negativity about their little journey holds any weight, this may be the last time he gets to see her.

Shutting the engine off, Billy lets the truck roll to a stop beside the curb. Before he can ask a question, JD is already jumping out of the truck to go see his mother. "Okay, since I didn't get to ask, I'll make the decision on my own." Judging by what JD has already told Billy, the son can't find a way to stand up to the father. That's okay; Billy is good at standing up for others who can't stand up for themselves. Without JD noticing, Billy slips out of the truck and makes his way over into the shadows of the yard beside the house.

"Mom," JD runs up to her and gives her a long overdue hug. "I know that we don't have much time, but I had to come by and let you know that I'm alright." JD pulls away from her and looks into her eyes, "I found my calling, Mom, just like you said I would. I wanted you to know that I am embracing it just like you told me to, mom, and I'm going to make you proud. I'm gonna make a difference."

JD's statement is interrupted by the front porch light coming on, startling both mother and son. Before his mother and JD could move a step, his father is standing on the front porch. "Madeline, I already took out the trash. You better not be wasting any trash bags! Those things cost..." Isaac's rant is cut off abruptly when his eyes fall on his son, "You!" Isaac comes off the porch as fast as he can and walks right up to Madeline who was shielding her son from the father. "Liar," he yells, and then reaches out and slaps his wife to the ground. Just as fast, the preacher draws back his hand again to take aim at his son. This time, JD doesn't sink to the grass to cower from Isaac's harsh discipline. Feeling disrespected, Isaac decides to carry out the threat. Surprise and then noticeable fear covers the man's face, as JD reaches out with swift reflexes to grab and stop Isaac's arm. The fear that the father feels stems from how JD instinctively draws back in a defensive manner to retaliate against his father's aggression.

JD just stands there for a few seconds fighting off the urge to lash out at his father for all of the years of abuse he and his mother have endured. A few seconds later, he lets go of Isaac's arm and lowers his own fist. "No, I'm not going to sink down to your level. But, if you ever touch her again, I'll come back for you, and it won't be God that you'll be begging for mercy."

This is the moment that Billy was expecting. He was right about JD's father, and he was right that JD would back down. The wife, nor the son, deserves such treatment. Being right about this, gives Billy the justification he needs to intervene. If JD can't do it, then maybe Billy can put the fear of God back into the man. If not that, then Billy will at least scare the hell outta preacher. From the corner of the front porch, Billy produces a small amount of energy, and launches it at the fuse panel on the side of the house. It's not enough to do any permanent damage, but the Johnstons will need to replace a bunch of fuses when this is all said and done.

"...worrying about your mother should be the least of your concerns! I'm calling the Police and the FBI!" Again Isaac's rant is interrupted by the entire house going dark. "What in the hell," Isaac turns around to investigate, only to be fear struck again by the vision of an unholy presence, standing on the front porch with glowing blood red eyes. "Mother of God," Isaac whispers as Billy's black form leaps from the porch to land in front of JD's father. Isaac's legs crumble underneath him as Billy reaches out and grabs the preacher by the collar of his shirt.

"You are a man of God. What gives you the right to abuse the ones who love you?" The energy around Billy's eyes intensifies, highlighting the snarled expression on his face. "If you ever lay a hand on another living soul again, I'll come back for you preacher man, and show you what hell on earth is really like!" Believing that his warning was well received, Billy releases his grip on Isaac's shirt, allowing the man to fall to the ground on his knees. When the preacher looks up, Billy was nowhere to be seen, having already disappeared into the shadows.

"JD, was that a friend of yours?" Madeline turns to JD hoping her fear could be comforted.

"Nope, I don't know who that was, mom." JD looks at his father to see Isaac crying and praying for forgiveness, "but, it looks like he got through to dad. Are you going to be alright?

"I think so, Jefferson." Madeline walks over like the faithful wife that she is, and helps her husband up from the ground. "You go on now, son, before the neighbors become too suspicious. You'd better stay in touch with me and let me know how this all turns out." JD walks over to his mother and gives her a hug and a kiss. Looking at his father, JD can't help but feel compassion for the sorrowful expression Isaac's face is displaying. Without another word, he turns and starts for Billy's truck, Madeline calls out to him one more time. "JD, if you run into him again, tell him I said thank you for not hurting my husband."

JD waves an acknowledgement back to his mom and walks around Billy's truck. Several neighboring lights had come on, probably due to people being awakened by the yelling. The last thing JD wants is to be recognized at his parent's house. By the time he's in the truck, his mother has already escorted his father back into the darkened house. Unknown to JD, the man and wife would spend the rest of the night together in a prayer vigil by candlelight. "You know, sometimes you can be pretty spooky, when you want to be." He closes the truck door and looks back to the front porch of his home to see if there is any sign of his mother. "Ya know, sometimes, along time ago, I would sit and daydream about the day when someone would come along and do what you did tonight. I always thought that I would feel better about it, after the fact."

"Yeah, well it's like we were talking about earlier. You're a nice guy, JD. You still listen to your conscience." Billy pulls out and heads north.

"Where are we headed now?"

"I figured we would crash at my apartment tonight, and then head out in the morning." Billy looks over at JD, "do you have something else in mind?"

"Naw, I'm willing to go anywhere that has no form of conflict taking place, and a soft place to lie down."

Chapter XVI

Back in New York, more specifically the lower Bronx…

Kaitlyn crawls down the side of a decaying building that houses a run down boxing academy owned by one Bruno Campano, who she knows nothing about. Once, it served as the haven for some of the upcoming stars of the New York boxing circuit. Now, it's nothing more than a hangout for Campano and his boys. Sure there are a few fighters who still come here to train, but they're all on Callistone's payroll one way or another.

Finding an open window on the fourth floor, Kaitlyn looks around the dark and eerie neighborhood before she crawls inside. By the time her eyes adjust to the pitch black interior of the room, her sense of smell is already detecting the stench of decades of human perspiration. To live in this building had to be torture for anyone to smell the rank odor day in and day out.

The apartment most likely served as a place for fighters who were just starting out, and had no other choice but to suffer the harsh living conditions. Using a small pen light she keeps tucked inside the legging of her boot, Kaitlyn shines the light around the room. She could see the promotion flyers and fight cards from the glory years of boxing, pinned to the walls, mostly to hide the plaster damage of age. "Well, I guess it was better than sleeping in the street," she thinks to herself. "What more could a guy really need than three hot meals, a cot and a squat," she adds, referring to how the kitchen and bedroom were one in the same, with the toilet and shower annexed by a ragged curtain.

Making her way over to the front door of the studio apartment, Kaitlyn is stopped suddenly when one of the floor boards creaks under her foot. After standing frozen for several seconds, she continues her path with a little slower speed, hoping that no one below heard the announcement of her presence. Stepping to the side a little, she opens the front door, offering another warning that she was there. The old and rusted hinges moan and scrape together, causing enough noise to stir the pigeons roosting in the stairwell in front of her. Her heart sinks a little as the birds take flight, creating a ruckus of their own. If anyone is in the building, they would surely be introducing themselves to her soon. This is something that she obviously wants to avoid, so she reacts, almost instinctively, leaping up to the underside of the stairway landing above her, to seek the safety of the shadows. What she doesn't expect is her disturbance to the surface of the ceiling causing the plaster to give way, and sending her and the large portion of plaster back down to the landing below with a loud crash. Staring up at the apartment door she just exited a few minutes before, Kaitlyn can't help but express her frustration. "Jesus Christ, can't anything go right for me tonight!"

Down the stairwell, chunks of plaster, and debris, ricochet around the banisters and stairs, causing Kaitlyn's anxiety to grow even more. Rolling over, she stares down between the bars of the hand railing, watching for any sign of someone investigating her chaotic reconnaissance. Her worst case scenario would have her dodging bullets as she made her way back out the way she came. Right now, that's an easy one, being that she is less than thirty feet away from her exit. The problem increases for her the deeper she goes into the building. Within a split second, she ponders the thought of calling all of this off. After a few minutes of staring into the blackness of the lower floors, her curiosity overwhelms her anxiety. "Why would Jonathan be interested in this place anyway?" Seeing no signs of life, Kaitlyn picks herself up and begins her trek downstairs. When she reaches the door to the gym on the second floor, her nose picks up the intensity of the malodorous stench that awaits her inside.

Pulling the door open, the expected smell rushes out to greet her, as if warning what awaits her inside. But now, she is detecting a second odor drifting in the air, one that she is unfamiliar with. Over in the far corner, a lone heavy bag is gently swinging because of the wind entering through a nearby broken window. The slow methodic squeak produced by the metal hook and chains supporting it only increases the eeriness of the old gymnasium. This and the occasional rat sighting gives Kaitlyn the reason she needs to quickly exit the large room and continue down to the first floor offices. Whatever it is about this place that caught Jonathan's attention must be downstairs. Either that or her father is definitely losing his touch. Even she can see that there isn't anything on the upper floors that would require a Federal Agent's attention.

Taking the stairs across the way, Kaitlyn goes over everything, which really isn't much, about what she knows, trying to come up with some reason why this place was on her father's list. None of it fits or makes sense, unless the assassin that Jonathan is chasing comes here to work out. At the bottom of the stairs, she can see the front door standing open slightly, suggesting that someone had been there using the door as their path of entry and/or exit. Down the hall towards the back of the building, she can see the flickering of a light in one of the offices. Her best guess is that somebody probably broke in to rob the place.

Slowly, Kaitlyn cautiously makes her way down the hallway approaching the office in question. If someone did break in, and are still here, she doesn't want to give her presence away. Chances are that if someone was in the building unwanted, she probably scared them away with the commotion she made upstairs. But, if they're still here, Kaitlyn's pretty confident that she could handle a couple of lowly street thugs intending on robbing the place. Stopping and standing beside the office door jamb, she peers into the room to see the flickering light was actually originating from another inside office. As she makes her way through the outer office, her eyes are focused on the swinging light of the next room. Then, with a crackle of electricity, the light falls from its mount and crashes to the floor. At first, she's like a deer caught in the headlights of a car, and then breaks the trance to hurry over to the doorway to see what she can see.

The street light outside casts its light into the room through the shattered windows on the far side of the office. What it reveals is a gruesome sight, of at least seven, maybe eight, bodies scattered about the room and draped over the furniture. This is the origin of the unfamiliar smell, coupled with the vision of death is enough to turn her stomach. Still, her curiosity urges her in to investigate more, but she is slowed by the fact that her foot was stuck to the floor. Using her pen light, she shines the beam down to see the floor covered in a thick gelatinous layer of human blood. So much blood; how could there be so much blood? Moving the light around more, Kaitlyn sees more bodies piled on the floor as well, bringing the death toll to fifteen, maybe sixteen.

Most teenage girls would be ready to break and run from a scene like this, but not Kaitlyn. She continues to scan the room with her small flashlight searching for clues. That is, until she sees the face of Bruno Campano. The expression of shock and fear frozen on the mobster's face for all to see warns her that this is a very bad place, in more ways than one. The light continues to move around, checking the face of each dead man to collect the same result. "These were men of power," she deduces. "Never in their wildest dreams did they ever suspect an attack like this on their home turf. The time is growing near for her to join the ranks of teenage girls. All of these dead bodies, in this spooky setting, are getting the best of Kaitlyn's bravado. Then, to top it all off, she thinks she sees movement over in the corner of the room. Moving the light over quickly, she finds nothing, but for a split second, she thought she saw a pair of red eyes looking back at her. It didn't matter if it was a big rat, or something else staring at her, Kaitlyn has already decided that it's time for her to leave, now.

Backing out of the room, she crosses the outer office and exits into the hallway, just in time to see Jonathan coming into the back of the building at the end of the hallway, "Oh this just keeps getting better and better!" For the moment, she's concealed her presence in the shadows of the stairwell, but Jonathan is making his way up the hall and he will see her if she doesn't move soon. One leap straight up takes her to the third floor landing. Now with her father added to the situation, her anxiety is beginning to peak. Looking around, she thinks that she sees another pair of red eyes. This troubles her as well, but before she can make her next leap, Kaitlyn does a double take to the doorway across the stairwell, thinking she saw another pair of eyes staring back at her. Were they the same eyes, or a different pair? Being that they were within the doorway, five feet off the floor is enough to send her on her way. Rats or not, she has no intention of tangling with anything man-sized with red eyes.

Up to the fourth floor landing she moves, scurrying up the wall, heading for her exit. She doesn't believe that Jonathan saw her, or at least he didn't call out to her. But, something was watching her and she doesn't feel good about it at all. Seeing the sight again inside the studio apartment, as she makes her way to the window, causes Kaitlyn to cast caution aside, and exit the building as fast as she can.

Downstairs, Jonathan hears the noise made by his daughter on the floors above, alerting him to another presence in the building. Slipping on her bloody footprint in the hall sends the unsuspecting agent to the floor, where his attention is diverted to the office massacre. Being an investigator for the FBI, Jonathan has dealt with the smell of a dead body plenty of times to recognize the stench. This obviously requires his attention more than a possible intruding vagrant. Entering the outer office, Jonathan draws his pistol, just to be on the safe side. When he discovers the death scene laid out in the inner office, he is set back in his thoughts and theories about this little covert investigation. Finding one of Callistone's top men used as target practice is the last thing Jonathan expected to find. But, there the bruiser is spread out on a poker table for the entire world to see. "I guess you weren't holding the winning hand, were ya Bruno?"

Another clue he wasn't expecting was the blood stain footprints leaving the room. Someone was in here, recently, and could have been the perp he heard moving around upstairs. The question from that is, "who was it, and what were they doing in here?" Judging by the size and shape of the footprint, it could have been a woman, or young lady. The thought of Kaitlyn spying on him crosses his mind, worrying him about what she could have witnessed. He pans the room with his flashlight from side to side, stopping briefly when he sees the small rebel flag sticking out one of the bullet holes in Bruno's chest. A lot of fire power was used for this, judging by the bullet holes riddling the bodies, and the empty casings littering the blood soaked floor. Hearing a scuffling sound over in the corner, Jonathan pans the light back around to where he heard the noise. When the beam of light stops on a blood soaked shirt of a man standing in the corner of the room, Jonathan stops, and is honestly surprised as hell. When the man growls and lunges at the FBI agent, Jonathan reacts with actions of survival, firing two slugs into the man's chest to send him back to the floor.

Jonathan shines the flashlight on the body taking notice to the exit wounds in the body's back and shoulders. Nine bullet holes means that someone shot the guy seven times before Jonathan pulled his trigger. He recognizes the man's face. It's lil' Al Campano, son of Bruno, a washed up prize fighter. Finding him here isn't surprising at all. With Bruno's eyesight and health waning, Alfred doesn't stray too far from his father's side. What is surprising to Jonathan, is when Al opens his eyes, glowing red, and lunges up at Jonathan again. This time, he doesn't hesitate to shoot three more times wanting to make sure the former boxer stays down for good this time.

Frustrated by the turn of events, Jonathan turns to leave as quickly as possible, without stirring up any more evidence. He's already contributed five slugs for ballistics to trace back to his gun. At the moment, all he's worried about is getting out of the building before anyone else shows up, or comes back to life. Lil' Al's actions were enough to shake up Jonathan's applecart but good. He's heard of instances where guys were strung out on dope so bad that they were too stoned to know they were dead. He wants to apply the scenario to this instance, but deep down inside something tells him that it's more than that. Regardless, he needs to add these new factors into his equations, and rethink his plans. Who is it that's this new player in this game? Has his target changed the rules of the game without telling anyone else? The rebel flag is a clue that needs to be investigated more. At the moment, he feels that his home will be the best place for him to do this. For whatever reason, he craves the comfort and security of his bed for the night. If nothing else, he'll have the opportunity to check in on Kaitlyn. Something is nagging at him that it's something he needs to do.

Kaitlyn rushes into her home via her bedroom window, pressed for time to be in before Jonathan shows up. There's no guarantee that he saw her in Brooklyn, or that he will or won't come home tonight. But, if he does, it'll be between ten and ten thirty, to make sure that she's in before curfew. His scheduled lifestyle is the one thing that she can always count on. Right on cue, she hears Jonathan's keys hit the lock on the front door, as she crosses the living room ceiling. Into the hall she scurries, dropping down into the doorway of her bedroom, just as the front door swings open. Her goal was to be out of her costume before he has a chance to see her in it. The downside to choosing to disrobe first leaves her vulnerable to the open bedroom door. With her top pulled up over her head, Jonathan scares her beyond belief when he calmly asks, "What are you doing?"

"Dad!" Kaitlyn covers her bare torso and runs over to slam the door in his face. She had hoped to avoid this situation, but never thought it would transpire like a peep show.

"Ya know that was kind of nice to hear you call me dad, but I had to wonder where you were, dressed like that." Jonathan almost falls into the room when Kaitlyn snatches the door open.

"What was nice, seeing your teenage daughter topless? You're a perv, Jonathan." With her sweat shirt covering her modesty, she pushes her way past her father. The reason she slammed the door the way she did was to give her a chance to come up with an alibi. "As for where I was, what does it matter? I wasn't out playing superhero, if that's what you're thinking." She stops and turns to face him when Jonathan offers no reply. "It is, isn't it? Well, just so that you know, I have a photo shoot next week, and I was at the gym down the street trying to tone up my legs." Heading straight for the kitchen, Kaitlyn makes her a cool down drink and proceeds to ignore Jonathan's disbelieving stare. "I thought you were gonna be gone for a few days or so. What are you doing back here so soon? I know that you didn't catch the bad guy already. You're good, but not that good."

"Thanks for your vote of confidence. Actually, I was missing your abuse, and being away from you more than four hours, so I decided to stop by the house so you could bust my balls a little, before I head back out." Pulling her door closed, he adds, "Good night, Kaitlyn. I'll see you in a few days." Off to his room, Jonathan leaves his daughter feeling as disconnected from her as he usually does. At least with her tucked away in her room, he can go through his files without disturbance or interference from Kaitlyn. The first thing he grabs from the cabinet is his stash of bourbon and takes a swig straight from the bottle. That was to calm his nerves a little, after his episode with lil' Al, back at Bruno's gym. Never in all his years with the Bureau has he seen anyone take that many bullets before he stayed down. But it is more than that. The entire incident made Jonathan's skin crawl. Every fiber of his being was screaming that there was more going on, something unnatural. The problem is that Jonathan doesn't want to hear it, or believe it.

The last thing Kaitlyn wants to do right now is interfere with Jonathan any more tonight. An hour ago, she was following one of Jonathan's leads. Each face frozen with the look of fear, as they watched the gunman end their lives, haunts her thoughts. Blood was everywhere, on the walls, on the ceiling, and washing over the floor. Never in her life did she ever think she would see so much blood at one time. The sight was such a surprise and blow to her psyche that she had to come home for the night. Not because she was worried about Jonathan, but because she wanted to lie down and cry from the emotional strain of it all. This wasn't what she expected, when she made the decision to follow her intuition. She wishes that Toby hadn't turned his back on her. He always knew how to make her feel better in times like this. Maybe she'll try again tomorrow, and it will offer her better results, or at least fewer dead bodies.

Jonathan has no idea that he has found exact same crime scene Kaitlyn stumbled across, of Bruno Campano and his lieutenants gunned down around the poker table. The toy flag is the giant question mark of the night. Is it the calling card of some new player that making a move for dominance? The other thing that didn't fit the picture was the single footprint in the blood, resembling a woman's shoe. Was this new hitman actually a woman? Being the paranoid father always suspecting Kaitlyn of treachery, he thought about his daughter for a moment, wondering what the odds were of Kaitlyn being at the crime scene. Of course, he was glad to find her at home, which eases his mind a little. He may never know that she is sobbing herself to sleep because of the traumatizing sight she saw. He might not ever see the faint footprint of blood on the living room ceiling. All he knows for now is that she is safe and sound here at home.

With that thought process resolved, he can now focus on what he knows about Bruno Campano. Finding him and his boys slaughtered like that even took Jonathan by surprise. Why there, and why like that? This seems like a piece from a different puzzle all together, as in it doesn't fit. Who had the balls to take out Antonio Callistone's strong arm? This changes the perimeters, which means that Jonathan will need to change his tactics to compensate, if he's going to get to the bottom of this. The one unresolved issue was lil' Al's actions. As far as Jonathan is concerned, he's willing to leave it that way to focus on the other problems at hand. He can contemplate the actions of a dead man after Crossfire is behind bars for life.

Frances Callistone sits at his private table, in his son's ritzy Manhattan nigh club, waiting for the rest of his men to sit down. "Something's not right in the big apple, boys." I'll be the first one to shoot the guy, who disrespects my brother, but even I have to wonder what is going on with him. Now, I know that the loss of Darien was a blow to him…"

"Yeah, but not the organization, right Pops?"

Frankie gives his overzealous son a scowl, and then continues with his train of spoken thought. "…but involving Margaret with matters dealing with the corporation is beyond me. The other problem I'm having is that Valleccio informed me that someone has gone into De Luca's, and gunned down him and his boys, all in one fell swoop."

Sitting over in the darkened corner of the booth, Uncle Anton leans forward to retrieve his fresh drink from the table. "Tell me Frances, how do you think that Margaret is involved with Carmine's demise? Is it that, or do you fear the thought of her taking over permanently, when Antonio hands the Corporation over to her?"

"I'll tell ya what I think," Johnny sits down to explain his theory, "I think she paid to have De Luca knocked off, to make it look like my pops is making a move for the seat. Everybody knows that Carmine was Mr. C's leading man, and could never be swayed otherwise. That way, she could blame pops sayin' that he was making his move." Johnny takes a drink of his Scotch and sets the glass onto the table. "Personally, I think it's what should happen any way. Don't get me wrong, Carmine didn't deserve to go out like that. I'm just saying that the leader of this organization, and the corporation should carry the Callistone name, and be able to carry on the family name, that's all."

Anton stares at Johnny for a moment, and then throws his martini into Johnny's face. "You talk too much," Anton turns his head and looks at Frankie, "and you talk too much to him."

Frances Callistone couldn't agree with his uncle more, but on the same hand, Johnny is partially right. "Yeah, well the problem is that if my thick headed son could come up with the scenario, then the chances are that the same thought may be rattling around in my brother's head as well. I'm going to set up an appointment with him tomorrow, and talk to him personally about De Luca. Until then, I want all of my boys to watch their backs and be on guard for anything like that coming our way."

Anton motions for the hostess to bring him another martini. "So tell me something, Frances. When did you and ol' Sergio Vellecio mend bridges and bury the hatchet, so to speak?"

"Let's just say that we came to a mutual agreement, for the sake of our interests in what's going on." Frankie chugs down the rest of his watered down bourbon and motions for his son to go get him another.

"Keep an eye on that boy of yours, Frances. We don't need him stirring the pot right now." Anton's phone rings distracting the aging mobster. To his surprise, the caller ID reports that it is Carmine's personal cell phone calling. "What?" He looks at Frank and Johnny, before answering the call with a question, "De Luca, is that you?" Frank and Johnny look at each other, completely baffled by the words coming out of Anton's mouth. "Yeah, no I understand.. Of course, I will inform Antonio about it in the morning. Very well, I will see you then." Anton hangs up the phone and then stares at Frankie and Johnny. "I don't know what the two of you are doing, but someone is going to have some explaining to do."

Chapter XVII

Billy and JD cross the New Jersey state line closing in on their target. "Listen," Billy spouts off, interrupting the silence inside the truck, "I'm hungry, and want to go over our plan for tonight." He glances over at his sleeping passenger looking for a response. JD had dozed off hours ago, after not sleeping much last night. Billy nudges him with an easy punch to JD's shoulder and asks, "Hey are you with me?"

JD sits up straight in his seat, rubbing and batting his eyes while facing straight ahead. "Yeah, yeah, food sounds good to me too." He stretches his back and shoulders the best way he can trying to work a kink out of his neck. Then, he notices the unfamiliar landscape and the fact that the sun was setting in the west. "Wait a minute; I didn't think you had a plan yet. You said last night that you were going to talk about it and put it together while we drove. Where are we, any way?" It's then that JD turns in his seat to face Billy. What he sees is a little unnerving to say the least. Billy had maps and papers scattered across the dash and console, and had a notebook wedged into the steering wheel.

"Yeah, I know, but I didn't have anything to do while you played sleeping beauty, so I worked it all out myself. That's why we need to go over it while we eat." Billy scans a passing billboard searching for signs of an eating establishment up ahead.

"Uh huh, I can see that, but do you really think it's safe to be driving while you do that?"

"Oh hell, this flat road ain't nothing! You should have been awake when we were going through the mountains while ago. I'll tell you what; there was a couple of times that involved some serious STF!" Billy chuckles to himself recalling the said incidents and then breathes a sigh of relief.

"Okay, judging by the added gestures, I'm probably going to regret this, but what does STF stand for?"

"Sphincter tension factor," Billy replies with a smile.

"I was right," JD admits. He really didn't want or need to know that. In fact, he should probably be happy that he slept through the hair raising events, and is happy to leave it at that. "Hey, there's a McDonalds up at the next off ramp. "What time is it, any way?"

Responding to JD's declaration, Billy sends the truck across two lanes of traffic and heads up the off ramp in search of sustenance. "Almost seven o'clock," Billy answers pulling into the McDonalds parking lot, gathers his collection of paperwork and shoves it over into JD's lap. As they pull into the drive thru lane, Billy begins to lay out the gist of what he had so far. "So, here's what I was thinking. I'll drop you off at the location on the map marked number one. All we're worrying about is recon for information. In fact, I don't even want you going near the building until you're absolutely sure that it's clear to do so. While you're there, I'm gonna go up the road to the location marked number two. We gather what information we can, and then move on to locations marked three and four." Billy pulls up to the window and waits for the girl to take his order. "Yeah, how ya doin'? Let me have six Big Macs, two large fries, and two large cokes." Once he drives away from the window, he feels comfortable to continue his explanation. "You'll need to take a copy of that map with you, so I can drop you off a couple of blocks away. That way you can hoof it in like you did at the Chism estate, without getting the truck too close to the target to be seen by the bad guys. What we are looking for most of all is fire power. Guaranteed, the place that has the most guns at it will be the location of where Taylor and the others are being held. If you run into any problems, 9-1-1 me and I'll get back to you as quick as possible. The trick will be to avoid problems so that you don't need to call for help."

He drives the truck up to the next window, where the attendant is happily waiting with their food order. After graciously thanking her for the service, Billy pulls away leaving the young woman swooned by his southern charm. Pulling around to the back, Billy points out a parking spot at the back of the lot, and hurries over to get it, as if someone else might be interested. During this mad rush for the open space, JD is doing his best to organize the papers in his lap before they are sent to the floor by Billy's erratic driving. Drawn in by the specifics of it all, JD finds himself scanning over more and more of each page he stacks. "How could you possibly know so much about all of these places, when you said earlier that you've never been to New York?"

"My dad's notebooks, he kept records on everything. When he first started tracking down leads on Callistone, his quest began in New York. My mom was just starting out with her private practice, and my dad was just promoted to Senior Inspector. It was when he learned of Callistone's desire to relocate to Atlanta, that prompted my father to transfer to the south as well, where he finished out his career." After thinking about it for a moment, Billy edits his statement, "actually, I guess you could say that his career finished him." Finishing off his first burger, Billy takes a long slurp of his coke to wash it down, before continuing his explanation.

"I knew that all I had to do was find a Callistone property within each of the circles to give me a target to search. I knew that they could all be long shots, but, it's all that we have, so we have to go with it. When you look at it kinda sideways, they'd be a good place as any to begin our search." The monster inside needs food, prompting Billy to unwrap his next burger and continue his feast.

He's impressed, "I bet no one ever expected you to have this kind of information. I can see now how this could be very beneficial to us." JD starts into his first burger and looks over to see Billy finishing off his third. "Dude, are you gonna be worth a shit after eating all of that junk food?"

"Yeah, no problem, in fact I was thinking that I should have ordered another one," Billy replies, eyeing the sack beside JD. "I always have to pack it on like this to have enough energy to support my accelerated metabolism. Besides, I always eat when I'm on the edge. It calms me down," he adds, shoving a handful of fries into his mouth. "Man, no matter where you go in this country, McDonalds always has the best fries." Billy picks up his coke and has it standing by to wash the potatoes down. "Getting back to your other statement, maybe he does, maybe he doesn't know. If you're right, and he doesn't, then we have to take full advantage of every situation. This guy that Callistone has hired is an outsider. If we're lucky, the plan was his to make, and that could lower the odds against us a little. But, that also means that he and his men are well financed and very experienced. Antonio never does anything cheap, and he usually gets his money's worth. If I'm right about this guy, he would want no involvement from Callistone's men and want to handle the situation personally." Billy's taken back a little when JD starts rotating his head from side to side. "What are you doing?"

"I'm trying to see your sideways point of view. No offense, but I think it works, and I see what you're trying to say. I have to admit, Billy, it sounds like you've pretty much got the bases covered the best you can. I guess we'll both find out how right or wrong we are, in a little while." JD reaches for his next burger, and then opts out, offering the food to Billy. "Personally, I hope you're dead on about this, and everything goes as smooth as silk." JD sits back and continues to read Billy's notes while the driver of the truck finishes off the rest of the food. "Brother, I can't believe you ate five of those things."

"Yeah, well I can't believe you only ate one!" Saphyre had made a similar comment about Billy's food intake. He hopes that she is alright, and regrets the fact that she has been dragged into this.

Saphyre awakens to find herself in the grips of two men, dragging her through some kind of industrial building. There is no way of her getting away, so she decides to keep her consciousness a secret from her captors, at least for the time being. "This has got to be the most elaborate plan the boss has ever run, don't you think?" One man asks the other.

"Yeah, but from what I've heard, this is supposed to be the biggest score, and that's what requires the intricacies that have been put into play," the other replies as they wait for the elevator to reach the first floor. "Remember, the boss is expecting the primary target to be here soon. Whatever you do, don't let your guard down, or this guy will take you apart and leave you dead, before you know what happened."

"Uh huh, and like that's gonna happen. With the fire power in this building, this rebel vigilante doesn't stand a chance." The elevator doors open allowing the two mercenaries to enter with Saphyre's body. She remains lifeless as she watches the gunman push the button for the second floor. At least she can assume that she isn't going to die just yet. Otherwise, she would already be dead. The down side to that is the possibility of upcoming torture to find out what she knows. Nothing would be the correct answer, but if she is going to be tortured and held captive, these men aren't going to give up that easy.

The elevator doors open again, revealing the second floor in front of her. Actually, it's a short hallway that leads down to a room where bright lights are flashing within, lighting up the hallway via the frosted window in the door. A woman's scream echoes from the room, causing Saphyre to tense up in the grasp of her captors. "Oh good," one of the men says, "you've woke up at the perfect time. Wait until you meet Mr. Smith. He's a scream." The two men laugh as the woman in the room screams out again.

A rap against the door by one of the gunmen signals the occupants of the room to open up. Saphyre's heart is filled with terror, as she gazes into the room at a young woman strapped down to a table, being electrocuted as a form of torture. "Ah good," A man states as he takes notice of Saphyre's presence. "It's always nice to know that we have plenty of test subjects. "To emphasize his point, the man raises the levels of electricity being administered, as if he was trying to make a point. "My name is Mr. Smith. It is a pleasure to have you, my dear. Bind her against the walls with the others," he instructs, pointing to the rest of the hostages shackled to the wall across the room.

Saphyre looks over and recognizes Billy's mother, but at the moment, she feels it's best to keep that to herself. For now, she must recall all of her father's words of wisdom for a safe life, if she is going to survive this.

"Now then Ms. Lewis," Smith says, leaning over Taylor's face, "Are you ready to confess to the truths I have listed for you?" Like a sadistic madman, Smith wipes away a tear rolling down Taylor's cheek. All she can do is grit her teeth and try to catch her breath while this vile bastard gives his spill about her signing a confession. "I'll tell you what, little lady; I'll let you think about it for an hour or so." He turns to face his associates and says, "Shut it down for the evening, boys. We'll see what she has to say in a little while."

"No need to wait," Taylor says, still trying to catch her breath. "I can say it now. Go to hell, you sonofabitch!" Mr. Smith and his men laugh at her remark and simply exit the room, shutting off all of the lights to leave their hostages in the pitch black dark.

Chapter XVIII

Leaping and bounding through the New York skyline, Kaitlyn arrives at her first target of the night. Already, last night is a distant memory to her, with Kaitlyn writing it off as a learning experience. Tonight is different. Tonight, she will move with more caution, and definitely not take any chances. What good would she be in her defense to Jonathan, if she gets herself killed? Now if she would only stick to this train of thought, Kaitlyn might do alright tonight. The problem is that she is already reverting back to her normal thought processes, finding something to complain about to make her hurry through what she is trying to accomplish. The serving for the night is the hideous aroma of the Fulton Fish Market mingling with the stench of the East River. It's enough to turn Kaitlyn's already nervous stomach, but she refuses to admit it.

Tonight, she is in luck, or so she believes. Her target is the building next door, but the men occupying the roof she's on, crouched down behind its parapet wall, give her plenty of notice that something is going down. The gunmen are all gathered along the west side of the building facing the river, but she doesn't doubt that there is a few more roaming around for security. For now, her cover behind an air conditioning unit has her hidden from prying eyes, but she knows that she can't stay in one place for too long. Reaching down, she opens the only storage container on her belt. As the bottom flap door swings open, Kaitlyn retrieves a roll of spearmint breath mints. "This was the best idea I had, when I designed this little outfit." Popping several mints into her mouth, she returns the roll to her belt, and hopes the taste of spearmint can ease her stomach, and her olfactory senses.

To either side of her are rows of air conditioning units that would serve as a nice path of travel. Kaitlyn also knows that it would be a perfect place for an ambush if she isn't careful. Tonight, careful is her middle name. The main thing is that something big is happening and Jonathan is going to miss out. This of course is based on a phone conversation that Jonathan had late last night. Someone else who is missing out is Amanda and Henry. Toby is missing out too, but he didn't run off and leave everybody behind, just Kaitlyn. Still, with the three of them watching her back, Kaitlyn could be a little more adventurous with her tactics, but at the moment, she has to watch her back, front, and both sides. "Running solo kinda' sucks," she admits. Of course the fire power of this magnitude is something far worse than not having her friends around, so Kaitlyn is more than willing to stick to her plan of simple sightseeing.

With her course plotted, she checks on the gunmen one more time and then readies to depart, right up until a lone gunman steps out in front of her, stopping to light a cigarette. Before he has an opportunity to turn and look her way, Kaitlyn is already leaping high into the air. The gunman is completely unaware of her presence, and helpless to her descent. A crunching in his neck and a thud against the roof is all that is heard, when she makes contact with the gunman's head and shoulder. Kaitlyn checks on the men along the wall, and doesn't continue her trek until she is certain that no one was alerted to her actions. She takes off again, making her way to the building next door, thankfully without any more intrusions.

As she bounded over the alley between the buildings, Kaitlyn could see more armed figures lurking about the two waterfront properties. Whatever is happening is illegal, and that creates a small desire to call her father right now, to get him over here to handle this. Then, after a moment of clarity, she puts on her big girl panties and readies to continue the task she laid out for herself. Common sense tells her that if she placed a call to Jonathan right now, she could actually be putting his life in jeopardy. Of course, that's like a basket of mixed fruit, when it comes to how she feels about Jonathan. One could say that she fears the thought of giving up her hand, and reveal what she's doing.

On the lower roof next door, she's surprised to find that the only thing occupying this roof deck is three rows of air conditioning units, and a large neon sign at the front of the building. "Wow, no one's interested in this building, at all." Did Jonathan miss his target by one building address? No, she knows that her father is a better detective than that. Whatever's going on next door is completely separate from what Jonathan's working on. That however doesn't mean that she can't see if there is anything interesting happening while she is here. Using the parapet wall to conceal her presence, Kaitlyn makes her way to the west side of the building. Peering over the edge, she can see more men stationed amongst the containers, as if waiting for the guest of honor to arrive. A long black car turns the corner around the building at the end, and slowly drives down the docks after turning its headlights off.

Could this be going down right now? If so, Kaitlyn would much rather be inside the building hiding, instead of on the roof where stray bullets could be flying. After seeing what happened to Bruno and his boys last night, she wants to avoid gunfire as much as possible. After scanning the roof, she sees that the only roof access door is at the opposite corner of the building. If she tries for the door from where she stands, the men on the roof next door would surely see her. The only choice then is to skirt the parapet wall and moves back to the front of the building to avoid detection.

Hunched over, she makes her over to the rows of a/c units and meanders between them, closing the gap between her and the access door. When she reaches the last roof top unit, all that's left is fifty or sixty feet of open roof. "Okay, so what do you do, when you can't become invisible?" The full moon shining bright overhead doesn't help matters much. She's got two choices; the safety of the shadows, or what's in the box? One leap could put her at her target with no problem. To cross a distance like this, the height she would need would put her just about at eye level for the gunmen on the roof of the adjoining building. Well, she can either go for it, or sit there playing the guessing game, wondering when would be the right time to go. Kaitlyn looks around one more time to make sure it was clear to go, and then she leaps into the air.

You should always look before you leap. It's one of those "words of wisdom" catch phrases that always seems to apply in situations like this. If Kaitlyn had, she would have seen one of the steel support cables that secure the large sign to the roof, running right through her path of travel. Catching her across her midriff, the cable slings her back down to the surface of the roof with awesome force. Panic stricken, Kaitlyn tries to right herself and get her legs underneath her. She's able to succeed, at the very last moment, but the roof itself is incapable of handling the impact. One leg goes right through rotted roof decking, while the other one folds up underneath her, sending Kaitlyn's right knee up under her chin, knocking her out cold. Unconscious, the aspiring superhero falls back lifeless on the rooftop for all to see.

Behind the building, Salvador Gambenni's limousine rolls slowly down the west side docks, a few minutes early for a scheduled appointment. Rule of thumb; anything dealing with Antonio Callistone's men, and appointments scheduled "after hours", usually isn't a good, or legal, thing. For Sal Gambenni, the night is the favorite time for him to operate his business endeavors. "I want you to make sure that the guys are in place. I'm not a big fan of the way things are being run around here, and I don't trust little Ms. Margaret one bit. From here on out boys, all we worry about is Mr. Callistone's interests, until he is back in control again." Gambenni lights his cigar and looks out the window at the moving river to his right. "I don't buy this crap that if this transfer happens now, two weeks ahead of schedule, it will be delivered safe before anyone can move on it. Does she really think that anyone has the guts to make a move against us?" Gambenni steps out of the car and looks around the docks. He motions for his men to spread out while two stay close at his side.

On cue, a Delivery truck pulls around the corner at the opposite end of the docks, and continues to drive slowly towards Gambenni and his men. As it closes in on them, the headlights flash, signaling that the other party had arrived. The truck stops twenty feet away, with the cab doors swinging open to allow six armed men to quickly exit the truck. In a matter of seconds, the six men dressed in black fatigues walk right up to Gambenni with no sign of what their intentions are. The leader of the group steps forward to address the mobster with distain sounding out in his voice. "What's the meaning of this, Gambenni? A shipment like this shouldn't be moved without adequate protection serving in the convoy!"

"It will be alright," a voice replies from behind the group. What follows next is a maelstrom of bullets flying in all directions. Gambenni's men fall from the shadows. They fall from the rooftops, and stacks of cargo containers. The six men from the truck are cut down without having a chance to return a shot. Gambenni's bodyguards fall at his feet right before the aging mobster takes a bullet to the throat and then another to his forehead. With his gun stored away in its holster, the mystery man walks over and lays a toy rebel flag across the mobster's head, gently patting it into the pool of blood of the gunshot wound, just to keep it in place for others to find. Without a sound, the man turns and walks away, casually tossing a grenade into Gambenni's car.

At the corner of the lower roof, Jonathan Justice can't believe what he's just seen. He was originally climbing up the secondary roof ladder from the front of the building's lower section. He thinks to himself that before yesterday, he never in his wildest dreams would he have seen Kaitlyn here, but after the events at Campano's boxing academy, Jonathan really isn't surprised. Pissed as hell, yes, but not surprised. Then, to top it all off, there was some kind of major gun fight behind the building on the docks, that he can't investigate because of his downed daughter lying on the middle of the roof. For him, this entire plan has just gone sideways because of his Kaitlyn's unwavering attempts to enter his world. How stupid is he? Did he really think that she was going to be cooperative and compliant with his wishes? Now he has to sacrifice weeks of investigation to see to her safety. One thing is for certain; Kaitlyn is going to be in deep shit, for a long time, if the two of them survive this little episode.

At best estimate, Jonathan's got about a hundred feet between him and his daughter. But with the gunmen on the roof next door dispersing from their hiding places, he would surely be seen if he was to run out to Kaitlyn. Jonathan knows that he needs to get to her, but drawing attention to her would only put her in further jeopardy. Taking the best, but longer route, he moves along the parapet wall, until he reaches the framework of the massive company sign. "What in the hell was she thinking? Maybe she does still blame him for the loss of her mother, deep down inside, and wants to reunite the family." He slips out of the shadows of the sign works and hurries over to Kaitlyn's side. "Come on, baby, wake up for Jonathan." He gently taps the side of her cheek with his fingers trying to revive her. "Come on, Kaitlyn, it's time to wake up and go home."

Suddenly, Kaitlyn's eyes open wide, recognizing the pain registering in her mind, from her wounded leg. When her foot created the hole in the roof, the splintered wood decking was embedded in her leg. "Daddy?"

Unknown to Agent Justice, two of the men occupying the building inside are moving around directly below him and his daughter. "I'm telling you, Vinny; I heard a noise, or something, over here."

"Yeah, and I'm tellin' ya that there ain't nothing over here but this little bit of trash on the floor." Vinny shines his flashlight around the perimeter of the warehouse, but sees nothing of concern.

Davie isn't buying it, "Well what about the gunfire we heard? Doesn't that make you a little paranoid? When Mr. Gambenni called, he told us to stay inside and guard the shipment no matter what, but he never said anything about a fire fight." Just as he is about to walk away, a small drop of fluid hits Davie on his nose, "Vinny, what just hit me in the face? Please tell me it wasn't rat piss."

Blinding Davie by shining his flashlight at his partner's face, Vinny sees right away the drop of blood running down the side of Davie's nose. "Holy shit, Davie, that's blood," he explains, shining his light up at the ceiling of the warehouse.

Before Davie could respond, a stranger walks right up behind the two thugs and shoots them in the back of their heads with no remorse or concern. "Get up there, and find out who that is," the man commands to his troops. His British accent is thick, almost guttural, but his attitude his overwhelming with arrogance. Keying up the microphone on his headset, the man reports to his cohorts, "Shalimar, m' love, the inside is secured, we can begin our set up, as soon as I check out a little disturbance on the roof."

As part of said disturbance, Jonathan looks into his daughter's eyes and tries to be as caring as possible when he says, "I'm gonna pull you outta there on the count of three. It's probably going to hurt like hell, but I've got to get you away from here as fast as possible." He pulls away some of the roofing materials around her wounded leg, and then grabs her under her arms for the extraction. "Take a deep breath and hold it, kiddo. One, two, th…" His countdown is rudely interrupted by gunfire riddling up through the roof from inside the building, around the father and daughter. Hit by one of the bullets, and grazed by another, Jonathan is sent falling back, ripping Kaitlyn up back through the roof. She screams out in agony, falling back down to the roof deck beside her father.

Rolling over, Jonathan sees Kaitlyn writhing in pain, but at least she's conscious and alive. There's no doubt that their presence has been compromised, and they need to flee immediately, but it's already too late for that. On cue, the roof access door flies open as half a dozen men rush out onto the roof deck with their weapons aimed at the father and his daughter. Right away, they split up, with three covering Kaitlyn and the others focused on Jonathan, as the mystery man from downstairs exits onto the roof. "Well now, would you look at this, mates? We've got ourselves a two for one sale! Sometimes, I even surprise myself," the leader declares, kneeling down beside Jonathan. "I guess you know now why they call me Checkmate." The man slaps Jonathan's gun free from his hand, "See, that's me name; Danny 'Checkmate' Muldoon, but you know who I am, don' ya Special Agent Justice?" Muldoon looks over at Kaitlyn, "Do you lass? Do you know why they call me Checkmate?"

Jonathan gives the hired killer a hateful stare, "yeah, I know who you are. In fact, it's your boss that I'm looking for. You wouldn't want to tell me where he is, would ya?" Jonathan sees an opportunity and seizes it. Kicking Muldoon's feet out from underneath him, Jonathan yells at his daughter, "Kaitlyn, get out of here!" Before the hitman can catch his balance, Kaitlyn is already bounding away from her captors, sailing high overhead. Her wounded leg is painful and distracting to her focus, but it's nothing like the effects of the tazer that Muldoon hits her with, as her path of travel carries her over him. He didn't aim, look, or even move, except his arm when he raised the weapon and pulled the trigger. "It's because I always know what my opponent is going to do, before they do," he declares, walking over to Kaitlyn. He giggles slightly, watching her lying on the roof, twitching and convulsing. "I knew you were going to do that too." Muldoon stares at Kaitlyn for a second, and then looks back at Jonathan with a big smug smile, "what are ya doin' out here, Jonny boy, training another one for the slaughter?" Muldoon keys up his headset microphone, while keeping a watchful eye on his wily hostage. "Shalimar, we're coming down with one of the party crashers." He motions for his men to gather Kaitlyn up, giving Jonathan reason to try and stop them. Before Jonathan can get up off the roof, Muldoon is already holding his pistol pointed right at Jonathan's head. "Ah, ah, ya surprise me, Jonny boy. I didn't think ya could move that fast with the chunk o' lead buried in your leg." The Irish born British assassin gives Jonathan an evil grin, "Don' be worryin' about the lass, just yet. Ya need to be worryin' about your own needs first. After all, what good are ya to her, if ya bleed out here all over the roof?"

"I'll be coming for you, Muldoon, you piece of shit. Don't you worry about that."

"I knew you'd say that," Muldoon declares. Then, just as quick, he lowers the pistol slightly and squeezes off a round, hitting Jonathan right in the stomach. "Crossfire will be happy to know that you're gonna come calling. I just don' want it to be an easy task for ya." Even gut shot, Jonathan still has enough left in him to try for Muldoon again. With no worry of threat, the hitman simply raises his tazer and embeds a set of electrocuting prongs into Jonathan's chest. "Lay down for a minute boy-o, before I put you down permanently. Pressing the button on his microphone, Muldoon calls down to his partner one more time. "Shalimar, m' Persian love, are ya hearin' what I'm sayin' to ya? The girl comin' down with me boys, I want her put in a car and readied to transport. I need to go see Crossfire and tell him about this new wrinkle."

A female's voice responds through the headset, warning him of her distaste for his lack of respect, "Watch your tongue when you speak to me, Irishman, or I might cut it out and serve it to my jackals, for dinner. Crossfire is in a meeting with Callistone. After that, he's headed to the main facility." Her voice is cold and deadly, like the desert night that brought this heartless woman into the world. For her, killing is a simple act of will. Man, woman, or child, matters not, when it comes to who dies by her hand. One, ten, or a thousand victims, life means nothing to her but something to extinguish like the flame of a candle. Soon the true rise of power will be made, and she will take her place beside the true leaders of this world. "Remember our orders,

Muldoon. We are supposed to remain here until Crossfire states otherwise."

"Don't fret yourself over it, lass, if ya knew what this little morsel means to the boss, you'd understand why I need to deliver the package in person, and as soon as possible."

Chapter XIX

Uncle Anton walks into his room wearing a silk house robe and slippers, carrying a bottle of fine wine, and puffing away at the sweet tobacco in his pipe. Waiting for him is a harem of attractive middle aged women who cater to the seventy year old Mafioso with pleasure. Anton knows how to treat the ladies. "Ah, I bid you good evening, ladies. Tonight, I will be reading from my collection of Pablo Neruda," he declares as he runs his fingers through his silver mane. The gathering of ladies applauds the choice as Anton sits down on the edge of the bed and begins to pour the ladies their glasses of wine. As he climbs up and adjusts his pillows at the head of the bed, the ladies take their place at the foot and enthusiastically waits tonight's reading.

Before Anton can begin his reading, a man dressed in black, complete with a mask, steps into the room. The ladies are startled by his appearance, but know the company that they keep. Anton Callistone will protect them. Anton uses his class and sophistication to quiet the women, slowly waving his hand to hush the murmuring. "So, you're here for me, are you? Then be a gentleman and let the ladies leave. They have no part in this."

"The girls are safe from me, Anton. I don't kill women." With that, the gunman raises his weapon and fires a single bullet into Anton's heart. The ladies on the bed scream out in horror at the sight of their benefactor murdered before their eyes. When they look back to the killer to determine their fates, they find that he is gone. In his stead is a young woman dressed in black and grey camouflage, holding an automatic weapon complete with silencer. With a smile on her face, Den Mother opens fire, killing Anton's ladies in a matter of seconds. Satisfied that the job was complete, the woman walks over and lays a small rebel flag between the bodies laid out on the blood soaked sheets. Police sirens sound out in the distance, responding to Anton's compromised security system. By the time they arrive the pair of killers will be long gone.

In Union City, the man known only as Mr. Smith walks into what looks like the modified examination room, ready to resume his work for the evening. On the table, in the middle of this room, lies a certain red headed young lady, against her will, with he arms and legs stretched to the ends of the table. "Ah, Ms. Lewis, how are we doing now?" Smith walks over to the console attached to the side of the table and throws the master switch, bringing the electrical equipment to life. The flow of tears resumes from Taylor's eyes, knowing what comes next is painful and traumatizing to say the least. Even sadder still is the fact that even with her awesome strength, she is still helpless to Mr. Smith's tools of his trade. While under the employ of the CIA, Smith's Methods of information extraction became so severe that he was forced out of the government agency, allowing him to seek work with Crossfire's team. Breaking Taylor's strong spirit is a pet project he's waited for, a long time.

The torture device that holds Taylor in place is one of his designs. The thick steel cables that are shackled to her hands and feet run right through the holes cut in the floor, and down to the room below. There they are connected to two hydraulic winches, readied to perform their duty. The slightest body movement activates the hydraulics basically to pull her apart, by doubling the strength that she applies. But this is only a small part of Taylor's suffering. The steel table that she is lying on is basically a low voltage electrocution tray, lined with rows of small electrode buttons. Strategically placed, they feed a low dosage electrical shock to her body when contact is made. Once the table is activated, Taylor must use her shoulders, hips, and ankles, to keep her body suspended above the table's surface for as long as she can. It is an effort on her part that is usually short lived, as expected by the man conducting the torturous experiment. When her body tires from the strain, it makes contact with the electrodes, causing the electrocution to take place. When Taylor moves, brought on by the electrocution, the hydraulic motors engage to counter her strength. The more she pulls, the more they pull her apart. Once the torture reaches this point, Taylor usually passes out shortly afterwards.

"You monsters; is torturing women the only thing your good at?" Sarah McBride sits against the far wall of the room with the rest of the hostages, with her hands shackled to the wall above her head, like the rest of the victims taken against their will. Taylor hears Sarah's voice, during her suffering, bringing the young woman some measure of comfort in knowing that she is not alone.

Mr. Smith looks over at Sarah and just stares at her for a second, determining if the question deserves an answer. "No, Dr. McBride, I find pleasure in torturing men, children and animals as well. Trust me, dear woman, I will find the most pleasure when I introduce you to this exquisite machine of pain and torment." He turns on the bright, hot, blinding light that is stationed right over Taylor's face. The shock of the introduction of light to her eyes causes her to cringe. As expected, she is delivered a small jolt of electricity, while the cables tighten slightly. "Now then, Ms. Taylor Lewis, of Alexander City, Alabama; are you ready to confess to the crimes that you and your boyfriend have committed? Look at you, Taylor," he leans over her face so that she can see her reflection in his mirrored sunglasses. "I think it is obvious to everyone present that this is something you are not enjoying. All you have to do is say his name, and you can end this once and for all."

"No," Taylor objects, not wanting to give in, but she knows what comes next.

Mr. Smith smiles at her answer, resembling the devil himself behind those mirrored glasses. Oh, how he loves a challenge. "Are you getting hungry? You haven't eaten in days." Smith presses a button on the console, causing two small vents to open on either side of her head. "Wouldn't a nice, thick, juicy, T-bone steak and potatoes be good right now, with a lusciously large lobster tail to go with it? That would be delicious, wouldn't it?" The aroma of the meal he just described begins to drift up from the vents and float around her face to torment her even more. "It could all be yours, if you would just give me what I want."

"No," Taylor cries out in defiance. Then, she starts to cry even harder knowing that the inevitable is near.

The cruel man motions for one of his assistants to enter the room. "I really thought you were going to come through for me, tonight, Taylor. You remember Mr. Black, don't you? He's going to help us try something new." Smith motions for Mr. Black to set the metallic case he brought into the room onto the table near Taylor's head. As soon as Smith turns off the table, Mr. Black opens the case and removes a head piece framework and stations it around Taylor's face. Smith crosses his arms resembling a proud father seeing his new born for the first time. "Now this is something I really think you can appreciate. Just the principle of it alone is sheer genius. Mr. Black, if you would hold her head, I'll apply the eye drops." Morbid that he is, Smith actually strokes Taylor's auburn hair as if trying to comfort her.

Taylor can feel the clammy rubber gloved hands of Mr. Black clasping the sides of her head. Her only recourse is to close her eyes as tightly as possible. Of course, this doesn't sit well with Smith at all. "No, no, no, this won't do at all." Smith throws the switch on the table's controls, sending a low voltage current flowing throughout the table's surface, while intermittent spikes of electricity hit her randomly in different areas, while the overall voltage continues to rise. Finally, after a few more seconds, Taylor finally concedes to his will, crying out in agony. "That's my girl," he says drawing the narcotic out of the small bottle with a syringe. "You wouldn't believe how expensive this stuff is, for just a drop, not to mention its potency. So not only do we not want to waste any, we don't want you to die, either." He lowers the tip of the needle down almost touching her iris, and administers one drop to one eye and then the other. "There now, we'll give that a few minutes to go to work, and then we'll give this a try."

Taylor can feel the narcotics burning its way into her brain. Her vision is the first to go, for obvious reasons, with it blurring a little, before the color spectrum is blocked from her perception. Then slowly, her body begins to feel as if it's melting out to cover the entire surface of the table. Seeing the effects showing in her eyes, Smith returns the framework around Taylor's head and attaches a visor to cover her face. With the setup locked into place, he plugs the cord into the console and leans down beside her ear. "You'll love this," he whispers. "The terrorists held at Guantanamo, thought that this was a hoot."

The small screen lights up inside the visor, allowing Taylor to see the image of her nude body, even though she knows that she is fully clothed. Then a gloved hand of a surgeon comes into view, holding a razor sharp scalpel. When the hand slowly drags the blade against the skin of her thigh, the electrodes in the table send the sensations of being her leg being sliced open to her narcotic induced thoughts of her brain. Seeing the blood run down her leg begins her psychotic episode, as she is forced to watch the hand continue to slice away at her leg. Whimpers form under her breath, as the outline of a rectangle is carved into her skin. She tries to see the face of the person doing this to her, But she is forced to look only at her leg.

The cuts that make up this four sided box of flesh are deep, seeping blood at the edges of the cuts standing open. Then, her whimpers become cries, when the surgeon jabs the blade of the scalpel under one of the corners, and viciously works it around under the tissue. With the hand drawing away, Taylor is given a moment of reprieve, while her mind struggles for a reason behind this madness. As if on cue, the hand returns to her field of vision with its mate holding what looks like a pair of pliers that have shallow flat jaws. She yelps out in fear as the pliers are clamped down on the flap of skin. The one hand gives a tug on the utensil, as if testing the resilience of her skin. Taylor can't believe her eyes, causing her to slip into a brief moment of shock, as she is forced to watch the skin of her thigh being pulled away an inch, or so. When the shock of it all subsides, the pain of the sensation causes her to scream out at the top of her lungs.

Smith leans in close to her again and whispers, "We're in luck. I just received word that your boyfriend is on his way here. I can only imagine the sadness you will feel in your heart when you see his broken, bloody, lifeless, body for the last time."

Even in her narcotics induced state, Taylor holds onto the hope that Billy is coming to save her. This hope is shattered when she watches two hands grasp the pliers, and then with one strong pull, rip the entire section of skin away from her leg. The reaction is too much to bear, as the other hostages are forced to watch Taylor's torture. With one last gasp for hope, she screams out Billy's name before passing out. Mr. Smith smiles at his comrade, realizing that he had succeeded in winning this battle of wills.

"Why are you doing this to her?" Saphyre asks. New to the mix, she doesn't understand any of this, "why are you doing this to me? I don't have anything to do with these people!" Her will is broken and she hasn't even been subjected to Mr. Smith's vices. Saphyre does what anyone would do, and breaks down and sobs uncontrollably from the strain of her captivity. She lays her head against Sarah's shoulder and asks her, "I didn't do anything wrong, did I?"

"No child, you didn't do anything wrong." Billy's mother watches as the sadistic violators pack up the tools of their trade, with their job completed for the moment. Their job; the sick bastards, this is too enjoyable for them to be referred to as a job. She says a silent prayer for Taylor that she can find a way to hang on, and that Billy gets the chance to give these men their just desserts.

Chapter XX

Antonio Callistone stares out at Central Park from his New York Penthouse. His distaste for this situation keeps backing up in his throat, leaving a bad taste in his mouth. "The further this plan of yours moves forward, the more I don't like it." The aging mobster turns around and faces Crossfire, who is sitting comfortably on the plush sofa. "Ryker, do you know why I detest hiring you?" He looks down at Crossfire's boots propped up on the furniture, and demands, "Get your feet off my table." Grabbing his drink from the bar, Antonio walks over to Crossfire and Margaret to continue his statement. "It's because you don't respect me or my position." Antonio drinks from his glass taking notice to how his left hand is trembling again. To hide his concern, Antonio returns his attention to his daughter and the hired assassin, hoping to keep them from noticing his ailment by badgering them to death. "I'm tired of being kept in the dark about this elaborate plan the two of you are working on. I want to know what it is that you are doing, and why I am being held hostage in my own home." He directs his attention to Margaret, who seems to think that he is making a big deal out of nothing.

"Oh, daddy dear," Margaret peels herself off the sofa and slinks her way over to Antonio, "first, you need to relax and finish your drink. Remember your condition and try to calm down. You are getting yourself all worked up for nothing." She nudges Antonio down into the chair and walks around behind him to massage his shoulders. "You were the one, who wanted to see this upstart tortured and killed in front of you, after he has watched the same thing done to his family, right?"

Margaret, I know what I said." Antonio closes his eyes, feeling the need for one of his little pills coming on.

"Then you have to understand that a task of this magnitude requires careful planning. Your demon, as you call him, is in route, or may already be here, and Crossfire's men are ready to spring the trap. The reason you must stay here is simply to keep you out of harm's way. You will have the opportunity to watch him die, and his reputation forever ruined. When this is all over, your rebel vigilante will be found as America's most wanted, and your empire will continue its thriving progression."

"You make it sound like there's a chance he could get away. Otherwise, why would you smear his reputation?"

"Mr. Callistone, nobody is perfect," Crossfire stands and walks over to the bar and tosses his empty water bottle into the trash can. "Even I'm bound to miss a shot sooner or later. Since I don't know when that will happen I like to make sure that there is an effective contingency in place."

Antonio shakes his head at the remark, "I know what it is. I don't like your arrogance most of all."

Crossfire strolls back over to the sofa and retrieves a box of files and paperwork. "What you see as arrogance, I claim as confidence and experience. A thick headed brawler doesn't collect information like this. You think that he just doesn't know when to quit. I say that he wasn't just going after you, but your entire syndicate. Darien wasn't the first to fall. He was just the next. I think you've underestimated your adversary this time, Mr. Callistone. I don't plan on making that same mistake, that's all. Lucky for you, your daughter was willing to pay my price and bring me in to rectify the situation for you.

The elevator dings, signaling that the car was at the penthouse. The doors open, revealing Sergio Vellecio and his boys inside the lift. Vellecio steps out and motions for his men to wait in the foyer while he walks over to Antonio. Anxiety is displayed all over Sergio's face, enough for Antonio to notice and become alarmed. After dismissing Crossfire and Margaret, Antonio escorts Vellecio into the study. Margaret sidesteps over to Carlton and whispers in his ear, "go ahead and give him the information."

"You and I need to talk," Carlton declares, disapproving of her subtle display of affection towards Ryker.

Sergio sits down in front of Antonio's desk, after waving his men into the room with him, escorting Tony. "Antonio, please understand that it grieves me to come to you with this news. I know that I should have gone through proper channels with Margaret, but I felt that this is too personal a matter, and we should keep as many outsiders out of the picture." Vellecio snaps his fingers signaling for his men to sit Tony down in the chair beside Sergio.

Antonio stares at Tony G with utter contempt. "So, this is the man who claims that my brother's son is conspiring against me?"

Tony G sits straight up in his seat, realizing that he has been accused of a crime carrying the death sentence. "Whoa, Mr. C, I didn't accuse anybody of nothin'! All I said was that Sally M. said with his dying breath, the gunman fingered Johnny C! I swear on my mother's grave, that's all that he said."

Smiling at the response, Antonio reassures the young man that he is not the one on trial here. "Relax, Mr. Gidducci, you haven't been implicated in any way of wrong doing. In fact, Mr. Vellecio has already informed me of your value to the organization. All I want to know is who else heard what Mr. Moreno said?" Antonio opens the side drawer of the desk and retrieves a cigar and a lighter.

Relaxing a little, Tony leans forward and offers to light Callistone's cigar, and then sits back trying to get as comfortable as possible considering the situation. "No one, sir," Tony swallows hard. "Bobby and the other guys were in the hallway. By the time they entered the room, Sally was already dead."

Antonio looks over at Vellecio for confirmation. Vellecio swallows hard knowing that his son's life could ride on his answer. "That is correct, Mr. Callistone. My boy Bobby is who Tony is referring to, and I asked him personally what happened. Bobby said that Tony was standing over Sal's body, but didn't hear anything said between the two. In fact, Bobby told me that he was pissed with Tony, because he clammed up and wouldn't say a word."

"Good, let's see to it that it stays that way, because I don't want this getting out, until I know what's going on." Antonio produces a pistol from his lap, complete with silencer, and fires two bullets into Tony's heart. "Sergio, my friend, I think it's time for your son to relocate to Atlanta until this is all cleared up. I appreciate your loyalty, Sergio. I hope your son appreciates what I'm doing for him. Who were the other two men that accompanied Robert and Mr. Gidducci?"

Sergio sits up, concerned where this was going. "New guys, boss, who were friends that Tony brought into the fold."

"I want them to disappear as well. If my dear brother is making a play for my chair, I don't want him to know that I already suspect him of such treachery." Antonio looks over at Carlton, who was patiently awaiting Antonio's next request. "I don't want Margaret to know about this. Is that understood?"

"Yes, Mr. Callistone," Carlton knows that this meeting is adjourned, and begins prepare Tony's body for transportation by laying out a small roll of plastic sheeting.

"Watch your boy, Sergio, and make sure he doesn't put himself in another position to end up like Tony here. I'd like to know that his loyalty is to me, and which side he stands on, because he makes it crystal clear to everyone." Once everyone had left the room, Antonio returns the pistol back to his desk drawer, and quickly grabs his prescription bottle. The syndicate has had a line drawn in the sand, for some time now, dividing the loyalties between Antonio and Frankie. Suddenly, for whatever reason, Antonio sees that line blurred, and begins to wonder about his own mortality. "The hell with one," he states, popping two of the pills into his mouth, and impatiently waits for his heart to calm down.

Chapter XXI

"Okay JD, are you ready for this?" Billy finishes off the last two cans of spray paint and tosses the empties into the trash can, while JD pulls the rest of the newspaper and masking tape from the truck windows. When Billy said that he could have the truck painted in less than fifteen minutes, JD thought that his new friend was out of his mind. Obviously, Billy Ray McBride is full of surprises. "Okay, as soon as I get this license plate on over mine, you open the door and we're outta here. With the screws tightened to hold the "borrowed" plate, Billy tosses the screwdriver over onto one of the work tables of the out of business garage. "Okay, raise the door, JD, and then get in." Billy climbs into the cab of the truck and starts the engine. He too is impressed that he succeeded with his boastful claim.

Thirty minutes ago, Billy stopped at a store and purchased a case of black spray paint, claiming that he could paint the entire truck in less than fifteen minutes, once they had it prepped. This made JD a little curious, wondering what it is that Billy had planned, but he held his question to see what is unveiled. Then, when Billy declared that he was driving around looking for a certain location, JD's curiosity gradually gave way to concern. But when Billy stopped in front of a closed garage and climbed out of the truck with a pair of bolt cutters, JD quickly became apprehensive about their actions. Fifteen minutes; that's all he needed was fifteen minutes. Fifteen minutes to prep the truck, covering all of the windows and chrome, and fifteen minutes to spray it all down.

Under the cover of night, Billy slipped out into the rear lot and "borrowed" a New York license plate from a junked car, while JD was left in the garage to start masking off the glass. He did as he was asked, but that doesn't mean that JD's anxiety levels weren't peaking the entire time, worried that breaking and entering would be the charge on their arrest report. When Billy returned from his task, He catches two cans of paint that JD had shaken, and begins his efforts at speed painting the Toyota. In thirteen minutes he had finished his task and was ready to depart. JD looks over at him and asks, "Should we at least close the door?"

"Only if you want to walk the entire way to your target," Billy puts the truck in gear and speeds off down the street. Once he's confident that their getaway was successful, Billy begins to explain the next leg of his plan, as they cross the Jersey state line into Staten Island. "Okay, check out that street map I've marked as number one. I'm gonna drop you off at the location marked with an X, but first we're gonna drive by the building and get a visual to see what we're up against."

"Ya know, I was wondering what brought on this wild idea to paint the truck."

"Duh, would there be any other reason? Any way, according to my dad's old notes, the building was used for freight storage for one of Callistone's export companies. We'll loop through and around to test the waters so to speak, and then I'll drop you off before I head over to Newark. Remember, we're just collecting nuts and berries on this go round. Avoid any and all conflict, unless absolutely necessary." Billy takes the I-78 off ramp and steps on the gas to merge with the oncoming traffic.

"I have to admit that I can see how you and your lady made such a good team. It may seem like you have a terrible habit of keeping people in the dark, but you just choose to carry the load of the weight so that your companions can keep a clear head, right? That's cool and all, especially if that person has all the faith in the world in ya. But what do you do when your mind becomes too clouded? As the leader of your team, you need to learn how to have faith and trust in the ones who follow you, giving them the opportunity to carry their share of the load. That way you can remain focused to serve them as their leader."

"JD, let's get one thing straight, okay? In no way was I any kind of a leader and all my intentions did was get everyone I love involved with this life or death situation. I didn't share my knowledge or information, simply because I never planned to work with anyone in the first place. Taylor's involvement was of her own doing, just like Bobby Sox. In both instances, I was forced to scrap my plans and improvise. I honestly think that me and Taylor just got lucky, which allowed her to walk away," and then he adds, "at least for a little while." Billy sits there silently for a moment pondering his thoughts, and then ads, "Come to think about it, now you've been drawn into this as well."

"Yeah, I love you too, but seriously Billy, I think you're missing the point. When the situation arose, you put the needs of others before your own. That's what makes you a great leader."

Billy shrugs his shoulders trying to dismiss JD's statement, and then has an overwhelming desire to try and dispute it. "Here's the problem; a leader is usually someone who wants the job. I, on the other hand, was forced into the situation against my will. I didn't change my plans by choice. I did it because I had to."

"Maybe, but you still did it. You say that you didn't have a choice, but you could have walked away and continued on with your quest for revenge. If anything, you care too much about people, to be this hard nosed uncaring person. At least, that's what I'm picking up, but what do I know." JD checks out their surroundings, noticing how when you get right down to it, there isn't much difference between Atlanta, Miami, LA or New York. City streets are just that, city streets.

Feeling the need to change the subject, Billy slows the truck down as they enter the neighborhood of JD's target. "There, on the street corner, the man at the bus stop, wearing the suit and tie. He's a point man keeping an eye on the south perimeter." They drive on through with Billy's suspect appearing to be uninterested in the black truck moving passed the bus stop.

"You're not being a little paranoid, are you? I know it's like 8:30, or so, but a guy in a suit, at a bus stop, doesn't appear to be that out of place, that much." JD looks back at the bus stop one more time, just to see if Billy saw something that JD might have missed.

He can't help but laugh at JD's response. "Come on, karate kid, didn't your teacher teach you anything? What's his pet peeve? Be aware of your surroundings at all times, and the people occupying those surroundings, right? One thing I've learned in this little endeavor is that everybody has to be seen as a suspect. Being at the bus stop this late at night, isn't out of place for anyone, especially a man in a suit. But, when the guy in the suit is wearing military issue combat boots makes him a prime target for my attention. Once around the corner, and out of sight of the bus stop occupant, Billy pulls over to the curb and asks, "Last chance, are you sure you're ready for this?"

"No, but if I back out now, it'll be a long walk back to Auburn, so lets get this over with, and take your family home with us." JD opens the passenger door, but looks back at Billy once more before he gets out. "Just remember that I'm counting on you to come back and pick me up, so don't do anything stupid, okay?" He climbs out of the truck, and looks up the alley way. "It's one block over and one block down, right?" Billy nods, and then JD closes the door to slip out of sight into the shadows.

He stands there for a moment, watching the tail lights of the truck disappear around the street corner, as if he can't believe that he is actually doing this. Here he stands, in New York no less, possibly presumed dead by the authorities in Alabama, helping a stranger try to save friends and family who were brought here against their will. Why JD is doing this is not open for discussion. He's made the decision and he is going to follow through with it to the end, for several reasons. Nick has trained him for this moment, this opportunity. The dream about Master Masamoto has JD convinced that it is somehow connected to Billy, and he plans on showing everyone that he is the right man for the job. The recent events in JD's life would affect changes in any man's life, but JD has grown and matured, directly because of those experiences. He has the abilities to help others, and these new found beliefs insist that he does so. After folding up the papers that Billy had given him, JD stuffs them into the inner pocket of his shirt and prepares to leave the safety of the shadows.

Just as JD is about to step out into the alleyway, he sees a man on a stoop across the street trying to light a cigarette. At first glance, the loner doesn't seem to be any kind of a threat, but that's what JD thought about the guy at the bus stop too. After watching a few seconds more, he sees the man lean an automatic weapon against the stoop he was sitting on to try and light the cigarette again. It seemed a little brash to be flaunting a weapon around like that in public, but at least now JD knows the man's purpose of being there.

The guy at the bus stop, the smoker on the stoop, anybody that JD sees could be a lookout for whoever's inside the building. "Okay, so I guess walking up to the front door is out of the question. Well Nick, I suppose this is where we find out if I was paying attention to you or not." Sticking to the shadows, JD maneuvers around the outlying buildings of the neighborhood to make a round about way to his target. His senses are strained, with every little sound catching his attention. Every movement that catches his eye causes his movement to stop, until he is certain that it's safe to continue on.

There's an old saying that you can't see the forest for the trees. Well, sometimes you can't see a single tree, because your focus is on the entire forest. Case in point; JD is so busy watching his surroundings that he walks right up to another gunman who was standing in the shadows. The man is so shocked that JD had gotten the drop on him that it causes him to fumble around trying to pull his automatic weapon out from under his coat. Of course, JD is also surprised by the man's presence, but is still able to recognize the man's dilemma and takes advantage of the brief window of opportunity. "Hi," he says softly, and then delivers a good old fashioned upper cut that knocks the man out. In a way, JD's a little surprised at the result. He stands there and watches the man crumble to the ground, and then wonders what he should do with the guy. He can't just leave him lying around out in the open for someone to find.

Now it is JD who faces a dilemma. If the guy comes to, and alerts the others to JD's presence, he could be the one in jeopardy. Laid out in the street is a sure giveaway, l should one of his buddies come walking around. Nick told him once that there is always a chance for a person to face the kill or be killed scenario. It doesn't mean you have to like it, but you do have to face it head on when it arises. The only other option is to lie down to die. "Sorry pal, but you're not supposed to know I'm here."

Hearing the garbage truck making its way up the street towards him gives JD an idea. Just across the narrow alleyway are several dumpsters that would appear to be on the truck's route. "All I can say is good luck buddy. If it is your lucky day, then you'll wind up on one of those garbage barges that I've heard about." With the body cast off into the dumpster, JD returns his focus on the building across the way.

From this vantage point, JD could see two sides of the building, and the bus stop down the street, a few blocks away. Seeing this explains why the point man was positioned there. It also tells JD where he needs to cross over, realizing that the other point man doesn't have a clear line of sight on JD's position. "Alright, I already know that there was three men staked out around the building's outlying perimeter as an early warning system. This leads me to the next question of what's in the box." If there is a need for an early warning system, could this be where the hostages are being held? If so, JD has to be sure to watch every move he makes. He looks around as the garbage truck picks up the nearby dumpster, and wonders if the truck driver could be a lookout as well. Just to be safe, JD steps back further into the shadows until the truck moves on down the road.

"Okay, JD, are you ready for this?" Billy's words echo in JD's mind as he stares at the building. "Obviously, with the front lit up like the fourth of July, no one would make a forward assault, at least no one who didn't have suicidal tendencies. There will probably be a sentry at every entrance and exit, and on the back side of the building is the river. JD's seen movies about the New York waterfront, and doesn't want anything to do with a scenario like that. Either way, he's not going to have an easy time getting inside to know the whole truth. Billy thinks that it is just a set up to lure him in. Still the question remains, what's in the box?"

After checking the buildings and streets several times, He looks at the window beside him to see his reflection and asks himself, "are you ready for this?" Again he's surprised, this time thinking that he saw a woman standing in the alley behind him. Spinning around, he has to know how she could have gotten the drop on him like that. There's no way anyone could have walked up the alley without him seeing her. Satisfied that there was no one else out in the night with him, JD dismisses the incident and looks at his reflection one more time. "Okay, here goes nothin'."

Checking the streets once more, JD sprints out across the deserted road, with his destination being the shadows of the building's monument signage. From there, he slips around the perimeter to an alley that accesses the building's loading docks. Here in the alley is where JD encounters his next opposition. Stationed at the bottom of the building's roof ladder is one man, no gun, and no misleading attire. The guy is obviously Chinese, or a Bruce Lee fan. Believing that he has the drop on the guy, JD slips up behind the man and prepares to take him out. His plan is to try the same move that he used on the lookout across the street. To JD's surprise, the man suddenly spins around to confront him, taking a defensive martial arts stance and motions for JD to give his best shot.

JD happily obliges by deploying his force field to drive the man's head up against the wall. Sure that the guy was out cold, JD walks down the alley a little further where the building jogs inward creating a small truck yard in front of the loading docks. From where he is at, JD sees three more guards standing on the loading dock speaking to another man on the ground, in what sounds like a Chinese dialect.

Suddenly, his heart sinks a little as he is forced to relive his little excursion to the orient by the sounds of their voices. If that wasn't enough, JD really gets uneasy when all four men turn and look in JD's direction, with their eyes glowing blood red. Now this is too much like Japan for my taste," he thinks to himself, as he senses the attacker approaching from behind. It sucks that he's breaking Billy's number one rule of no conflict, but JD's sure that if Billy was here, he would do the exact same thing.

At the last second, JD sidesteps the approaching man and slings him into the granite cornerstones of the building. It's the second time he's introduced the man's head to the side of the building. He hopes that the guy will stay down this time. Mainly because JD is about to have his hands full with the other four men charging towards his position, and doesn't need any more outside interference.

There is no time to debate the right or wrong aspects of this moment in time. JD accepts the challenge and takes on each man one at a time as they approach. There is no thought about ethics or morality; there is no worry about Nick's pride or honor. JD simply does what he must do. The first man is sent to the ground hard and fast, with the second rushing up to take his comrade's place. This continues until JD has sent all of his opponents to the ground, giving himself a chance to catch his breath. Feeling good about the moment, he says, "If you want me to give you a few minutes, I'll let you run inside and get some of your buddies to back you up." Why did JD just say that? "Why did I just say that?"

Four of the five men stand up ready to face JD again. The first of the five will not be standing up again. "We don't need the others," the ringleader declares. "We are capable of taking care of you ourselves." With that, the foursome of Chinese fighters allows their darker sides to show, allowing their demon possessions to reveal their presence. "Even though your efforts may be futile, we cannot allow you to interfere with our master's plan, student of Landry."

The last part of the man's statement troubles JD the most. Here he is, not a hundred feet from the East River, in New York, and a China man just referred to JD as the student of Landry. How is this possible? With his fear quickly dismissed, courage takes over JD as he pulls a small baton from his waste sash and charges towards the four men. Pressing a small button on the baton causes the ends to extend outward, until a full length bo staff is created. Burying one end of the staff into the ground, JD uses the weapon to pole vault over his opponents' heads. Flipping his body over, JD springs off the wall behind the men and uses the staff to clothesline two of the combatants. Following through, JD hits the ground and rolls up to his feet and then twirls the staff around his head before pointing the end at the other two men. Before they can react, JD jumps into the air and kicks one of the men in the side of his head, while driving the staff into the other's chest. Both go down, but just like the other two, all four stand and dust themselves off to ready for battle again. This time, they let their full demon forms appear, as if it offers them some sort of added protection.

He's seen this before, sort of, during his battle with Sonny's followers in Miami. These "men" however seem to be taking on a different appearance with less human characteristics than Sonny's victims. Still, the long claws and gnashing pointed teeth are familiar and obviously something that JD wants to avoid. Releasing his psychic force field with tremendous force, he eliminates the threat and dispatches the demon spirits that inhabited the unfortunate ones. This time, JD doesn't suffer the agonizing headache from his action. This time his deployment was intentional and controlled. He's learning.

As for the demon spirits entering the building, JD already knows enough to determine their retreat is not a good thing. What he needs to do is bail out of this scenario and regroup with Billy so that he could fill his new friend in on what JD knows and what he's seen. From the rednecks after the game, to the guys at the Chism estate, and these guys here, are all involved in a lot more than just Billy's little skirmish. Billy needs to be shown the big picture, and that there is more going on than just the abduction of his friends and family.

With his mind made up, JD has a revised plan and he is going to move forward with it. Just then, another one of Nick's old sayings comes to mind. "You never get what you want, but a smart man knows how to make do with what he has." Okay, so it really doesn't quite fit the situation, but it's what JD thinks when he sees a small strip of cloth tied to a bolt, hit the ground at his feet. Looking up, he sees the form of a person draped over the top of the parapet wall, just before it falls back onto the roof.

Immediately, he picks up the piece of cloth to see the word help rubbed onto it in blood. "I'm starting to see what you mean, Billy." JD's already determined that the building is not an option, but someone up there needs JD's help. The roof ladder has to be his method of travel. Once he's investigated the rooftop, then he'll call Billy for pick up. Around the corner, into the cage and up the ladder he climbs, hoping to get to the top before anyone knows where he is. Just a few more rungs and he's there. Three, two, one; he's made it.

Stopping at the top of the ladder, JD watches as a sentry runs around the side of the building, searching for any sign of JD's presence. Stopping at the bottom of the ladder, the man looks around, and then up, but JD is already moving across the roof. At least up here he has more room to move and defend himself, than he did inside the ladder cage. To his immediate right is the roof access door, and further down the parapet wall is a man who is either dying, or already dead. Before he could make his way over to determine which theory fits, the access door swings open, revealing three more combatants in matching tunics, rushing out onto the roof.

The three men were sent up to the roof to investigate the activity on the roof. Obviously, they didn't expect to find JD standing right there in front of them. Taking advantage of the opening, JD kicks all three men with a single spinning wheel kick. The first opponent is sent face first into the parapet wall, where the collision releases the demon spirit possessing the man's body. The other two are sent sliding across the rough pebble surface of the roof deck. One appears to be out cold, and the third guy is only dazed, struggling to get to his feet. He has to be JD's first concern, sending the young man back flipping across the roof to sweep the man's legs out from under him. The opponent lands flat on his back driving the air from the man's lungs. It's time for the kill shot, as Nick would put it, and JD follows through with an elbow to the man's chest. To finish him off, JD grabs the man's shirt, and then flips over the combatant to launch the guy into the parapet wall.

Turning around, JD isn't surprised that the last of the threesome is readying for battle again. The guy appeared to be knocked down a notch or two, but when he reveals his extensive knowledge of Kung Fu, JD still has to turn up the burners to match his opponent's skill. Within seconds, the two combatants are caught up in an actual mixed martial arts battle, blocking each others attacks, and occasionally landing a punch or take down, but neither gains the upper hand.

JD knows that he can't let this continue any longer. He needs desperately to get in touch with Billy, but first he needs to check on the guy lying on the roof. Of course, to do that, he has to finish off this guy, before any more of his buddies show up to join in. For a split second, JD's thoughts betray him, distracting him from the conflict and giving his opponent the upper hand. Grabbing JD, the man flips him down to the roof deck, where JD lands with a painful thud. JD has less than a second to act, as his adversary is already leaping into the air, with his leg poised to land a crippling stomp to JD's head.

Act he does, deploying his force field above him as the man descends to crush JD's skull. Not only does the psychic energy field halt the man's trajectory, it sends him flying off to bounce around within the framework of the massive roof top sign. He knows that the fight is over when he sees the demon spirit dispatched from the man's body fly off to seek refuge elsewhere. Now he can focus on the true reason that he's on the roof, in the first place.

Before he even gets close, JD hears the sound of a pistol being cocked, as the mystery man rolls over and points the weapon at JD. "I suggest that you state your intentions, before I pass judgment with a rash decision," Jonathan declares, grimacing from his wounds.

JD just stands there for a second, knowing that he has to make a decision. He could surprise the man by deploying his force field to disarm the man and take the advantage back into his court. That would surely defeat the purpose of coming up here to offer assistance, if the man was further injured by JD's action. "Easy friend, you're the one who sent me the message for help."

JD raises his hands to show that he's unarmed, and slowly starts to walk over to Jonathan, while holding the cell phone in his hand that just sent Billy the 9-1-1 message.

Chapter XXII

Billy's approach is much different than JD's. Where his new friend prefers the shadows, Billy plans on taking the straight on approach, walking right up the street towards the building in question. The cold air feels good against his face, as he tries to sort through the mountain of thoughts stacked up in his mind. There is still a doubt alive inside of Billy that eats at his conscience about involving JD in this mess. While part of him worries about JD's welfare, the other part is happy to be separated from his new ally. The war inside of Billy has come to a cease fire between the facets of his personality. For the moment, he is in control and feels no need to unchain the monster inside of him.

The conditions of this mental arrangement are simple. As long as he and JD are working together, Billy will remain in control and stay to the guidelines of their plan. When Billy is alone, he can act accordingly to the situation that he faces, but still must maintain some measure of control, at least, until JD takes everyone to safety. Then, Billy is free to unleash the monster inside to exact his final revenge for all involved.

Parking the truck a block away, he watches the property for any activity while he prepares himself for this little jaunt around the block. Looking into the rear view mirror, he says to himself, "Remember, you left a man who's counting on you to return and pick him up." Is it necessary for him to remind himself of that? Probably not, but this time Billy has to maintain control over the monster inside, for all the people that are counting on him in more ways than one. So, even though it isn't necessary, it doesn't hurt to keep it on mind either.

Climbing out of the truck, he grabs his cowboy hat and trench coat and starts to walk towards the construction site in question. The wind blowing at his back whips his hair around his face, and blows the front of his coat open, revealing his alter ego's costume underneath. To fight the wind's effects, he shoves his hands deep into the coats pockets and holds the lapels closed the best he can.

Yo, homeboy, what'cha doin' walkin' our street at night?" The leader of the four gang bangers walks right out of the alley to confront Billy, getting right up in his face. This makes it easy for him to see Billy's mask under the cowboy hat. Before the hoodlum could react or give warning, Billy grabs the young man and slings him at the other three, driving all four back into the alley.

As a professional wrestler, Billy's persona was known for his expertise in the battle royal and handicap matches. His opponents tonight have no such experience. In a matter of minutes, he has left the four gang members stuffed into garbage cans and lying in water puddles, with Billy none the worse for wear. "That's pretty good," a voice behind him declares, "but how do you think you'll do against the rest of us?"

Billy slowly turns around to see fifteen or sixteen more young men, ranging in age from fifteen to twenty. Each one was gesturing as if they wanted a shot against the champ as well. "Shouldn't y'all be in bed right now?" Not expecting a response, his attention is drawn away by the sound of his cell phone buzzing, "Hold on a second, guys. I have to take this real quick." The street gang suddenly stops as Billy raises his hand as if motioning for a time out, while pulling his phone out of his pocket. Unsure what to do next, the gang members wait for Billy to answer the call. Billy acts like this is no big deal holding off the gang like this, which sets the leaders off. With his signal, their eyes light up bright red, as they begin their charge again down the alley. Howls and screams echo in the alley while Billy looks at the view screen on his phone to see JD's 9-1-1 message. He isn't happy about it. "Christ, man, I haven't been gone for thirty minutes yet, and you're already in trouble?" Billy looks back at the street gang, who were already making their move to cautiously approach their intended victim. "Look guys, I would love to hang out with you, and whoop your asses all over this alley, but my buddy seems to have gotten himself into a pickle, and needs me to go bail him out."

Without warning, Billy produces and unloads an enormous energy blast at point blank range; eliminating any threat that the gang may have posed. The darker side of him wants to continue on and unleash the same kind of pain to the people occupying the construction site, but the rational side of him wins out, with JD's needs being the deciding factor. Regardless of how Billy thought that JD could take care of himself, Billy gave his word that he would go if JD called. It doesn't mean that he has to like it any. It's frustrating, and aggravating, but Billy follows through with his word that was given, and takes off for the truck. Besides, after personally seeing the property and the remodeling taking place, Billy is able to scratch it from his list of hostage possibilities. Whether or not it was listed as a distraction or possible trap doesn't matter. This guy he has come to face, doesn't really expect Billy to fall for every little trap and ploy, does he?"

Chapter XXIII

Jonathan Justice eases himself back against the parapet wall, as JD inspects the wounds. "I'm gonna ask you something, son, and I want you to be honest with me. After twenty years with the Bureau, it's not hard for me to see that you're not from around here, so what are you doing here tonight?"

This man is dying and there's nothing that JD can do to help, and both of them know that. At least he can honor his father, and tell the man the truth. Pulling his mask off, JD offers his explanation of his and Billy's plan, with his face visible to proclaim the truth, "Okay, but this will have to be the condensed version. A friend of mine is in town with me, and we're here, believe it or not, to rescue his friends and family members who were brought to New York to lure Billy here. He took up the mantle to avenge his father's murder, but I guess you could say that it blew up in his face. So, we're here to clean up the mess, and maybe make a little of our own."

Jonathan scoffs at JD's statement, "What are the two of you supposed to do? You do know that this is a mob owned property, right? You don't look like you've got the balls to take on the mob, kid." He pulls his hand away from his side and watches the blood surge from the bullet hole with every beat of his heart.

This is what JD was hoping to avoid. He hates when people sell him short and never give him enough credit. Pulling the map out of his inner shirt pocket, JD waves it in front of Jonathan's face as if it was prime evidence to back him up. "Yeah, that's exactly what we're gonna do! Billy's got enough information from his dad's files for us to pull this off. Once we have his mother Sarah, and the others freed, Billy's going after the head honcho, to make sure this doesn't happen again."

There is something very familiar to Jonathan about JD's story. In fact, it is so familiar that the Federal agent doesn't like it one bit. He has one response, and it can only be, "McBride."

Well that one sure came out of left field and knocked JD for a loop, so to speak." I'm sorry, what did you say"

Jonathan Justice hasn't survived this long with the bureau by being short sighted, or obtuse. The answer he was looking for is written all over JD's face, whether the kid likes it or not. "Your friend is one William Raymond McBride; age twenty two, with blonde hair and blue eyes. He stands about six foot, two inches tall, and weighs around two bills. Oh, and most importantly, he has a knack for finding trouble. Ya know this makes those crazy reports coming out of Atlanta a lot more understandable now." Having his hopes dashed like this is more than Jonathan can take. When he first saw JD down below on the ground, Jonathan thought there might still be a chance to save his poor daughter. When he saw the way JD took care of the goon squad on the roof, Jonathan's hopes rose even more. Then, to find out that it all rides on one Billy Ray McBride is just too much to bear. "Well, now I know it's time to use this, I just hope that they can get to us in time."

Jonathan pulls a small transmitter from his coat pocket and then presses the button to activate it.

"Okay, I'll bite, what's the gadget do?"

"It calls for some old friends, if this little scenario were to have ever taken place. It calls for their help with Crossfire." He coughs a little tasting the blood in the back of his mouth. "Now, let me tell you about this little excursion of yours, and what your friend has gotten you into. Mr. McBride has ruffled the feathers of one of the most powerful men in the world. I say this because Callistone would have to be paying a small country's ransom to get Simon Ryker to return to the United States to do a job. Ryker, who once called himself Crossfire, is one of the deadliest, and heartless, killers in the world."

"How is it that you fit into this picture?" JD asks, while using one of his leg sashes to tie off Jonathan's shoulder, and then the other is folded up to serve as a compress for Jonathan's side. "We really need to get you to a hospital."

Jonathan coughs again, this time expiring small drops of blood into the air. "My career has been dedicated to the fall of the Callistone syndicate, with only one little hiccup along the way, when my wife was killed by the same man you've come to face. For the past fifteen years, I have waited patiently for this day to come, to have the chance to put the guy behind bars forever."

"Really? See, I figured you'd want revenge like Billy."

"What, and kill him? No, Simon Ryker would suffer countless times worse, to be trapped behind bars like a kept animal, kinda like Billy.

"Since you know so much about me, why don't you tell us who you are?" Billy's sudden arrival causes both Jonathan and JD to jump. Only, Jonathan reacts by pulling his pistol and drawing down on Billy. "Do you really want to pull that trigger, or not?" He charges his eyes and hands with enemy trying to look as formidable as possible, while ready to retaliate against Jonathan's actions.

"Whoa, hold on now you two!" JD jumps up and steps in between the two, needing to end this stand off as soon as possible. "Let's not let this get stupid. Number one; none of us have time for this! You're bleeding to death," he adds, pointing out the obvious, "and you have a job to do! Now help me take care of this guy so we can get on with it." Looking back at Jonathan, he motions for him to lower his weapon, "I could have left you up here to bleed out all over the roof, so put that piece away so that we can help you.

Billy grabs JD by the arm and pulls him over to the side. "What is going on here, JD?" He glances over at Jonathan and then back to JD, wanting to hide the fact that JD's new friend looks familiar for some reason. "All you had to do is scope the place out and tell me what you find. Avoid contact and conflict unless there is no other way possible. From the looks of things, you just marched in here and started kicking ass all over the place! Hell, it wasn't hard to figure out where you were, with all of those bodies falling off the roof! In fact, why don't you just go ahead and call 'em up to tell Callistone that we're here!"

"Are you done yet? I told you before that we didn't want to go down this road again, so let me stop you before you reference the word stupid again!" JD steps right up in Billy's face, still feeling the rush from his earlier battle rekindling inside him. "Adapt and improvise, is what we're supposed to do, right? Well, that's what we have to do. I told you before that I'm not going to leave an innocent man down, and that's…"

JD's statement is interrupted by Jonathan whistling as loud as he can. With both Billy and JD turning to look at Jonathan, the Federal agent gestures with his pistol that he's the one in charge at the moment or at least he thought. "Now, if the two of you are done, I'd like to be moving on from this location as quickly as possible. If I'm not mistaken, there are quite a few lives in danger right now, and my daughter is one of them. What are your intentions McBride?" Jonathan's question causes Billy to glance over at JD, blaming him for the information leak. "Don't look at him, Billy. Hell, I should have known it was you all along. What I need to know is what have you gotten Sarah into, and how you expect to save her by dishing up a blood bath of your own, all over New York?"

"Mister, I don't know what you're talkin' about, and from where I stand; you're in no position to be demanding anything." He stands there for a second, staring at the stranger who knows who he is, and who his mother is. "Who are you?"

"What, you don't remember me?" Jonathan lowers his pistol, finding that it's easier to breathe with his arms down at his sides. "The name's Jonathan, Special Agent Jonathan Justice." Instantly, he sees the effect of what he said spread out all over Billy's face. JD snickers to himself, wondering who his partner is, Liberty, or Freedom? "That's right, Billy boy, it's a small world after all, isn't it? Jonathan coughs again, alerting Billy to the extent of his gunshots. "Here's the crash course on what's going on, because I now understand the hows and whys. The guy hired to bring you to New York is the same guy I've wanted to get my hands on for a long time. Unfortunately, he knows this, and now my daughter has been dragged into this mess, and I don't want your hotdog antics risking her life any further. Now get me outta here so we can compare notes and make our move." When Billy and JD don't jump right away, he looks at the both of them and says, "Now, gentlemen, I can hear the sirens getting closer.

Billy knows the name; that one is for sure. He just never thought he would meet the man, much less have him point a gun at him. "Okay, Agent Jonathan Justice, we will drop you off at the nearest hospital, on our way to the Bronx. We have a few more places to check out, but if we run across Kaitlyn, I'll be sure to tell her where you're at." Billy motions for JD to move to the other side of Jonathan, so that they can help him off the roof.

JD asks with skepticism, "How are we gonna do this, Billy?"

"Down the stairs; there ain't nobody inside the building to worry about. Hell, ya'll already took care of that." Billy slips his arm under Jonathan's shoulder and waits for JD so that they can lift in unison.

"How can you be so sure?" Jonathan grimaces as he is lifted from the roof deck.

"Because, that's how I got up here in the first place. Ya didn't think I'd climb the roof ladder, did ya?" His brash and uncaring attitude about their surroundings continues as they descend through the building, as if he didn't worry about anything. JD on the other hand is constantly scanning every shadow in the building for any signs of trouble that he expects to see. What he and Jonathan didn't expect to see is how many dead bodies there was scattered about the warehouse floor.

Right away, Jonathan knew that some kind of sweeper team came through here and eliminated Gambenni's men, but judging by the blood trails, most of these bodies were brought in from somewhere else. Jonathan knows where. These had to be the bodies from the gun fight out on the docks that he heard, when he discovered Kaitlyn's presence. The question now is who is supposed to be the ones to find them.

They make it outside and to Bill's truck with no further conflict, where Billy unloads Jonathan's weight onto JD. Moving around the truck to the driver's side, Billy opens the door and grabs a piece of paper from the dash. With pen in hand, he crosses off the first two addresses on his list of places to see in New York. Climbing into the truck, Billy looks over the back of the front bench seat and suggests, "Do me a favor and try not to bleed all over the upholstery."

Jonathan has remained quiet until now, mainly due to the pain inflicted by their hasty retreat and departure from the building. "Where are we headed?"

"Well, I want to go to Brooklyn, I think, but the nice guy in me still thinks we should get you to a hospital." He can hear the emergency vehicles closing in, causing him to start up the truck and put in gear, before JD is inside all the way. You do understand the dilemma I'm facing, right? What do I do with you?" Billy stomps on the gas as JD closes his door, leaving the scene as quickly as possible.

"I'll tell ya what, Sport. Why don't you give me that list of yours, and maybe I can help you out with this. Jonathan looks over the list of properties, using the map to cross reference each location. "Billy boy, you're being set up for a lot more than you know about," Jonathan starts down the list to make his point. "This guy here is dead, found in the back of his restaurant, along with all of his associates. This address here is your mom and dad's old house, and this one is mine and Kaitlyn's. In fact, I've checked out all of these addresses myself, and found nothing but dead mobsters. I found Campano and his boys slaughtered in Bruno's gym. De Luca was found in his restaurant. Anton Callistone was gunned down in his bedroom with his harem of ladies. Hell, I'd be willing to bet a year's salary that Gambenni was gunned down out back on the docks, while me and Kaitlyn were on that roof. From the looks of things, all of Antonio's supporters are falling like dominoes, and the only evidence is little rebel flags left at the scene of the crimes."

"How do you know all of this, if you've been running the rooftops?" Billy inquires.

"I had a smart phone, until a little while ago. You have modern technology down south, don't you?" Jonathan lets out a cough, and then tries to press on with his instructions. "There's only one place left on both of our lists, and it has to be where they are holding Sarah, Kaitlyn and the others. You do understand that this is going to get messy, right?"

"Ain't it kinda funny how you always find what you're looking for, in the last place you look?" The question is a little corny, but JD meant for it to lighten the mood a little. He can sense the anxiety in Billy about Justice's condition, as if a major moral debate is raging within his new friend.

"Okay, so I'll bite, and ask what you think I should do." Billy pulls the truck into the parking lot of an all night convenience store, as if it was a planned event.

"To be honest with you son, everything you should, or need, to do goes against everything my badge stands for, but I don't see you having any other choice. This guy you're up against knows a lot more about what he's doing, than you do about what you face."

"No he doesn't. If he did, he would have never taken this job to stand against me." Billy grabs his wallet out of the truck's console and hands JD twenty dollars. "Go get as much first aid stuff as you can, and hurry back even quicker." Once JD is out of the truck and on his way, Billy turns around in his seat to face Jonathan. "You know you're gut shot, right? Your window of surviving this is closing on you. Don't you want me to take you somewhere that can give you the chance to see Kaitlyn again?"

"No, I want you to help me get her to safety. Billy, I know my time is short, but I have to see this through, now for her safety more than revenge. You can relate to that, can't you? The main thing is that I need you to promise me to take her with you when this is over." Jonathan looks at Billy closer taking notice to the strong resemblance of Jonathan's old partner. "Ya know you look a lot like him, Walter that is. Granted, a young version of the man, but you're his son, there's no doubting that. Now do what you have to do, just like he would."

"Why don't you just lean back and relax, until JD gets back. The last thing I need right now is a walk down memory lane." Billy checks the front of the store for any sign of his friend, wanting to have some interference to avoid the oncoming discussion.

"Yeah well, due to recent circumstances, and since I didn't see you at the funeral, I want to say that I'm sorry for your losses and current situation. In a way, I guess you could say that I'm the one who's responsible for it all. It was me who infected your father with the ambition to bring down the Callistone Empire." Jonathan could see that he has touched a nerve with the subject, watching the anger welling up in Billy's eyes. It may have hurt to hear the words said, but Jonathan had to say them none the less.

"Oh good, JD's back. Now let's see about getting those holes plugged." Billy jumps out of the truck and grabs a roll of duct tape from the truck bed, before climbing in to the back seat of the crew cab. JD, seeing Billy's movement, opens the rear passenger door, and holds out the bag of gauze and bandages. Billy simply waves them away for the moment, and tears off two strips of duct tape. He then lays them down on the seat, slightly overlapping, and sticky side up. "Okay take out some of those gauze pads, stack 'em together, and put some of that antibiotic crème on the center." Pulling off his glove, Billy looks at Jonathan and gives him a patronizing smile, as if he were a doctor giving a child a shot. "This is gonna sting a little, but I know it'll stop the bleeding, at least on the outside." Drawing up a little energy at the tip of his index finger, Billy then touches his finger to the grazing wound in Jonathan's leg to cauterize it shut.

Jonathan's eyes roll back in his head, as he tries to endure the excruciating pain. With no other alternative, he lashes out and punches JD's shoulder. "Hey, what the hell was that for? He's the one setting you afire!"

"I know, and I'm sorry, but I couldn't reach him with my right arm."

Billy takes a rag from the floor board and wipes off Jonathan's shoulder around the wound. Sure that the area was clean and dry, Billy places the makeshift bandage over the wound, sealing it shut. With one hole plugged, Billy adjusts his attention to the hole below Jonathan's ribs. He looks up into Jonathan's eyes, but doesn't bother to say a word. He doesn't have to, because Agent Justice already knows. "Just do that trick again to keep the rest of my blood in my body, so we can finally move on," Jonathan suggests as he prepares for the ensuing pain. Billy obliges his father's friend, but this time it takes everything Jonathan has to keep his senses while Billy seals the wound from inside out. Still, JD tenses up his shoulder muscles just in case Jonathan has the urge to lash out again.

Seeing that Jonathan isn't going into shock, yet, is a good sign that Billy can get back into the driver's seat to continue this mission of his. Trying to stay focused, Billy blocks out the chaos taking place around him. Every distraction, every delay, forces him to struggle more and more to stay in control. "So, since you eliminated all of my prime pieces of real estate to investigate, do you know where we should go?"

"Union City, that's where they should be holding Sarah, and the others. To be honest, it's the one place that I haven't checked out yet, because it was next on my list." Jonathan checks his coat pocket and realizes that he doesn't have his cell phone, "hey, one of you let me borrow your phone. I need to call my partner, just so that someone knows what's going on."

"Do you trust him?" Billy looks in the rear view mirror to see Jonathan's reply.

"Pete's been my partner ever since your dad was transferred to Atlanta."

"Yeah, but do you trust him? Dad's partner got him killed."

Chapter XXIV

Pete Del Gato walks around Kaitlyn's bedroom, looking for answers pertaining to where the girl could be. When his phone rings, the Federal agent smashes the screen of the young lady's laptop computer, frustrated to no end by her security access features. "Hello? Jonny, hey partner, I didn't expect to be hearing from you tonight." Del Gato reaches down and grabs Kaitlyn's friend, Toby, from the floor beside Kaitlyn's bed and tosses the young man across the room. "Huh? Oh that, I'm moving some stuff around, and just dumped a book shelf in the floor."

With Toby out of the way, Del Gato begins to rifle through the drawers of Kaitlyn's desk, bound and determined to find something that will help him out of his problem. "Listen; why don't you tell me why you called me, so I can get finished with this mess." He squats down and rifles through the final drawer, and then stands straight up, not believing what he has just heard. "I'm sorry, she's what?! Oh man, what was she thinking? Better yet, what were you thinking? Ya know you could lose your badge and pension going after the guy on your own like this. Yeah, yeah, I know, just tell me where you are and I'll come get you." He grabs a piece of paper and pen from the desk top and waits for the address.

When it comes through the receiver, he just wads the paper up and throws the pen out the opened window. "Yeah, I'm at home. Where do you think I'd be moving furniture around? Give me fifteen or twenty minutes and I'll be there as fast as I can." Del Gato hangs up the cell phone and gives Toby a devilish grin.

Toby wanted nothing to do with Kaitlyn's little scheme, right from the start. But, being the loyal friend that he is has brought him right into this dangerous situation. The only reason he came here is because he hasn't heard from Kaitlyn in the past few days. He thought for sure that she had gotten over herself by now, and would have been by his place to scheme her next little adventure. Never would he have believed that Kaitlyn would have gone off on her own. Toby never really thought she had what it took. Sure she talked a good story, but deep down inside, she could never back it up. That's why he's here. Believing that she might be in trouble, Toby thought for sure that Kaitlyn would have left him some kind of clue as to where she was going. Finding Del Gato there looking for the same thing is not what he expected.

Now he has more trouble on his hands than he ever expected. If he could just get to the window, he could fly to safety. While Del Gato is distracted, Toby rolls off the dresser only to fall to the floor. This only draws Del Gato's attention to the young lad, sending the crooked agent heading for Toby again.

Del Gato reaches down, grabs Toby again by the back of his shirt, and slings him into Kaitlyn's closet. The collision with the clothes and closet organizers brings all of the contents of the closet down on top of Toby in the middle of the closet floor. "Looks like you held out for nothing, Champ." Del Gato screws a silencer onto the barrel of his pistol. "It turns out that she has already been picked up by some associates of mine, and her loving father is hurrying to her rescue, as we speak."

"He was you partner. How could you betray him like this?" The voice is low and muffled by the mountain of clothes covering Toby's face, but the question still hits home all the same.

"You shut up!" Del Gato pulls the trigger, sending a bullet whispering into the pile of clothes and accessories. Then, he does it again two more times. "You don't know what you're talking about!" Again he pulls the trigger, and then waits for any sign of movement. "Stupid kid, ya shoulda' kept your mouth shut." It wouldn't have made a difference any way. Acting as if nothing had happened, Del Gato retrieves his cell phone and dials another number. "Hello, yes ma'am, it's Del Gato. Tell your man that his secondary target is heading over to the place in Union City. Yes ma'am, I told him that I would meet him there in twenty minutes. No, thank you, ma'am."

Margaret hangs up her phone, and then quickly dials another number. "Yes lover, Justice is heading your way. Del Gato is meeting him there in twenty minutes. I'm going back to my father's to be with him. You make sure that everything goes off without a hitch. I want this to be over for him, tonight."

She hangs up the phone and looks at the rear view mirror, and sees the reflection of another woman, THE other woman. The woman Margaret calls mother, and the one who has promised Margaret the means for unlimited power. "Mother, everything is transpiring as you have foreseen. This plan of yours is so intricate. I fear that if one miscalculation is off, the entire plan could unravel."

"Remember, my child, what I said. All of this is but a means to your, or should I say our, end. You have already admitted that everything is taking place as I said, did you not?

Remember, the most important thing is that our unlikely ally must be lead to New Orleans to serve our bidding. Then, and only then, can you receive what I have offered you." A car horn blowing behind Margaret's Bentley interrupts the conversation. Realizing that the traffic light had changed in her favor, Margaret speeds off heading back to her father's penthouse.

Across town, in her father's penthouse, Frances Callistone sits in his brother's office, nervous about the outcome of this meeting. For too long Frank has stood at his brother's side, to see the family organization unravel like this. Somehow, he has to find a way to convince Antonio that they aren't standing on opposite sides. "As soon as I heard about Anton, I had to come see you as soon as possible. Antonio, I need you to believe me that I have no interest in making a move against you."

"Forgive me dear brother; if I don't run to you and take you into my arms, but at the moment, I have no measure of trust left in me for anyone." Antonio lifts his drink, revealing the shakiness brought on by recent events. "Too many of my boys have taken the ultimate fall, and that leaves too many fingers pointing in different directions, with most being pointed at you. You are my brother, Frank, and that's the only reason that we are still talking about this, other than at your grave site. I'll tell you this much, I don't think it's you, but I still have to ask; what's your boy Johnny been up to, lately?" One of my pigeons told me that Anton insulted Johnny at his night club. Is that why 'family' has been added to the hit list?"

Before Frank could answer his brother's question, Margaret walks into the living room, where both men in the office are made aware of her arrival. Playing the role of the caring daughter, she marches right into Antonio's office to check on his condition. "Hello, Uncle Frank, I didn't expect to see you here." Moving right over to Antonio, she walks up and stares at her father's face. "Daddy, you look pale. Are you feeling alright? I really think you shouldn't push yourself so hard. I was worried about your condition, so I came back to check on you."

Antonio isn't so quick to buy into her concern for his health and welfare. That's all fine and well, Margaret, but I am having a meeting with my brother at the moment, so please, go and wait for me in the other room. I have a few issues that I need to discuss with you as well, when I'm finished with your Uncle Frank.

Margaret gives her father a kiss on his forehead and honors his request by slipping out into the living room without any more interruption. On her way out of the room, she makes eye contact with Carlton and motions for him to join her. Once she's out of the room, Frankie returns his attention back to his brother. "Antonio, I have to warn you that there's mumbling within the ranks, and they're saying that she is the one behind these hits on our boys. Others say that it is you who is to blame, believing that this nemesis of yours has brought this war to you, here in New York."

"Do you see? That's the problem with people today. There is always talking going on, but never are the right people having the conversation." Antonio knows that he is pushing his limits with his health, but he has to make his way through this to put his mind at ease. "Some say that this rebel assault is simply someone using my troubles in Atlanta to cover up their own agenda. Those same people are the ones questioning family loyalty."

"So, you do think that it's me!" Frank stands up to express the appalling nature of his brother's accusation.

"I'm sorry, but this is where I feel like I'm intruding." Carlton excuses himself and leaves the office, walking out into the living room. His true urgency is for finding Margaret to find out what she knows about what's going on. "Joining her out on the living room balcony, he walks right up to her and asks, "Margaret, I need to know more about what is really going on, and what you're planning." Carlton stops for a moment to admire her seductive form highlighted by the moonlight.

She turns around as if she expects Carlton to hand her the world, like he owed to her in some way. Sipping from her glass, Margaret wets her lips and smiles at Antonio's right hand man, "Hello lover, I was hoping that you would join me out here. You definitely don't want to be in the same room when those two get going at one another." She walks over and meets Carlton half way across the balcony to drape her arms around his neck and gives him a long and passionate kiss. "There, does that quench your thirst for now?"

Antonio looks into his brothers eyes, "I have to admit that this is the hardest thing I've ever done. All of our lives, we were raised to believe that the family values were the back bone of this organization. And yet, here I sit questioning my own brother's motives. How do I…" Antonio's question is interrupted by a mysterious intruder stepping from the shadows in the corner of the room. "So this is how it ends."

Before Antonio's armed guards could draw their weapons, the masked man cuts them down with his automatic machine pistols. When Antonio's personal body guard, Douglas, leaps into action, the mystery gunman pulls another weapon from his side, "This one is especially for you!" The small weapon erupts with the roar of cannon, blowing Douglas Deadlocke back across the room, and showering Antonio and Frances with the bodyguard's blood. Pointing one pistol at Frances, and the other at Antonio, the mystery man smiles and asks, "How are y'all doin' tonight?" He walks out into the light revealing a costume similar to Billy's alter ego.

"You're not him. Guns aren't his style," Antonio declares as he sits back in his chair, trying to relax as best as possible to keep his heart from beating its way out of his chest. Pills, he needs one of his pills.

Frankie sits up in his chair, unwilling to show any fear. "My boy Johnny will find you and cut your heart out for doing this!"

"Johnny? No, pal, you've got that all wrong. Ya see, I just left John-John sittin' in his office of that high class night club of his. Now, I could be wrong, but I think he was having trouble getting that champagne glass stem out of the side of his neck." The intruder lowers his weapon pointing it right at the middle of Frank's chest. "Just so that we are clear on this, the Callistone family line comes to an end tonight." With that, he pulls the trigger, loading Frank's chest full of lead. "Now then, where is that daughter of yours? I know she is hiding around here somewhere." The intruder suddenly raises the other gun up and points it at Antonio's head, and pulls the trigger while yelling, "BANG!!!"

Antonio's system can't bear the strain of what is happening. This must be what it is like to be scared to death. One thing is for sure; it's not a quick process. He doesn't know if he is having a heart attack, or a stroke, but the result is some kind of paralysis that forces him to watch the gunman laugh at Antonio's changing condition.

Margaret clings to Carlton, "No, don't go back in there! Please, I'm begging you to stay with me!" Looking towards the balcony door, she sees the killer approaching. This causes her to pull away from Carlton, backing away believing he would be the next target. When the mystery man turns his aim to follow her, Margaret becomes genuinely concerned about the current turn of events. "Wait, what are you dong? He's my father's right hand man! I'm nobody!"

"I know that, toots. That's why he gets to live, so he can pay me everything I've got coming." The intruder pulls back the slide, loading a bullet into the chamber of his gun. Pointing it at Margaret's head, he gives her a smile goodbye. But before he can pull the trigger, Carlton hits the man with a bullet of his own, right between the eyes.

Margaret rushes over to her savior and throws herself into Carlton's arms. Then, once she has regained her composure, she looks into his eyes and asks, "Can you check on my father and the others inside now, for me?" With Carlton doing her bidding, Margaret walks over to the fallen killer and pulls the mask and wig off the man's head. "Sorry Paulie, but it wasn't supposed to go down like that. Or at least that's not what I had planned."

Chapter XXV

"Ya shouldn't be so quick to write us off." Billy is tired of Jonathan's condescending comments about Billy and JD's inadequacies for the job at hand. "I've handled my fair share of Antonio's goons. My partner here, along with a buddy of ours, fought their way out of Japan, leaving over a hundred guys in their wake. I think we're qualified enough for this."

"Yeah, well that's your problem, McBride; you only think you're good enough. Simon Ryker, a.k.a. Crossfire, isn't just one of your ordinary, run of the mill, gun toting goons. He's the half brother of Commander Steven Ryker, of Darkside Command, and the one who betrayed the original Task Force Zebra team, leaving his brother to die. Kaitlyn's mother was the medical officer of Ryker's team. She was recruited for her uncanny healing talents. That's why Simon took it upon himself to end her life, so that she couldn't save the rest of the team. The sad thing is, Julie was able to save members of TFZ numerous times, but couldn't save herself in the end. Obviously, the guy is a heartless, ruthless, killing machine, who is the best at what he does. He's since pooled a number of high dollar hit men, assassins, and mercenaries together to create an organization for hire. If you need to overthrow a government, and kill the President's staff, Crossfire's team can do it on multiple levels." Jonathan makes eye contact with Billy through the rear view mirror, "You two are going to have your hands full."

"Thanks for your vote of confidence," Billy replies, stopping the truck for a traffic light a few blocks from their target. He looks over the map one more time before the light turns green, and then glances over at JD who seems a little unnerved, "Are you alright, brother?"

"Yeah, I'm just having one of those realizations. Ya know what I mean?" JD looks over at Billy, trying to hide the nervousness that is building inside him.

"How's that working for you?" Jonathan coughs again, tasting the blood in his mouth. Has he let himself slip into the same situation Billy is in? Both of them hold a grudge. The only difference is that Jonathan has had possession of his longer. Now, like Billy, the only family he has left is being held with her life on the line, and it's all because of him.

"I'll get over it, guess," JD responds, as he turns to face Jonathan in the back seat. It's just that when Nick and I fought our way out of Japan, I don't know; it was different. This time, not only do I know what I'm facing, I'm walking into it on my own free will. I guess I just need a few more minutes to cope with that."

Billy turns the truck onto the next cross street, thinking about what JD had just said. Sure, Billy acknowledged the risk of what he's doing, but has he truly come to terms with his decision? When the chips are down, can he give himself up to save the others? In some ways, there is no way for him to know, until that time comes. He thinks he has what it takes. Then he remembers what Jonathan said earlier about 'thinking' he's good enough. If he stays the course, he can make sure it never gets to that point and get everybody out. "You've got to give me the low down on this guy, Agent Justice.

There has to be something that you know about him and how he works." Billy's focus in the rear view mirror changes from Jonathan, to the car back down the street that just stopped trying to stay out of view. Someone is checking them out. The no headlights routine is a sure giveaway.

Shifting in his seat, Jonathan tries to find a more comfortable position. "Well, if you're hoping to find a chink in his armor, good luck. This guy covers every base, and doesn't miss anything. Hell, you'd be better off just walking up to the front door and ringing the bell."

Billy sends the truck turning up the next alley on his right, and speeds up to the next intersection. After abruptly stopping, he looks over at JD and says, "Get over here and drive the truck up one more block, turn off the lights, and wait for me there. I'll be back in a few minutes." Billy climbs out of the driver's door, not giving JD the chance to question Billy's actions. Mainly because Billy never took the truck out of gear, leaving JD rushing to gain control before it hits one of the buildings.

Up the fire escape he goes, finding the third floor landing a suitable perch. Right on cue, the car can be seen slowing down quickly to turn onto the alley. Up ahead, JD was doing as he was told, stopping the truck and turning off the lights. For a second the car drives slowly up the alley, as if monitoring the truck for any signs of movement. Then, the mystery vehicle begins to speed up. The driver has no idea that Billy is above the car. From his perspective, there is no way of him seeing what is about to happen. Billy leaps over the railing and drops three stories as the car passes underneath. Just before he makes contact with the car's roof, Billy produces an energy blast below him. On impact, the blast flattens the roof down onto the seats and doors, and sends Billy flying off into the air. Landing on his feet, Billy takes off running towards his truck as if he had practiced the move too many times.

Jonathan is the first to question Billy's actions. Again he comes across with a disapproving tone, "What the hell was that all about, McBride?"

JD chimes in as well, when Billy gets inside the vehicle, "Dude, I have to admit that your little stunt was pretty freakin' awesome. When did you pick up on that tail?"

"While captain fat mouth was back there short changing us," Billy starts up the truck again, and then looks back at Jonathan. "Just so you know; I'm not flying Kamikaze tonight, so that suggestion about the front door is out of the question." Slapping his friend across the chest, Billy directs his attention to JD, "We scout the perimeter first. I want to know what my feet are jumping into, before they leave the ground." As they reach the main street ahead of them, Billy slows the truck down again and points at a building up the street. "JD, do ya see that dark grey complex, two blocks up, and on the left?" Before JD can answer Billy turns the truck in the opposite direction and speeds off again. "That's the place we want."

After another two left turns, Billy pulls the truck into a darkened alley, a block away from their target. Grabbing the necessary map, he starts to go over his plan, "Okay, JD, we'll head this way, which will bring us to this point here." Billy traces their path with his finger for visual reference to make sure his directions to JD are crystal clear. "The complex perimeter is close to two miles in length. You go this way, and I'll circle around the other. We'll meet at the opposite corner and go over what we see, before we continue on, retracing each other's paths to verify what we've seen, or see if anything has changed, or was missed. As quick as possible, I want us to regroup back here, and with captain courageous helping us, we'll determine the best route in. You can do a mile in five minutes, right?"

Jonathan climbs out of the truck feeling like he has been left out of the planning a little too much. "Hold on there a second, McBride. You were the one crying about not receiving enough credit while ago. Don't go doing the same thing to me. I'm still functioning enough to help you save my daughter."

Billy turns around and scoffs at Jonathan's remark. Letting his alter ego handle the situation with the Federal agent, Billy's reply is laced with sarcasm of the highest form. And yet, everything he says is true. "No offense, pal, but you're nothing more than a liability to me from here on out. The help I need from you is information about what I see. Wounded, and dying, there is no way you can keep up with him and me. Do us all, including your daughter, a favor, and sit back down in the truck. Stay here, quit aggravating your injuries any more, and wait for your partner to show up with the cavalry. We'll be back in ten minutes." He waves JD on, and the two disappear into the shadows of the alley.

Jonathan Justice can't, or won't hear the logic in Billy's words. To him, he thinks that Billy's arrogant and egotistical outlook is underestimating the severity of the situation, and Jonathan's abilities that still exist. The old man may be slowed down by his wounds, but he can still move good enough to aid the two would be heroes. If nothing else, his pistols could offer Billy the back up he's going to need. With his mind made up, he takes off towards the building wondering where his partner is, and what happened to the back up he called for, while ago? He pulls the transmitter out of his pocket and looks it over to make sure it was still working.

Suddenly, a car with no headlights pulls up in front of him, causing Jonathan to drop the transmitter and kick it over to the curb. Drawing both pistols and aiming them with shaky hands, he's surprised to see that the driver is Pete Del Gato. "Damnit Pete, what the hell are you doing? Hell, if I wanted to be seen, I would have walked on over to the front door!" Jonathan shoves the pistols back into the waistband of his pants, and breathes a little easier knowing that it was his partner, and not the enemy of the moment. His strength is starting to fade, faster than he thought it would. Doubt starts to creep in, making him wonder if Billy might be right.

Del Gato chuckles at Jonathan's statement, "Actually, that's not a bad idea. Get in the car, partner. You don't look like you could walk all the way over there." Del Gato can appreciate Jonathan's hesitance for the situation. That doesn't mean he approves of it. "Get in the damned car, Justice!" To emphasize the necessity of the request, Del Gato points his pistol at his partner, aimed right at Jonathan's head. "Don't even think about reaching for those guns again, because I will shoot you if you do. I swear to god I will do it!"

There is no way this is happening, is it? Has Jonathan lost too much blood? Is he delusional, or is his partner really pointing a gun at him? He knows that he was starting to feel a little light headed, but he thought it was nothing he couldn't handle. Then, before he can question his partner's loyalty, Jonathan feels the barrel of a gun being pressed against the back of his Kevlar vest. "Easy there, mate. Don' be goin' and doin' something foolish. The things this baby spits out will cut right through that vest of yours." Danny Muldoon reaches around and retrieves Jonathan's pistols. "I have to admit, me boy-o, I really didn't think you would have made it this far. That little chickie of yours must be more important to ya than I thought. Now get into the car, ya bloody cocker." The rear door of the sedan swings opens signaling Muldoon to hit Jonathan in the back of his head, sending the betrayed agent falling into the back seat.

After checking the streets for any signs of witnesses, Muldoon climbs into the car shoving Jonathan across the bench seat. "Get us over to the building, Del Gato. I'm sure you will be wanting to collect your pay."

Keying up his headset, the hitman known as Checkmate calls in to his boss, "Crossfire, do you copy me, m' boy-o?"

"Muldoon, what's the status? And, don't call me that again," Crossfire responds.

He smiles at Del Gato, who was looking back through the rear view mirror, "Copy that, boss man, we've got him, just like our new friend said we would. There's no sign of the little bastard from down south, but I'm certain he's around here somewhere. We're coming in to drop off this package, oh and, Agent Del Gato is looking to receive his retirement for a job well done."

Crossfire's voice comes through the radio headset one more time, "Roger that, we'll be ready."

Del Gato lets a smile cross his face, knowing that soon he will be heading to the tropics where he can live out the rest of his miserable existence in style. Feeling the need to quiet his conscience, Pete tries to strike up a conversation with his new associate, "So, that head strong partner has really made life tough for your boss, huh?"

"Soon, Agent Del Gato, it won't matter to anyone."

Chapter XXVI

JD runs up the street to the alley where Billy designated for them to meet. In a way, he's a little surprised to see Billy there before he is. It's a little more surprising to see him standing out in view like this, "Billy, we've got trouble, bro., and we need to act fast! I think the bad guys just rounded up Agent Justice!"

"Yeah, well if you don't calm down a little, the sniper on that building over there is going to hear you." Billy looks across the street and points the gunman out.

"Okay, but if we move fast enough, we could probably cut him loose before they get him inside the building." It isn't hard for JD to pick up on how Billy seems disinterested in Jonathan's peril. Would he so easily dismiss JD as well, if he were in Jonathan's shoes?

"Listen to me, JD. Jonathan is involved in this mess for a different reason than we are. The last thing I want to do is jeopardize the hostages by showing our hand trying rescue Deputy Dawg. He knew what he was doing, when he left the truck. The longer they think I'm out of the picture, the better." Billy pulls JD back into the shadows as two men circle the perimeter in a company security jeep. "Come on, I think I know how you can get into the building."

Billy leads JD back around the building, pointing out the various men stationed around the building. Being the multitasker that he is, Billy contemplates Jonathan's actions, while heading to the office building of the complex. Just inside the perimeter fence, the side of the glass tower facing the street has an abandoned window washing rig positioned just above the first floor. Both JD and Billy assume that it was abandoned when Crossfire's team took control of the complex. JD just stares at the rig, and then looks back at Billy, "Are you serious? What if there are guys on the roof?"

"Then I guess they'll be as surprised as hell when you get to the top. Besides, you can take care of yourself. Use some of that ninja shit that Nick taught you." Billy pats JD on his chest, as if saying that he had all the confidence in the world in JD.

JD's earlier thoughts of Billy writing Jonathan off make him wonder now if Billy is setting him up as a distraction. "What will you be doing while all of the bullets are flying my way?"

"Sitting in the truck, and waiting for you to get back. It's freezing out here." The look on JD's face states his dislike for Billy's sarcastic humor. "Okay," He gives JD a devilish grin with his energy highlighting his eyes. "I'm gonna take Justice's advice and walk right through the front door. From the looks of things, I would say that I've got about as much of a chance to get in that way, as I would any other." Billy looks around, and then stares into JD's eyes. "Judging by the glass panels, and comparing it to the main building, this puppy is only five stories tall. The fourth floor is connected to the main building by a sky bridge that carries over to the other building's roof deck. Be ready when I give the signal."

"So, marching right into the building to place yourself in his waiting arms, is your big plan?!"

"Easy, chief," Billy suggests, recognizing JD's growing anxiety, "Remember, JD, my job is to give you cover while you gat the hostages out. You can worry about me when you're done with that, okay?"

"One question before you take off. Why do you keep referring to them as the hostages?"

Billy looks at JD and gives him a confident smile, "That's easy, bro. It keeps me from letting this get too personal. If I lose control this time, I lose everything. "I'll see you in a little while." Billy turns away and disappears up the dark alley.

"I hope so, Billy," JD replies before leaping over the even foot fence.

"Special Agent Jonathan Justice," Simon Ryker walks into the lobby of the main building and begins to survey his wounds. "You, my friend, have caused me great financial suffering over the past fifteen years. Because of you alone, it took me nearly three months just to get my team across the US borders, so we could do this job. I figured, since we were in town, I would look you up and have a two for one sale." Crossfire hits Jonathan in the ribs with a stun gun to incapacitate the agent, who was just coming around from his last assault outside. "Put him in with his daughter, and let me know when he wakes up. Alert the guards to be on their toes. Judging by that dressing on Justice's shoulder, he had help getting off that roof, where you said that you left him. I think our guest of honor may have already arrived. Crossfire turns away to head up the hallway, to go ready himself for Billy's arrival."

"Uh, Mr. Crossfire," Del Gato steps forward to address his issues, "What about my money for my retirement?"

Ryker stops for a second, but doesn't bother to turn around. "Checkmate, retire Agent Del Gato for me."

Del Gato freezes, realizing the double cross has been played. He hears the report of Muldoon's pistol, as the killer mumbles, "I knew you'd say that." A burning sensation envelopes Pete Del Gato's chest when the bullet leaves a clean, half inch, hole through Del Gato's torso. His treachery has been repaid, sending the corrupt investigator crumbling to the floor in a lifeless heap. "Checkmate," Muldoon declares as he and another guard gathers up Jonathan's lifeless body.

At the corner of the building, Billy scans the area for any signs of guards, thugs, hoodlums and cameras. With the area looking clear, he walks right up to the front doors where he can see Del Gato's body lying on the marble tile floor, in a puddle of blood. He doesn't know who the man was, so to Billy Del Gato is just one less man he has to worry about. The other thing he doesn't know is that the laser sight of a sniper's rifle is hitting Billy right in the middle of his back.

JD slips up behind the gunman and quietly deploys his force field around the sniper, just as he pulls the trigger. As expected, the bullet exits the barrel of the gun, only to fall to the roof top a few feet away. The sniper takes his eye away from the rifle's scope and stares at the bullet lying on the roof deck in front of him. So shocked by the occurrence, he forgets to call in the report of Billy entering the building. The silencer does its job, so no one was alerted to the gunfire. Frustrated by his failed attempt, he loads another shell into the chamber and takes aim before Billy moves out of range.

Unfortunately, the sniper doesn't get the chance to pull the trigger, with JD making his presence known. In a matter of seconds, JD reduces the gun man to a lifeless heap, with just a few well placed punches and kicks. "You're all clear," he mumbles, watching Billy disappear inside the building. "I'll see you on the inside, partner." Down the street JD runs, returning to the window washing rig. This may have put him behind schedule, but Billy wouldn't have made it inside, if JD hadn't remembered the guy he saw when this first started.

Chapter XXVII

In the holding room, the lights turn on causing Taylor to start her regiment of tears for the inevitable torture that's to come. Sarah McBride looks up and is relieved to see that it isn't that dreadful Mr. Smith. Checkmate and his fellow goon enter the room dragging an unconscious Jonathan Justice, and dump him at the feet of his daughter. The armed men quickly exit the room, allowing everyone to breathe a sigh of relief. Taylor on the other hand breaks down and starts to cry. How much longer is this going to last?" Her greatest fear now is that she is teetering on the edge of oblivion, and that she doesn't know how much longer she will last before welcoming death over this torturous treatment.

It isn't hard for Sarah to recognize Taylor's condition, "Taylor dear, you have to be strong. My Billy will be here soon, and he will put an end to all of this for us." With the lights left on, Sarah knows that this trap is being set for her son. At least with the room illuminated, she can see the condition of the other captives. Her assistant Josef, from her clinic appears to have had a nervous breakdown, mumbling chaotic gibberish about seeing men with red eyes. The young man next to Josef is unfamiliar to Sarah; making her wonder if he is another of Billy's friends, who have been dragged into this mess. One thing for certain, is that he hasn't moved since they brought him in. On the other side of her, Isaiah's granddaughter is quiet but watching everything as if looking for a reason to join Josef in his mental state.

From across the room, Sarah stares at the young girl laid unconscious on the floor. She can't put her finger on it, but there is something about her that is familiar to Sarah. Then, as Justice rolls over, with the effects of Crossfire's stun gun wearing off, Sarah is able to connect the dots. It only takes her a second to recognize the man that ruined her marriage, and ultimately her life. After that, it's easy for Dr. McBride to see the resemblance between Kaitlyn and Julie.

There's no way anyone could have made the connection between Billy and Jonathan, is there? No, this has to be Jonathan's doing with his quest for Julie's murderer. With that line of thought, for everybody's sake, Sarah must not let on that she and Jonathan know each other. Already, the guard at the door is taking notice to how Jonathan appeared to be waking up. Whatever is going to happen will take place real soon. "Be strong son. There are a lot of people counting on you," Sarah says as a silent prayer.

JD crosses the roof of the building and quickly eliminates the opposition stationed around the parapet walls and a/c units. Ten of them in all fall to his talents, but he isn't keeping count. JD's actions are precise and methodical as he moves along. Nick would be proud of his student, and how JD was handling adversity. No alarms have been triggered, and not one of his opponents had the chance to call for support. Once on the other side of the roof, JD looks over the short wall to see the sky bridge that connects one building to another.

"So, student of Landry, you have joined the crusade as well, yes?" The sound of a woman's voice sends a cold chill down JD's spine. How is it possible for her to be on the roof without him seeing her presence? Better yet, who is she, and how does she know who JD is? Of course, her knowing who he is could give a clue as to where she came from.

Spinning around, JD lays eyes on Shalimar just as she is about to lash out at him with a handful of claws. "Whoa, bitch, I can't let you do that!" JD blocks her attack, and then delivers a straight punch right to her nose.

Shalimar simply shakes off the result as if the attack to her face never happened. "Good, I was hoping you wanted to test me." The Persian terrorist strikes with a series of blows and kicks, only to have JD defend them with ease. "I do hope that you are not letting a small thing like chivalry come between us. I did hope to have some measure of challenge with you."

"Naw, you just haven't pissed me off enough yet, but be careful what you wish for. You might not like what you get." JD motions for her to take another shot at him, knowing that he doesn't have time for this. Shalimar literally growls at him before accepting the challenge, with her angered even more by his display of arrogance. Again, he is ready for her, and defends her assault, until she manages to land a single blow, raking her claws across his cheek. "Now you've done it," he explains, touching his cheek to assess the damage. Then, with surprising speed, JD lashes out at her delivering two punches, a kick and a karate chop to the base of her neck. Down she goes to one knee, angered by this mortal whelp that has bested her. As she rises to face him again, he waits like a cobra ready to strike, and he does. One kick, right to her chest, sends Shalimar over the short parapet wall. JD rushes the edge of the roof and looks over, expecting to see Shalimar sprawled out on the ground below. To his surprise, she had landed on the roof of the sky bridge and was now looking up at him.

Shalimar knows that she has to end this conflict with Landry's student immediately. JD leaps from the roof to join her on the bridge, feeling the same way about the situation. Deploying his force field below him, a trick that he saw Billy use, JD impacts with the bridge structure, ready to battle some more. He knows that Billy is already somewhere inside the building, readying to be the distraction, so JD can make the extraction. JD knows that he can't miss the opening, but can't allow Shalimar to reveal his presence either.

Feeling the most urgency about the situation, Shalimar decides to end this right away, charging at JD with full intention of slicing him up with her claws. Before she gets within three feet, JD deploys his force field with enough intensity to send her flying off the sky bridge and screaming through the air.

Crossfire enters the holding room with several of his cohorts following, "Look around, Jonathan. It's a goddamned reunion." He scans the hostages to see how many of them were paying attention. I have some good news, and I have some bad news. The good news is that we believe your savior dressed in grey will be arriving soon. The bad news is that this will be over for all of you real…" His statement is cut short as Shalimar's body comes crashing down through the skylight over the room. "Sonofabitch!" He looks around at his lackeys who are just as surprised as he is about the turn of events. "I want you on the roof immediately, do you understand me?!" Crossfire glares at Checkmate, "What's wrong Muldoon? Didn't you know she was going to do that?" Glancing down at Jonathan, taking notice to how the Fed was adding a smile to his series of grimaces. "Why hasn't anyone made visual contact yet?" Crossfire kicks Jonathan in his ribs, "Don't worry Federal boy, I'll get back to you in a minute."

Crossfire's right hand man, Pantera hands the boss a radio. "Security says that he's in the building. The cameras showed him walking right in the front doors, but we've lost track of him on the inside. "The Australian merc offers Crossfire the radio one more time, only to have it slapped out of his hands.

"Don't hand that thing to me!" Crossfire turns and stares at Checkmate, "Wasn't it your man who was supposed to be watching the front doors?" Ryker pulls his pistol and points it at Checkmate's head.

"Hold on there a second, me boy-o. You were the one who told us to drag the meat sack in here..." Checkmate's defense is cut short by a bullet from Crossfire's gun, as it penetrates Muldoon's skull.

Facing his lieutenant, Crossfire instructs, "Get on the radio and lock this place down. Better yet, turn on that PA system and hand me that microphone." There was a time when Simon Ryker thought that he had every possible scenario covered. Only now does he see that something was missed. This will all change momentarily. "Attention; Mr. William Raymond McBride. Allow me to introduce myself to you." His voice echoes through the building, with his surrender demands carrying into every room. If Billy is somewhere in the building, he can't help but hear what Crossfire has to say. "My name is Simon Ryker, better known to my employers as Crossfire. Of course, I really don't expect you to know who I am, so I'll try to keep this short. I've been hired to kill you. If you need any proof of my intentions, I have a person in front of me of little interest. Actually that's not very true. He's been a thorn in my side for quite some time. Have you had the pleasure of meeting your father's first partner?

Crossfire pauses, as if he expected Billy to answer the question. Instead, a gun shot reverberates through the intercom system. This is followed by screams from the terrified hostages, including Kaitlyn who just woke up to see her father gunned down. "Go with Billy, Kaitlyn," Jonathan instructs, before another shot from Crossfire's gun ends Agent Justice's life.

"There now, he is no longer a thorn to anyone." Crossfire turns around and faces his captive audience. "McBride, you have two minutes to surrender, or the dead man's daughter gets the next bullet. Who knows, maybe I'll change my mind and target one of your loved ones instead. Personally, I think it's the intrigue that makes all of this so exciting, don't you? Who will die because of your unwillingness to surrender, innocent stranger, or ill fated loved one?" Just for kicks, Crossfire pans the room with his gun to draw out cringes and screams from the hostages. "You now have one minute and forty two seconds."

Setting the microphone down, Crossfire turns on every monitor in the building, to display the hostages for Billy to see. As Pantera steps over to Crossfire's side, his Commander begins to explain the next series of events, "I want you to get everyone in and around this room. This guy has to be subdued as soon as possible. The boss lady wants her father here for the execution. I will call her as soon as we have him, but not a moment before."

Chapter XXVIII

Billy doesn't need a video screen to see what is going on, being that he is sitting in one of the observation rooms above the hostages' holding room. This guy Ryker doesn't appear to be any different than the rest of the guys that Billy's faced. Crossfire is nothing more than a high priced thug who holds no value for life. Before, Billy would just release the monster inside of him and eliminate the threat. But, every time that has happened, it seems like someone he loves gets hurt. Now, everything he loves is in the same room with his prey. There is no way Billy can guarantee their safety. This is that time in question, where he is challenged to make a choice; himself or the others. Where is JD? Is he in place? Billy has to wait until JD is ready, before he can make his move.

"Time's up, vigilante, who should it be?" Crossfire looks around the room pointing his pistol at each hostage. He stops in front of Josef, Sarah's assistant. The young man with few masculine attributes is no threat to anyone. Hell, he has a hard time killing a little bug. Unfortunately, it is Josef's lack of masculinity that earns him the next bullet. Crossfire looks back at Pantera and explains, "What? I just couldn't stand the sight of seeing a grown man cry like a baby. Someone had to put him out of his misery."

Billy never cared for the CNA's feminine personality, but even Josef didn't deserve this kind of treatment. Still, Billy hesitates, and isn't sure why. Where is JD? Does he show a little faith and make his move, or debate a little longer until someone else is gunned down in cold blood?

Grabbing the microphone, Crossfire walks over to Sarah, who is grieving the loss of Josef. "Tell him; tell your son what just happened!" Crossfire looks over at Kaitlyn for a second as she suffers a hysterical fit over the death of her father. Seeing no threat, he returns his attention to Sarah, "Speak, or die." Glancing up at Pantera, he asks, "Any word on his location?" Pantera holds his hand up to his earpiece of his headset, and then shakes his head no.

"Billy," Sarah's voice is broken and halted, coming through the speaker system, due to her emotional state. What she is about to say, is the hardest thing she has ever done. Going against her own values of life, Sarah states these words, "Son, I expect you to take this sonofabitch down for what he's done!"

Crossfire snatches the microphone away from Billy's mother and steps back a couple of feet, angered by her resistance. Sarah stares back at her captor, and then displays her distaste for him by spitting at his feet, "You piece of trash. I know who you are, traitor. I know that you're the man who killed that young girl's mother, when you betrayed your team and country."

"Did you know that I'm the one who gunned down your husband too? Oops, now you know too much." Crossfire aims and shoots two bullets, small caliber, right into Sarah's abdomen. "There, now you and Agent Justice have something else in common. Tell me, Dr. McBride, how long will it take you to die from those bullet holes in your belly?" Justice managed to hang on for a couple of hours, but we both know he didn't die from being gut shot, now don't we?" Slipping his pistol back into its holster, he faces his right hand man and asks, "Did that bring him out of hiding?"

Sarah McBride's words have been embedded into Kaitlyn's mind. The man standing in front of her has been positively identified as the killer of both her parents. This knowledge begins to distort her thoughts and pervert her sorrow into anger.

Up in the observation room, Billy is overwhelmed by the shock and horror of what he just witnessed. How did this happen? Did he hesitate too long? Deep down inside did his subconscious keep him from sacrificing himself for the others? After all of his posturing and planning, and attempts to control his personality, his mother was just gunned down, because he didn't act. No, he won't take the blame for this. The man responsible is directly below Billy, and he is the one who will suffer the punishment for what has happened.

The cage holding the monster inside him gives way. Seething, soul eating, rage boils up inside of Billy feeding the beast's strength until it breaks free to feast on the ones responsible for crossing this line. Behind him, he hears a jiggling of metal against metal, as someone outside checks to see if the door to the room is locked. This isn't a warning to Billy. It's an announcement to the monster that the first recipients of his retribution have arrived.

Checkmate and a half dozen of his men wait outside the door for the signal to charge into the room. On the count of three, Muldoon swings the door open with all seven weapons firing into the room. They're quick to realize that their efforts are in vain, watching their bullets vaporize against the growing orb of energy that surrounds Billy. Before the gunmen can change their tactics, Billy releases the energy in all directions. All seven are quickly eliminated from life, along with all of the windows of the observation rooms surrounding Crossfire and the hostages.

Crossfire points at the room above while cowering from the shower of glass, "He's up there!" He aims his pistols at the shattered window and readies to open fire. With his attention focused on Billy's presence, Crossfire doesn't notice Kaitlyn's growing condition. As Crossfire and his men open fire on Billy, Kaitlyn expels a blood curdling scream, and then sends everyone and everything rising into the air. Then, just as quickly, everything comes crashing back down to the floor as Kaitlyn passes out again.

JD sees this as his opportunity to act. In the observation room across the way, Billy's energy blast had blown out the glass that separated JD and the hostages. This gives him a clear path to the floor below. Before Crossfire can recover from Kaitlyn's assault, JD leaps down and extends his force field around Sarah and the other captives. Now he has to keep them safe until Billy can provide them a way out.

Crossfire collects himself and jumps to his feet to face JD, who just stands defiantly in front of the assassin. "Who the hell are you?" The hired killer pulls the trigger several times; sending bullets ricocheting back at him and his men. Then, Crossfire realizes that JD's force field doesn't reach Kaitlyn. "Surrender Commander Kung Fu or the little girl eats a bullet." Crossfire draws down on the unconscious young woman, "silly little bitch."

If he had pulled the trigger at that moment, Simon Ryker might have gotten the shot off. But in the second that it takes for him to look back at JD, Simon Ryker, a.k.a. Crossfire, loses his opportunity for another kill shot. Like a wild animal, Billy leaps through the broken window, firing a multitude of energy blasts at Crossfire and his remaining men. The barrage explodes all around the mercs causing an entire section of floor to fall away beneath their feet. Now

Mr. Black and his associates are cut off from the only exit. Crossfire and Pantera fall to the ground floor below, avoiding death, but not Injury.

"Sorry about your girlfriend, Shalimar, old friend," Crossfire declares, as if stating the fact that they may never get the chance for this conversation again.

"Do not mourn for her, boss man," Pantera suggests. "She and I will meet again sooner than you think."

"Sidestep that sonofabitch, Pantera, and then meet me at the stairwell exit. Don't be late buddy. I'd hate to leave you behind." With that, Crossfire takes off limping down the corridor, because of his wounded ankle. Pantera simply steps back into a darkened doorway to await his prey.

Billy drops through the opening in the floor and collides with a number of tables and chairs before coming to an abrupt halt. Jumping up to his feet, he expects an attack from any and every direction. He sees Crossfire disappear at the end of the corridor, sending Billy on his dark pursuit. Hell bent to exact his mother's last request, Billy takes chase after his prey, ignoring anything and everything else. Of course, if his rational side were in control, he might recognize the fact that he was chasing one man, when two fell through the floor.

Before he can react, Pantera jumps onto Billy's back, applying a choke hold with one arm, and pulling knife from its sheath on his thigh with the other hand. In the ring, Billy's wrestling persona would drive his opponent back into the corner turnbuckles to break the submission hold. It should be noted that the wrestling opponent would not be wielding a large knife. That's okay, because this isn't a wrestling ring,

so Billy uses the next best thing, and drives the Australian mercenary through the corridor wall. Once they collide with the floor, and furniture on the other side of the wall, Billy finds that he was successful in breaking Pantera's grip. Pantera on the other hand isn't as happy as Billy, when he finds that he has been disarmed somewhere during the collision and impact.

With the playing field balanced, Billy takes the offensive. He could use his energy to end this quickly, but this is what the monster inside craves right now. Being the grappler, Billy lands several crippling blows and then backs off for a second. "Come on, lap dog, want some get some!" The merc, simply known as Pantera, is enraged by Billy's invitation, sending the big man rising up at Billy with his eyes glowing red. Unimpressed by the ominous appearance, Billy strikes at Pantera's wounded leg and shatters the man's knee. Immediately, the opponent is sent back to the floor, howling like an injured beast. The only thing around to break his fall is a toppled chair. Only, when he hits the tapered wooden spear, it forces its way into Pantera's chest, ending the bestial howls, and the man's life. "Stupid," Billy declares adding insult to injury. Finished here, he heads for the corridor to try and catch his prize.

Just as he reaches the debris littered hallway, Billy hears the sound of movement back inside the room. Stopping at the hole in the wall, he looks back in to see a horrific sight that should be unbelievable. Pantera's body was lifting itself from the chair leg, and then stares at Billy with blank and hollow eyes. "Stupid," the mouth moves, but the voice echoes from somewhere else. "Foolish mortal, I am Sytaine, second High Priest to our Queen Jezana! You have accomplished nothing here, but perpetuate the inevitable!" To accentuate the claim, a pair of translucent bony hands pushes their way out of Pantera's mouth. This is followed by the rest of the demon forcing its way out of the mercenary's body. Billy can only stagger back against the corridor wall not believing, and then denying what he just saw. Finding a way to move on, he leaves the scene not seeing Sytaine's spirit exiting the building right through the thick concrete walls.

A few minutes ago, when Billy blew the hole in the floor, the result damaged the equipment that controlled Taylor's torture bed. Evidently, no one is aware of this except her, and this is not a good thing, for the unknowing. For the past few minutes, she has been taking in deep cleansing breaths of air, rejuvenating her sore and tortured body. Mr. Smith and his associates believe they still hold the upper hand with her, and decide to play it right away, rather than face JD. "You, Ninja man, sit your ass down right over there, or I'll start to peel the flesh right off her pretty little face." Brandishing the scalpel over Taylor's face, Smith thinks that he is proving his intentions. His goal now, is to get out of this alive, and regroup to discuss compensation later on. He has no idea that Crossfire has already left the building and abandoned his team. Smith is clueless about the many pounds of explosives staged throughout the building. He has no idea what peril he and his men are about to face.

JD is unaware of the fact as well, believing that Smith did hold the better cards, at the time. "Easy pal, there's no need to be getting' all happy with that thi…" JD's statement is suddenly interrupted by Taylor as she shatters the shackles that bound her arms. Kicking her heels together frees her legs, allowing Taylor to kick her feet up over her head, embedding Mr. Jones and Mr. Black's faces into the wall.

Seeing her standing in front of him, scares Mr. Smith to no end, knowing the potential that Taylor possesses. Now instead of standing like a brave man, he falls to the floor to crawl away like some vermin in the night. Crawling backwards away from Taylor, Smith is unconscious to his movement for survival, and is unaware of his position in the room. Without warning, he wanders right off into the huge hole in the floor, surely falling to his doom. Maybe some other time, because him getting off easy like this doesn't sit very well with one Miss Taylor Lewis.

With reflexes of lightning, Taylor reaches out and snares the man in mid air, saving his death for her own reckoning. Lifting him back up, Smith begins to plead for his life. Her rage ignores his begging much the same way he ignored hers. Slinging his body up and then down, he lands on the table of torture with an impact that shatters most of the bones in Smith's body. Then, she grabs the visor he had used on her, and presses it against his face until the facial bones of his skull give way under the pressure. Was her tactics justifiable, maybe, maybe not? But, one thing is for sure. Mr. Smith will never abuse anyone else, ever again. Now, she can focus on finding Billy.

At the end of the corridor, Crossfire watches for any sign of Billy. Then, when the rebel vigilante comes into view, Crossfire knows what to do, when Billy stops in his tracks, wondering why Crossfire was just standing there. "I'm heading to Central Park, McBride. Here, catch, and then see if you can catch me." He tosses a hi-tech grenade at Billy that explodes right away, halting further progress. After pressing a button on his gauntlet, Crossfire clears his throat and speaks into the microphone of his headset. "Den mother, this is wolf one. I'm coming out. Initiate the contingency plan and pick me up out front."

"A woman's voice is heard on his headset, "You are supposed to lead him to the main site, not blow him up."

Crossfire looks back up the corridor, and sees no sign of Billy anywhere. Breathing a little easier because of this gives him the bravado to reply, "Just do what I said! If he's as good as they say he is, he'll find a way."

Thick metal plates begin to fall into position over the building entrances and glassworks. Hearing the clanging sound echoing throughout the building, Kaitlyn opens her eyes and looks up at the ceiling seeing numerous little red lights flashing slowly, but gradually picking up speed. "Uh, could someone please tell me that's not what I think they are?"

Taylor looks around the room with a wild gaze, taking notice of who she knows and who she doesn't, like JD. Recognizing this, he quickly pulls his mask off, and raises his hands to show her that he's no threat to any of them. "You must be Taylor. My name is JD. I'm here with Billy to set you free." She doesn't reply. Instead, Taylor rushes over and breaks the restraints holding Sarah and the others. JD motions for Kaitlyn to join them, who happily obliges by jumping over to JD's waiting arms. At the moment, she believes that there is strength in numbers, and this is certainly a time when Kaitlyn doesn't want to be alone. Turning to Taylor, and pointing out the explosives at the same time, he asks, "We need to get out of here as fast as possible. Do you think you could do that for us?" His question isn't intended to belittle Taylor in any way. It's obvious that she has been through more than most people can handle. He was just asking if she had enough left to oblige.

Taylor isn't offended at all. Just like JD, her first and foremost action is to get out of this nightmare as quickly as possible. Then she has to find Billy. Snatching the hydraulic hoist from its mounts in the floor below, she hurls the massive piece of equipment at the front of the building. In a matter of seconds, a nice clean hole is created right out the front of the building. With their exit established, Taylor rushes over and scoops Sarah up to take the lead.

JD motions for Saphyre to follow suit. Billy is right about one thing. Miss Saphyre Colton is definitely right up JD's alley. If they make it out of here alive, he might have to pursue the idea of getting to know her. "Come on, we have to go now! Follow her and the others while I check on the guy over in the corner. Whoever this is, he seems unaffected by what has happened as of late. Even with the room being torn up around him, the guy hasn't budged from his fetal position on the floor. With no other option to get the guy's attention, JD leans over and taps the young man on the shoulder, "Hey bud, are you going with us?"

His name is Clovis, and he is one of Scotty McAllister's friends. Billy would have known this if he was the one checking on everyone. Clovis would have recognized Billy's voice, being one of three members of the Billy ray McBride fan club. Surprising JD, Clovis suddenly rolls over and punches JD in the nose, muttering the words, "Want some, get some," in a deep, scruffy, voice.

"What the hell was that for? Get the hell outta here before I leave you here with the party poppers!" On cue, an explosion rocks the building, alerting JD that the first series of explosives had started, and accentuates his point.

Saphyre grabs Kaitlyn by the arm to lead her to safety. Unwilling to leave her father's body behind, Kaitlyn looks back once more, and then faces Saphyre to ask, "But, what about my dad?"

Another explosion goes off on the level below. This time smoke and debris enter up into the room through the hole in the floor. "Girl, unless you're planning on going back over there to lie down beside him, I suggest you go with us!" Wanting to run, but unable to leave Kaitlyn behind, Saphyre spins the girl around and looks into her eyes. "Listen, I heard your daddy tell you to go with Billy. Believe me, sister, in times like this, there isn't anyone else I'd rather be with than Billy Ray McBride."

"Let's move ladies!" JD suggests, ushering the two girls to safety, following Clovis. Just one more room and they will be clear of the building. JD sees the metal plating covering the glassworks of the building's exterior, except where the hoist exploded from the building. Twenty more feet and they will be in the clear. Then, Clovis stops at the shattered glass, causing the two girls to do the same. This delay crushes their chances of reaching safety in time, as another explosion goes off under the floor right behind JD. His only reaction is to deploy his force field behind him as he tackles the girls and Clovis out the opening.

Chapter XXIX

The Toyota comes to life with the turn of the key. Pulling another piece of paper from above the visor, Billy scans down the list remembering a specific address he had seen. He knows that this isn't over yet. He knows where Crossfire is going. Once the map is memorized between points A and B, Billy puts the truck in gear and speeds off in search of his prey. He knows that Crossfire is leading him to Callistone and it's exactly what Billy wants. The explosions heard behind him tell Billy that the first stage of Callistone's plan has been initiated. He says a quick prayer hoping that JD was successful before the building was demolished.

JD rolls over after lowering his force field, to assess the status of the others. Looking back, he's proud of what he's accomplished, but even he knows that they aren't safe until they are far away from this place. Yes, Jonathan and Josef lost their lives, and Sarah is mortally wounded, but he and Billy were successful in getting the rest out alive. The question now is, can they maintain that fact. He looks over at Taylor who is still holding Sarah in her arms. Walking over, he decides that now is the proper time to introduce himself to her, "You must be Taylor. My name is JD Johnston. How's Billy's mom? Is she okay to keep moving? We still need to get away from here." Before he can assess Sarah's condition, JD sees movement in the parking lot, out the corner of his eye. Believing that the hostages are still in his care, he takes a defensive stance and deploys his force field around the group. Arming himself with his two favorite weapons, JD pulls the two batons from his waist sash, and presses the button on each shaft, extending them to full length staffs. He wants to make his point clear that he is ready for whatever comes next. What comes into view is a group of armored warriors running towards JD. Taking a stab in the dark, he assumes that these are the back up that Jonathan summoned earlier. "You're a little late."

Commander Steven Ryker stops short of JD's force field as if he somehow detects its presence. "Where's Crossfire?" Ryker looks around and then motions for his team to secure the area. "You're gonna need to pop your bubble if we are going to help her, son."

For JD, he sees that there is no other alternative, and that these guys aren't a threat to him or the surviving hostages. So, with no other delay, he obliges the covert ops commander and lowers the force field. Right away, Ryker's medical officer moves in with her equipment to perform emergency triage. Using the talents handed down to her by her mother, she is able to stabilize Sarah, but knows that it is only temporary. "I've done all that I can for her. Dr. McBride has lost a lot of blood, Commander."

Ryker turns and faces JD, "Where's McBride? Since you seem like the one in charge of this motley group, why don't you fill us in on what happened and catch us up to speed."

Ready to fill the role Commander Ryker has given him, JD stands toe to toe with the war veteran, ready to give his bit. "Well, the wacko started shooting the hostages, with Agent Justice being the first victim. Then, all hell broke loose when your brother shot Billy's mom. Billy took chase, while

I got the hostages out to safety, just before the building blew up around us. To be honest, I'm not sure if Billy and Crossfire made it out or not."

"Sorry to disappoint you son, but I can pretty much guarantee that my brother was on the outside before his contingency plan went into effect." Ryker looks down at Sarah, who seemed to be regaining consciousness. "Is that all you have to say?"

"No way, this guy left his whole team in there, and pulled the pin himself!" JD's tone of voice starts to reflect the anxiety that was building inside of him. "The question I have for you is, what are you gonna do?"

Ryker kneels beside Sarah, "Believe me, Jefferson, I know what the guy is capable of doing. I'm sure you know by now that he did the same thing to my team fifteen years ago." Focusing on Sarah, he moves her hair from her face and asks, "How are you doing?

Even in her weakened condition, Sarah McBride is still able to laugh at his question. "Commander Ryker, I think we both know how I'm doing. It would appear that this is your brother's signature shots, since Jonathan Justice suffered similar wounds." A cough filled with blood interrupts her final conversation. Fighting back the pain, Sarah reaches up with her trembling hand and grabs Ryker's arm. "Find my Billy, Commander Ryker. Find him, and tell him the truth." She releases her grip on Steven's arm, and then releases her hold on life.

The sight of the dear woman passing away is too much for Taylor to handle. She turns away as Ryker clears out of the path of the medical personnel, but there is nothing anyone can do to save her. Stepping away from the scene, he keys up his microphone of his com-link, and asks," Ranger, have you got anything yet?"

"Negative, Commander, there is no sign of Crossfire, or McBride. We did find a place where it looked like someone cut their way out of the side of the building with a blow torch. My best guess would be that both of them are somewhere on the outside, loose in the big apple."

Ryker looks around, wondering about his brother's possible location, "So you're out and about with a deadly threat on your tail. Where do you go?"

"I know," Kaitlyn interjects between sobs. She pulls a piece of paper from the waistband of her costume and unfolds it. Using her finger, Kaitlyn draws a straight line from Union City to Manhattan. "This is the main building of the Cornerstone Corporation. I overheard my dad say once that Callistone has a penthouse at the top overlooking Central Park.

"Where is he?" Everyone's attention is drawn to the voice coming from the courtyard. Obviously, Commander Ryker's Team is here to help, but this new team of Darkside Command agents, dressed in matching red and yellow uniforms, appears to have other plans. The leader of the group is a fellow colleague of Ryker's, and former teammate of the original Task Force Zebra. Against orders, Commander AC Cannone has brought his team in to assist with the apprehension of Crossfire. This would be vital information for him to have offered upon arrival. "Where is he?" Commander Cannone demands again.

Unlike Ryker and his team, there is no way for Taylor to know who Cannone is referring to, but she does know who the clowns in the red and yellows suits are. Her mind quickly perverts what she knows to believe that they have come for Billy, and there is no way she is going to let that happen. "NO!" Surprising everyone, she bolts from her stance charging right at Cannone and his team.

His team knows AC Cannone to be a hard ass, with a will as strong as he is. His team of new recruits however doesn't have the field experience he does, or the ability to stand against the rampaging red head. Therefore, they abandon their leader diving clear of Taylor, but Cannone seems to be trapped in a gaze, seeing a resemblance from years ago. Unable to break the trance, he is the helpless victim of Taylor's onslaught, sending the DSC operative flying off across the parking lot with one mighty punch. Then, without even stopping, she runs off into the night to find her man.

JD is confused by the fact that he has one DSC team standing beside him as allies, while another is squaring off against Taylor. Though he has known her for a very short time, JD's alliance must remain with Billy, and therefore with Taylor as well. To give her a clean getaway, JD deploys his force field around one half of Cannone's team, with Kaitlyn using her ability to lift the other Omega Corps teammates into the air.

Deep down inside, there's a small part of Kaitlyn that is glad to do this, recognizing her friends, Amanda and Henry, in their fancy new uniforms. Another part is willing to blame them for her current affairs, because of the way they abandoned her in her time of need. Are they her friends, or new foes? Perhaps time will only tell. The question is will they get that time to find out? "Go get 'em, girl," she says, watching Taylor disappear in the distance.

Crossfire speeds through the Lincoln Tunnel, dodging traffic while dialing a number on his cell phone. "Yeah, I'm on my way. Nope, as a matter of fact, I'm sure he's not too far behind me. Is everything ready? Good, I'll be there in a few minutes." He hangs up the phone and tosses it over onto the blood soaked passenger seat. On the floor in front of the seat is Den Mother's head severed from her body by the steel cable that was connected to the Hydraulic hoist. When Taylor slung the hoist through the building, enough noise was made to give Den Mother fair warning of the approaching doom. Ironically, the hoist was no danger to her at all, but in side stepping the flying piece of machinery, she stepped right into the path of the frayed cable as it came whipping passed. Now she is no different than the rest of his team, expendable.

Soon, this will all be over, and Simon Ryker will retire a wealthy man, alongside the most powerful woman in the world. He pulls up in front of the Cornerstone Building and climbs out of the damaged Mercedes, surprising the bystanders on the sidewalk and street. Walking right up to the guards patrolling the perimeter, Crossfire gives an order that no one can misunderstand, "I don't care who it is, if anyone pulls up in front of this building, I want you to shoot them on the spot! One catch though; he has to be alive when you bring up his body to me." Simon isn't taking any more chances with this McBride fellow. This little change in plans may not coincide with Margaret's grand scheme, but the job will be completed with the same outcome regardless. He tosses the keys to one of the security guards, as if he expected the man to valet the car for him. Before entering the building, Crossfire stops to look around once more, hoping to catch a glimpse of Billy, before going inside.

Crossfire may not see Billy, but Billy sees him. Rational decisions have become a non issue for this young man. The monster has been set free, and all it craves now is retribution. Billy may be unsure about JD and the others' outcome, and who actually survived, but he is sure of one thing. They will not be in the way for what is about to happen. It's obvious that he has to get into the building before anything at all can happen. The question is how does Billy do it? The rational decision would be the covert approach, sneaking in without being seen. That is why Billy chooses the more direct approach.

Crossfire exits the elevator and steps into the penthouse foyer. The first thing he sees is Margaret standing in front of him, appearing as if she had been waiting for his arrival for hours, "Well?"

"Not to worry, my dear. He should be arriving any minute." Crossfire scans the room and then the rest of the penthouse, "Where's my little brother?"

Margaret snorts her reply, disgusted by the way Ryker's younger sibling tried to change the plan, "He's out on the patio. Did you know anything about what he tried to do?"

Laughing at her question, Ryker knows exactly what she is talking about, "Listen, if I would have told you about the little scare tactic, your response wouldn't have been genuine when it happened. Did IT work?"

"IT got him killed," she corrects, still brandishing the distain for the event. Her cell phone rings pulling her attention away from Crossfire, easing the stress he caused a little. "Hello?"

"Ma'am, this is security. A black pickup truck just crashed its way through the front entrance and into the building. There are no casualties, but there is no sign of the driver eith…" Margaret hangs up the phone and looks at Crossfire.

"He's here," the mercenary chimes in. By the way, where is your father?"

"The poor dear is sitting at his favorite window, staring out at Central Park." She's quick to take notice of Carlton's dislike for her tone of voice, as he walks into the room. Antonio doesn't deserve to be further disgraced. To antagonize him even more, she jumps into Crossfire's arms and gives him a long passionate kiss. When Crossfire sees Carlton's disapproving stare, he's happy to add his own little touch by grabbing Margaret's right butt cheek. Once Carlton has had enough and moves on, Crossfire releases his grip on her, who was ready to be free of his embrace. "Back off, lover, we still have a lot to finish before you get any more of me." After straightening her dress and wiping her mouth, the two walk across the penthouse to get out on the west balcony. Down on the street below, a DSC transport pulls up in front of the building. "Major Delaney, your goon squad had arrived." Margaret looks over at the end of the balcony, where Delaney was standing. "Are you okay? You don't looks so well."

Delaney throws his glass to the balcony floor smashing it out of frustration. He isn't a stupid man, just greedy. It's that greed that has drug him down this dark road of no return. When summoned for this little meeting, his only interest was to secure what he has earned with his dealings with Callistone. Now, that move has cost him everything. He knows now that he has been manipulated to take a fall for his contributions, and there isn't anything he can do about it.

Inside the penthouse, the foyer explodes as Billy opens the elevator doors his own special way. Security guards charge from the nearby stairwell, but all are quickly sent back into the stairs by one of Billy's blasts, before they could draw their guns. Stepping through the debris, Billy walks into the living room, and searches for any sign of his prey. Moving on quickly, he knows that somewhere on the top floor of this building is Antonio Callistone, watching over his empire like a god. Tonight, Olympus will crumble, and Valhalla will burn to its foundations. The deliverer of vengeance is here to dethrone the god, "Callistone!!!"

He enters the kitchen area ready to meet any opponent head on. The one question on Billy's mind is, "Where is everyone?" As he makes his way into the family room, Billy sees Callistone sitting in a small study, staring out the window at Central Park. This is a complete surprise for Billy; especially after everything he's experienced facing off against Callistone and his men. There are no body guards, no army of armed thugs. It's just the man seated at his favorite window. Caution takes control of Billy's actions as he enters the room to investigate. The little voice in the back of his mind screams at Billy to run away, but he can't resist. His prize is so close that he can almost touch it. The closer he gets to Antonio, the more recognizable the situation is for Billy. Someone has already stolen his thunder.

Antonio Callistone looks like he is barely alive, as if he has had a stroke or heart attack. It's obvious that the mobster is still conscious when he twitches at the sight of Billy standing in front of him. Why? None of this makes any sense. As much as he hates to admit it, the little voice is sounding smarter by the minute. Run!!! That's what he should do. He could sort this all out with Callistone at a later date, when they both feel more up to it. But the monster inside him still has a person to find.

As he exits the study, the great debate wages on, with his actions swaying towards finding Crossfire. He gets his wish turning to face the living room again, where Billy sees Margaret and Crossfire standing in the middle of the floor, in front of a stairwell that leads up to the roof. The confusing part is how they appear to be delaying their departure. Are they really waiting for Billy to see them? The little voice was right. He should have run. His thoughts delay his reaction time. Billy charges both hands with energy, but it's already too late. Crossfire pulls the trigger on his machine pistol, emptying the magazine of shells. All but three of the bullets are vaporized by Billy's energy, but the three remaining bullets find their mark in the big bull's-eye target on Billy's chest. All at once, everything seems to slow down, as Billy staggers back against the wall. What is happening to him?

His chest burns with agonizing fire, and breathing hurts even worse.

Real time speed returns to his consciousness when he feels a sharp jab into his shoulder. His head has already started to spin, and turning to face the new pain introduced only causes him to drop to one knee. It was Carlton Smithers standing beside Billy, holding a syringe in his hand. Talk about insult to injury. "There ya go," Carlton says, looking into Billy's eyes, "That should help a little. Don't go dying on us. Margaret isn't done with your services yet."

Margaret raises her pistol and points it at Crossfire. "Are you out of your mind, Simon?! I told you he had to live!" The look on her face tells Crossfire that he too is being betrayed.

"Hold on a second, Margaret!" Crossfire lifts his weapon as well, creating their own little Mexican standoff. "You told me that you wanted this guy to be framed for your father's murder, so that you wouldn't risk any opposition when you took over the syndicate. If you had other plans, you should have told me. Wow, I guess that is a two way street after all, huh?" Cutting his losses, Ryker squeezes the trigger of his gun, but the hammer falls on an empty chamber.

She smiles as if she is the devil herself, and says, "Oh lover, you're all out of bullets." Margaret watches Crossfire's panic spread across his face, right before she pulls the trigger of her own pistol, hitting her duped lover in the chest. He feels the bullet cut through his armor and bury itself deep into his flesh. "Wow, I guess you were right. These bullets do cut through your armor. Ya know, you probably should have never told me that." She smiles as she watches her Simon fall to one knee, and then roll over to the floor. Looking around, he acts like he can't believe that this double-cross has taken place.

"Carlton, love, is our friend going to die over there?" Instead of waiting for a reply, Margaret marches over to see for herself. She taps Billy on the shoulder with the barrel of her gun. "Listen, I don't want you to think I stacked the deck against you. My plan was never to have you gunned down like this. So, to make up for your unfortunate shooting, I want to give you this warning. There is almost as much explosives here, as there was at the facility in Union City. You better not hang around too long. Who is going to save your family and friends in the next round of battle, if you and my father both go out with a bang?" She grabs Billy's face and directs his attention to the balcony outside the dining room.

Carlton walks over, and stands beside Crossfire's dying body, gloating over the outcome. "I told you that it would cost you too much to get close to her. You should have listened to me Simon." He shoots Crossfire in the head just to make sure the merc stays down for good, and Carlton is justified in doing so, by his jealousy for Margaret's affection.

As Margaret walks over to Carlton's side, she watches Delaney stagger in from the balcony. Obviously, the narcotics in his drink were starting to take affect, "Hey, wait, what about me?" His speech is slurred and his eyes are glazed over, but he is still able to recognize a gun being pointed at him, "Wait, you can't just leave me up here!" Anxiety and paranoia are now setting in because of the drugs in his system. Why are Cannone and his team here? He knows full well that they were remanded to base and specifically ordered not to leave under any circumstances. Even in his panic stricken state, Delaney knows that his team is closing in. If he's found here, the implications would be devastating to say the least. This fact only feeds his paranoia to disturbing levels. "Please?"

"You're right, what was I thinking? We can't leave anything to chance." Margaret pulls the trigger, ending Delaney's woes, once and for all. Even his dying expression questions her actions, as he falls to the sofa before rolling off into the floor. "Carlton, do me a favor and call up to the pilot, and tell him that we need an emergency takeoff as soon as possible." Walking back over to Billy, she kneels beside him and leans in close to his ear. "By the way, you missed one. I'm sure that he is going to hope you get out of this alive. Otherwise, he and I will have a lot of fun together." She stands up and starts for the stairs adding, "Hope to see you soon, down South."

"Margaret, if McBride is supposed to live, don't you think we should assist him in some way?" Now it is Carlton who seems bewildered by Ms. Callistone's actions.

"No!" She commands, turning to look Carlton in the eyes. "She said that this is to take place this way, and I am not to interfere. Now, let's get out of here while we still have the chance!"

Billy rolls over trying his best to stand up. He isn't surprised by the outcome of his arrival at the penthouse. Billy always knew that it was always an either succeed or die trying crusade. It would be apparent to anyone that this is the end, and yet he still fights to carry on. It's that stubborn never give up, attitude that has always given him the most trouble. But in the same instance, it has kept him alive as well or at least until now.

Above him, he can hear the roar of the helicopter's main rotor as the private aircraft prepares to take off. The sound, where is the sound the loudest? Hurry Billy, time is running out. Over at the wet bar in the living room, he can see the explosives packages tucked away on the shelves. The chance for his survival appears to be slim at best, for the situation. He can't go up, he can't go down, and the blinking red lights behind the bar are a sure sign that he can't stay there. Charging both hands with energy, he unloads the destructive force at the ceiling above him.

His aim is accurate as the explosion erupts through the roof beneath the helicopter that is taking off. Debris is sent skyward, cleaving the tail section of the helicopter in half. Immediately, the pilot is sent into a fight for his life, as the wounded helicopter carries a helpless Margaret down to the green landscaping of Central Park. Even with the dire straights that he is facing, Billy smiles through the pain as he watches the flaming helicopter descend uncontrollably passed the penthouse windows.

Believe it or not, but this gives him a newfound reason to try to live on. If the enemies of his friends and family are gone, Billy may still have a chance at resuming a normal life. But first, he has to get away. The problem is that he never came up with a contingency plan for a situation like this. The detonators on the explosives keep tinging, ting, ting, ting, faster and faster with the little red lights keeping rhythmic time. He knows the rhythm. It matches the explosives he saw at the facility before chasing Crossfire from the building. How much time does he have left? Judge the rhythm; how fast, to how much time? The elevator's out of service; that's his doing. Did the hostages get out? What about his mom? He knows that he can't think about those questions right now. If he doesn't find a way out, none of it will matter any way. He has to stay focused. It's getting harder and harder to breathe. His chest feels tight as if he is going to explode. It's hard to stay focused. How much time does he have left?

Following Margaret's advice, Billy exits the penthouse, staggering out onto the south balcony, barely able to keep himself up. All around him is nothing but air. Below him, however, is the sloped glass rooftop of the building's pool and gymnasium on the lower tower roof. Why would she go to all of this trouble, and then tell him how to save his life? Suddenly, the hair on the back of Billy's neck stands up, and in that brief fraction of a second when the detonators ignite,

Billy hears the perfect silence that preludes the coming blast. Time's up.

There is nothing else for him to do, nowhere to go. Billy simply leans over the railing, as the blast reaches the balcony doors. The glassworks that frames the penthouse erupts with a shower of glass as the fires of the explosion chase him over the side. His last conscious thoughts are hoping that he is on target to hit the pool three stories below. Consciously, or not, he releases what energy he has left in his body and shatters the glass roof between him and the water. "God, help me," he mumbles. Splashdown; his body slaps against the surface of the water and then slowly sinks to the bottom. Lights out, Billy Ray McBride, the towel has been thrown into the ring.

"Everything is unfolding according to my plan," Jezana proclaims as she picks up a small demon creature from the floor of her prison's chamber. Stroking its neck and back, as if the abomination was some sort of pet, she continues, "Soon, those who oppose me will fall and I will be free to lay waste to the world of man." Taking her seat on a throne of suffering, she remembers why she hates man so much. "Soon my pet, the Devastator will be welcomed to this realm and mankind will truly know the end of times."

Be sure to catch Act II of this continuing saga in just a few months with the release of North & South: Mysery Loves Company.